Field of Dead Horses

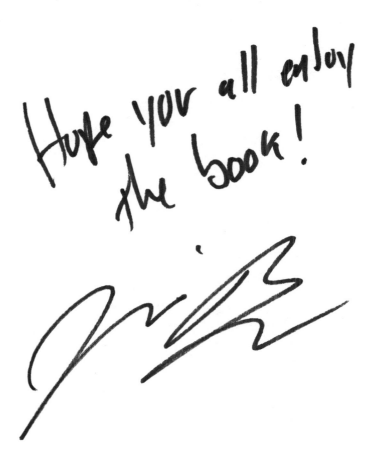

Field of Dead Horses

A Novel
by
Nick Allen Brown

HARROWOOD BOOKS
2012

Trade Paperback Edition
ISBN-13   978-0-915180-24-0
ISBN-10   0-915180-24-3

LIBRARY OF CONGRESS CATALOGING-IN-PUBLICATION DATA

Brown, Nick Allen, 1978-
  Field of dead horses : a novel / by Nick Allen Brown. -- Trade paperback ed.
     p. cm.
  ISBN 978-0-915180-24-0
  1. Horse farms--Kentucky--Fiction. 2. Fathers and sons--Fiction. 3. Women--Crimes against--Fiction. I. Title.
  PS3602.R722426F54 2011
  813'.6--dc23
                                    2011034004

10 9 8 7 6 5 4 3 2 1

First printing: May, 2012

HARROWOOD BOOKS
3943 N PROVIDENCE ROAD
NEWTOWN SQUARE, PA 19073
800-747-8356

PRINTED IN THE UNITED STATES OF AMERICA

*This book is dedicated
to my mother, Dixie Ann Brown
who encouraged my interests in cinema
and literature for thirty-three years.*

ACKNOWLEDGMENTS

I am indebted to the following people for their contributions to this book.

To Leslie Witty for your unwavering support. I am blessed to have you as a friend.

To Chuck Faulk for support, encouraging emails, conversations and reading whatever I gave you.

To Dr. James Farrage and J.D. Shoulders who read my manuscripts and gave me feedback.

To Mike Lauer for meeting with me at Churchill Downs and answering my questions. I admire your profession and am enamored by your ability to train thoroughbreds.

To Elizabeth Lauer, you were the first person I ever called for research and I thank you for answering my questions and thank you for introducing me to your father.

To Cari Small for reading the manuscript with an equestrian viewpoint and giving me helpful suggestions.

To Ellie Caroland, thanks for your assistance with my research at the Scott County Public Library. You are priceless to me and all the people who know you.

And finally, to my wife, Becky – who cheers me on every day.

1

GEORGETOWN, KENTUCKY, 1939.

Booley swung his wiry leg over the saddle and dismounted his horse. *Thwack!* His ankle-high work boots slammed into the damp earth beneath him before he righted himself and walked toward a loose section of the black, plank-board fence. The darkness of the night was retreating before the glowing illumination from the east, giving my eyes enough light to make out a cluster of birds in the trees. On the other side of Penny Creek, I could see several ponies fanning their tails and picking at the grass. They belonged to Mr. Grange who raised trail horses, ponies and obnoxious children. I watched as Booley determined the condition of the weathered, wooden plank fence taking notice that his face appeared to be as weathered as the boards we were inspecting. His frame was thin and gangly with movements appearing quick yet relaxed—like a marionette with a loose string. His eyes darted from the post to the rusted nails as he gripped the loose board with his cowhide gloves, which were noticeably worn at the knuckles. He nodded his head, satisfied with his diagnosis, and let the board loose from his grip. Removing a glove, he walked back toward his horse, Eros, whose name had come from a play written by Shakespeare. Booley had explained to me that Eros was a character who killed himself rather than obey an order. You could say he was more cultured than me as I had named my horse after a reference that pertained to baseball. With his ungloved hand, Booley reached into an old, tattered saddle bag with a broken buckle. The leather flap was long and flimsy enough to lay over the opening and heavy enough that it kept the contents from jostling out when Eros galloped over the pasture. The broken buckle would clang and ding sporadically as Booley navigated his faithful horse, with no intention of replacing anything that still had life in it. I watched as Booley fished out three box nails before removing the iron claw hammer from his thick leather belt. While holding two nails firmly between his lips and positioning the shank of the first nail against the wooden board, Booley reared his hammer back and struck the head of the box nail. That first strike caused the birds in the trees to erupt from their perches and move in a dark cloud across the pasture.

Along with the sounds of the creek, Booley's hammer and a rooster crowing in the distance, I could hear the thick, leather saddle tightening underneath me as I leaned to the left and reached out toward the fence to inspect it. The fence inspection consisted of grabbing hold of a board or post, trying to move it back and forth to see if it was loose. As I got closer to the embankment, I noticed something unusual from the corner of my eye. I saw an arm moving gently with the current of Penny Creek...my view was partially blocked by the embankment, so I slowly nudged my horse using the reins, my eyes captivated by the lifeless arm. As if the embankment were a dirty sheet slowly being pulled off an object to reveal the contents underneath, more body parts were uncovered. A woman's bruised shoulder could be seen along with a scratch on her neck bleeding onto her collar bone and into the clear flowing water. Once in full view of the body, I could see she was wearing a white nightgown, the right strap had torn loose and waved back and forth with the current. Her head was resting face up in shallow water and her eyes were closed. Her auburn hair was moving with the flowing water in a gentle, but eerie motion.

Never before had I been so scared to the point of disorientation. Time seemed to freeze. Seeing a dead body like that froze my thoughts and the part of my brain responsible for movement. Booley was still examining the fence, gripping a wooden board every few paces with his rawhide gloves, unaware of my discovery. The uneasy feeling that seemed to slide over my body was evident as my voice cracked, finally able to holler out to my assistant.

"Booley! Uh, you better come here," I shouted, never taking my eyes off the dead body. He trotted over on Eros.

"What is it?" he asked as he gently pulled back on the reins and brought Eros to a halt. I motioned in the direction of the woman. His eyes followed my pointing finger. Once his weathered eyes fixed in on the dead woman, he muttered "Awww...this ain't good."

My brain seemed to have thawed out from the initial shock and I remember thinking that I should make sure she was dead. I swung my leg over the saddle and put both of my boots on the ground with one swift motion before hurrying down the embankment. Booley watched as the gentle sounds of the flowing creek were immediately disturbed by the splashes of my awkward steps on the shifting rocks under my feet. A tall, skinny fella like me always has problems keeping balance, let alone walking on an unpredictable creek bed.

"Miss!" I called out loud—but no response. My heart was racing.

The flesh around her eyelids had a soft purple hue next to her milky-white skin. Beside her head, blood waved in a flowing pattern, mixing with the water before taking off with the current. Her body looked as if it had been raked on several rocks as she floated down the creek. The section of the creek that divided my property with Mr. Grange's was somewhat shallow. It seemed that her body had run aground like a ship at sea coming too close to shore. I bent over and reached out my calloused hand, extending two fingers toward the side of her neck. "Miss!" I called out again before pressing my numb fingers to where I thought her pulse would be. I could feel elasticity in her cold skin as I pressed on the vein with a faint purple hue just above her collar bone. The uneasy feeling became pure shock when I couldn't feel her pulse.

"Well?" Booley asked sitting high atop Eros. I looked up at Booley from down in the bed of the creek, still perched over the woman's body.

"She's dead!" I yelled back as I immediately stood up.

Booley jolted his horse with a swift kick and "*yawed*" to get Eros moving.

"Where ya goin?" I yelled. Booley pulled on the reins slowing his horse down and turned his head toward me.

"Dang it, Elliott! You know as well as I do a black man ain't got no business bein' around a dead white girl." He "*yawed*" once more and jolted his horse before galloping away from the creek. I couldn't argue. Booley was as old as my father, and he remembered the days of black men being killed for the crimes of white men. A "patsy" I believed they were called. Leaving the woman in Penny Creek, I took careful steps on the submerged rocks underneath my boots and reached the muddy, pebble shore before grabbing roots and handfuls of grass to assist me in getting up the embankment. Sliding my foot into the stirrup, I swung my leg over the Coggshall saddle and seated myself while grabbing hold of the reins. With a swift kick and a boisterous *yaw*, I started my horse, Catcher, in the direction of the main house. I intended to go as fast as my horse would go, riding past Booley's little house and heading to the front of my property where the main house was located.

There were only a few families that had a telephone in those days, but I would say we were unlucky to have one. Neighbors kept coming to the house asking if they could make a quick telephone call. My father once shut the door in Mrs. Connor's face as a response to her polite question—she never asked again. When anyone in Scott County made calls back then, the phone rang to a group of women in a central office who always spoke softly and melodiously. They would connect us to the person or business we desired and supposedly got off the line although it was rumored that they listened in on our conversations from time to time. This time I didn't care if they listened in.

"Central on the line," the soft voice answered.

"This is Elliott Chapel. Get me Sheriff Crease."

2

The year I found the woman in Penny Creek, I was 35 and it was the same year my farm and business in Georgetown, Kentucky had been turned over to me by my father. He built the Chapel Farm and the business by training thoroughbred race horses and breeding champions from champion bloodlines. Georgetown was home to many horse farms as it was situated between Keeneland and Churchill Downs and we always considered them our home tracks. Over the years, horse owners sought out my father, and I remember a few times he had to turn people away when he had too many horses on his roster. Turning clients away was a luxury few trainers experienced, especially in Scott County. My father's ability to get the most out of each horse was the reason for his notoriety within the thoroughbred community, even if his methods were unorthodox. Horses can be stubborn creatures, but my father was even more stubborn. On occasion, with a horse that was uncooperative, he would endlessly repeat a discipline until the animal just gave up and became like putty in his hands. I recall one horse named Big Six who wouldn't allow anyone to put a bit in his mouth. He would kick, scream and fight when anyone came near him with a bit in their hand. My father used three grooms and a stable boy to pin the horse to the ground using twisted fiber rope and their body weight. I remember watching Dad lay down with his craggy face about one foot from the horse's mouth. He was lying on his side on the dusty ground getting dirt and debris all over his clothes as the sweat on his lean, muscular frame formed damp, oval shapes on the front and back of his shirt. His bony, resilient hands reached out, and his eyes focused as if he were working on the brakes of our truck. He would take the bit and place it in Big Six's mouth and take it out over and over and over. He did this from mid-morning until lunchtime. After lunch, they pinned the horse down again and repeated the process. The grooms and the stable boy tired themselves to the point of exhaustion using all their strength to restrain the animal. Around two o'clock, Big Six got the point.

The farm started out relatively small, but by the time it was turned over to me, it had about three hundred acres and two barns. The smaller barn was located near the main house and had only five stalls, but by the time I took the farm over, instead of stabling horses it was mostly used to store our small tractor with its "digger" attachment (some years later, they developed these into "back hoes"). The larger barn had 20 stalls and was next to the track on the backside of our property.

In 1928, one of the horses my father owned won the Belmont Stakes in New York upsetting the Kentucky Derby winner in that race. Shortly after the big win, he purchased the Noland's dairy farm which expanded our acreage immensely. The Noland family lived in a little house close to Penny Creek and when they moved out, I remember my father asking Booley how long he thought he would work for him to which he replied, "I 'spose as long as you'll have me." Since Booley lived in town, my father thought it would be better if his new assistant was close by, so he gave him the little house—rent free. The very next year, the same horse that won the Belmont Stakes was sold to a breeder, which paid for the miles of fencing around our property. There wasn't much of our three hundred acres that wasn't fenced in and the only exception was the forty acres located off the right side of the main house. That section of our farm was heavily wooded and Dad would cut one tree down a year for firewood. Sometimes a single tree would last two years depending on how long the winter would last.

Booley had been my father's training assistant for over twenty years and in the winter of 1939, he became my assistant. His full name was John Boole, but he introduced himself as Booley and even spelled his name with a "Y" on the end. Never in my life have I heard anyone speak the way that man did. It seemed his brain held every phrase and saying imaginable. I remember when I was mad at my father and my face would inevitably show it, Booley would say to me, "Put your face straight before the wind changes." I still don't know what he meant. I once came back from the county fair after having spent some time with a girl on my arm. When I walked up our gravel driveway to the front porch with a smile on my face, Booley said, "There's Elliott, grinning like a jackass eatin' saw briars." I've heard him use that phrase a few times, most often referring to me. The other members of my staff were the Bennett family who lived about a mile away, but I will get to them later. Before I get back to the dead girl in Penny Creek, I want to tell you about my father, Paul Chapel.

Dad was married to a woman named Gracie who was described to me by people who knew her as "enchanting." By February 1939, I was thirty-five years old, and up until that point I had only seen my father smile once. He was "three sheets to the wind" as Booley would say and in his alcohol-induced haze, Dad picked up a photograph of my mother who was standing next to a 1902 Winton race car they saw on display in New York. Dad just stared at the photo and a smile came across his face that I will never forget. I believe that she was put on this earth for my father to love and everyone in Scott County thought the same. Many residents have told me the way Dad was before she died, always laughing and smiling, joking with my mother and making her laugh. They would go to Fava's on special occasions like Valentine's Day or on their anniversary for a piece of pie and ice cream. Before they would leave for the Kentucky Derby, he would buy my mom a beautiful dress with a matching umbrella and long white gloves. It has been explained to me that she had a hat custom made for her and Dad would have a local shop make her a dress according to the colors of her hat. He didn't even attend the funeral when she passed. Some of his friends came by our home and tried to talk with him, but they were chased out with unspeakable threats. After my mom's death, he drank a lot and buried himself in his work without speaking a word to anyone.

Several weeks after my mom died, my aunt moved in and stayed in the small downstairs bedroom. She took care of me while Dad traveled during the racing season. She was an oversized lady with bushy, brown hair and round glasses that were too close to her eyes. You could see her eyelashes scraping the inside of the lenses when she blinked. When I was eight years old, Dad found her next to the clothes line out back. She was face down in the green grass with a loose, white sheet trapped underneath her thickset body. The sheet was blowing in the wind unable to escape. Dad didn't go to her funeral either. That was when I began helping him on the farm, and it was about that time that Booley answered the help wanted sign which hung on the mailbox by the driveway.

My father rarely spoke to me as I was the cause of my mother's death. After I was born, the doctors couldn't stop the excessive bleeding. When I was two days old, she died and it seemed that my father died as well, but in a different way. Paul Chapel left this earth and was replaced by a petulant, troubled man. I had taken his life away from him. "Gracie," I had heard him say to himself from time to time under his breath often while doing a menial chore such as peeling potatoes or conditioning a saddle. I think his mind would escape to the time before I was born and images of my mom would float in front of him. I could almost see him dreaming of her as he held a potato in his hands. The knife would slide peel after peel off the thick spud, never cutting his thumb as he gazed out the window with the sound of the running water splashing into the metal sink.

The day my mother died, a gray cloud moved over our farm and there it stayed. When he retired, he handed the farm over to me and spent his days asleep in his chair in the living room or on the old couch on the back porch. The back-porch couch used to be in the living room and when it was replaced with a newer one, Dad insisted it be moved outside underneath the porch roof. It was upholstered in a yellow and brown plaid pattern with various stains from Dad spilling his favorite brand of whiskey. The couch would get wet if the wind blew the rain hard enough to reach underneath the roof of the porch, but for the most part the couch was dry.

My father wasn't completely cold hearted as he did have a dog that he took care of in those days. In 1927, a woman from a neighboring farm gave away four redbone coonhound puppies and we were lucky enough to get one of them. Dad didn't think so and told the lady if she left the dog with him, he would send it to the sausage factory. I was enrolled at the University of Kentucky when "Banner" the red-bone coonhound was dropped off at the farm and it was Booley that told me that Dad ignored the puppy for three days. He would go in and out of the house leaving the pup on the back porch. No food. No water. Booley once tried to take the dog back to his place, but Dad told him no.

"Leave that pecker-head alone," he growled.

Booley let him be and the puppy was doomed to starve to death on the back porch. I guess it was on the third day when Dad fed the puppy a few strips of bacon and on the fourth day, he let Banner in the house. When I came home from college, there were two bowls in the kitchen on the floor side by side and I don't think I ever walked by the bowls when there wasn't water or food in them—Dad was very meticulous about keeping them filled. Banner slept on several old quilts that were placed next to Dad's nightstand and it wasn't un-common to hear Banner in the middle of the night barking in his sleep. By the time 1939 rolled around, Banner was older than my fa-ther in dog years. Whenever he walked, his celery stalk legs shifted forward while his head hung low as if fatigue had taken up residence in his elderly canine body. As he aged, his skin had grown looser and his drooping eyelids exposed the reddened rims of his old eyes. His reddish, brown fur was turning a light gray on his ears, followed by the hair around his mouth and then on the top of his head. He took to sleeping for hours at a time by my dad's side and when I would walk by them on the porch or in the living room, Banner's tail would slowly wag as his eyes followed me. His head wouldn't move nor any other part of his body, just his old tail and eyes. Some people might think it is a cruel thing to do to a dog, but Dad would let Banner take laps of whiskey from the bottle. This was usually when there was only one gulp left and Banner seemed to enjoy whiskey. During the years when my father was away taking horses to various race tracks, Banner spent most of his time under the willow tree just off the back porch. He would stay in the shade during the day and at night he would curl up on the old back porch couch. People in town that had to deal with my father from time to time—a bank teller or the manager of the local feed store—generally disliked my father and never would have believed that he cared for a dog. Paul Chapel wasn't well liked in Scott County after I was born, but I suppose that the people around town who remembered how he used to be just felt sorry for him.

My father created a very successful business and treated people with a fair and direct demeanor. I think most people in the thorough-bred community saw him as a serious businessman and a remarkable thoroughbred trainer when really he was constantly grieving over the loss of the one person who made his life worthwhile. I often got the feeling that he would trade my life (if given the opportunity) in order to bring my mother back. I am sure he asked God to answer that prayer more than once. I live with the fact that if it wasn't for me, she would still be alive.

Now you might think that this story has to do with my pain and misery of growing up with a man like my father, but that story would not be worth telling. This story starts with the dead girl in Penny Creek; at least I thought she was dead when I found her.

3

Sheriff Crease and Dr. Thomas arrived at the scene followed by the director of the funeral home (we didn't have a coroner in Scott County back then). I was never a big fan of Sheriff Crease as he treated most people like they were beneath him, and he was notorious for his cruel nature. Doctor Thomas, on the other hand, was a very polite and kind man and the only doctor in Scott County who would make house calls. I was standing near the embankment with my arms crossed, watching Doc take careful steps as he walked down the steep slope toward Penny Creek. He had taken his stethoscope out of his black medical bag and was carrying it in his left hand.

"You touched her?" Sheriff Crease asked me without taking his eyes off of Doc.

"Yes, just to see if she was alive," I replied.

Everyone in town knew the story about the Howard dog. The Howard family had bought a Beagle puppy from a breeder in Lexington. When they brought it back to the house and placed it in the fenced in backyard, it barked several times throughout the night. Unfortunately, Sheriff Crease was their next door neighbor and he ended the pup's barking with a bullet to the head. He even bragged about it at Bullock's Barber Shop saying that he called the puppy over and it came running with his tail wagging. As soon as the puppy got close, he pulled the trigger.

Sheriff Crease took a few steps toward the embankment, taking his chubby hands off his thick waist. His left bear paw hand slid into his pants pocket while the other hand tended to the toothpick cradled between his tobacco stained teeth. The faint cloud that appeared in front of his face when he exhaled into the cold air smelled of mint and tobacco. Guthrie's General Store stocked Grey Wolf Chewing Tobacco on the account of Sheriff Crease's addiction. The tobacco was sold in small tins that caused a rectangle shape to protrude from inside Sheriff Crease's left shirt pocket. Along with his habit came the unsightly brown saliva that hung on his lower lip after he spit wayward toward the ground. He was a pudgy man who had an insatiable love for high calorie foods and it wasn't unusual to see him at the lunch counter at Guthrie's eating a big fat sandwich slathered in mayonnaise. I wasn't standing very close to Sheriff Crease, yet I could still hear a faint wheeze whenever he breathed air through his chunky throat that slightly constricted his windpipe. I looked at Crease briefly when I first heard the distinct wheeze before my eyes darted back to Doc wading in Penny Creek.

"You know who she is? She looks familiar," Doc yelled out.

"No, I don't think so," I said. Sheriff Crease and I watched Dr. Thomas as he made his way along the rocks partly submerged in the water with his arms stretched out to his side to help him maintain his balance. He wasn't as nimble as I was stepping on the creek bottom. The loose rocks shifted under his weight and he fell on his rear end with a splash.

"Shit!" he yelled. Sheriff Crease laughed while Doc struggled in the water.

"You just have yourself a seat anywhere you like, Doc!"...Crease wasn't known for his funny one-liners.

"Damn it! My ass is frozen," Doc yelled as he quickly got up.

Standing next to me and Crease was the funeral director of Georgetown. His name was William Cooper although it wasn't unusual to hear him referred to as "Cooper" or "Coop." His old jalopy of a hearse had somehow made it all the way from our driveway to the back of our property. Mr. Cooper was a kind-hearted man that I only knew from running into at Guthrie's or at Fava's. He was a tall man and dressed like a gentlemen, always wearing a tie and a hat that was always clean and maintained. I once asked him about the hat he was wearing and he told me it was a "Dobbs Dutton style hat with a wide grosgrain ribbon." I wasn't sure what he meant by all that but he always took pride in the hats that he wore. His thin, gray moustache always reminded me of a fuzzy tent caterpillar. I could have easily convinced a child that a critter wiggled its way onto Cooper's face and parked itself above his top lip.

Sheriff Crease and I watched as Dr. Thomas put his stethoscope on her chest. Mr. Cooper was pulling the stretcher out of the back of his hearse. Doc listened and readjusted the worn silver disc on her chest.

"She's alive!" Doc Thomas yelled. His eyes were as big as dinner plates.

"What?" I yelled.

"Yeah, what?" Crease added before spitting tobacco infected saliva toward his left.

"How can that be? She wasn't breathing when I found her," I said.

"Well, she's alive now! You wanna help me or stand there and try to figure it out?" Doc replied.

We had her up and out of the creek and into the back of the hearse within a minute or so. Doc and I crouched next to her draping our coats over her body.

"Damn, her skin is so cold," Doc said doing his best to tuck the folds of our coats around and underneath her arms and legs. "Her heart rate is very slow. She may not make it," Doc said before closely examining the wounds on her head.

"We going to the hospital or the Chapel house?" Cooper asked from the driver's seat. I peered out the front window as the vehicle bounced and jostled over the uneven terrain. The loud rattling sounds came from the old ramshackle dashboard in the front and the jostling wheels from underneath the gurney as we hit every bump and shallow hole in the ground.

Doc noticed smoke rising from Booley's chimney and dissipating into the morning sky. He shouted out to Mr. Cooper, "Better park it in front of the cottage there. We need warmth and we need it now!" Doc used his thin index finger to open the woman's left eye. He peered into it as if he was inspecting the flaws in a gem. "Chapel, were your fingers numb when you checked her pulse?" Doc asked as the hearse took a hard bounce, forcing us to brace ourselves by pushing up on the roof of the bouncing vehicle.

"I guess. I wasn't wearing gloves," I answered and I continued to brace myself for the next severe jolt. As the rattletrap hearse rolled over the uneven ground, the interior continued to shake and clatter making it difficult for Doc to check her pulse and examine her wounds. When the hearse came to a stop outside Booley's little house, Coop moved as fast as his tired, worn body would let him. He got out of the driver's side of the hearse and then moved swiftly to the back, opening the big swinging back door. Sheriff Crease parked his police car just behind the hearse and cut the engine.

Booley was reading a book at his small kitchen table when we burst in with the limp woman on Mr. Cooper's tattered stretcher.

"What are you doin' bringin' that dead girl in here?" Booley asked as he stood up. Instead of answering him, we hoisted her body up off the stretcher. I had her arms while Doc had her legs.

"Be careful. Don't bend her joints if you can help it," Doc said. "I don't know why, but I am sure I read that in a hypothermia article somewhere," he said as we set her down on the soft cushions of Booley's couch.

"Hypo what?" I asked, but I never got a response.

"What is this dead white woman doin' on my couch?" Booley asked as his face scrunched together in a puzzled expression. Mr. Cooper took the stretcher back out to the hearse and Sheriff Crease closed the door behind him.

"She ain't dead Booley," I said. Doc then started to push one corner of the couch closer to the fireplace and I followed by pushing the other side.

"Booley, give me all the blankets you got!" Doc yelled out. Sheriff Crease opened the door, letting Mr. Cooper back inside and quickly closed it, keeping the cold air from wafting inside. Doc looked at me as if he was my superior. "Elliott, keep that fire going. More logs," I picked up two logs from the side of the fireplace and threw them on top of the flaming stack of wood.

"Isn't this Mayor Evans' wife? It kinda looks like her," Dr. Thomas asked as he took an arm full of cotton blankets from Booley and threw them onto the plank wood floor next to the couch. He bent over taking the first blanket and unfolded it in a hurry.

"She kinda looks like Ellie Evans, now that I see her close up," Mr. Cooper said. "I just saw her a few days ago at the store."

"Yeah it's her," Sheriff Crease confirmed. He had taken off his lawman's hat and I could see the graying hair that had been concealed underneath. I suppose back then he was in his late forties, perhaps early fifties. I distinctly remember the way Crease confirmed the woman's identity when he said it was the mayor's wife. The way he said it led me to believe he knew it was her the whole time.

"I have treated her before, but she looks different, and I think she cut her hair. I treated her about a year ago," Dr. Thomas said as he positioned the blankets over his near frozen patient. "Someone should notify the mayor. Could you go call him, Sheriff?" Crease immediately pointed his pudgy finger at Doc.

"Hey! I don't work for you. You don't tell me what to do!"

"Sorry, I just…" Doc tried to explain.

"Everybody stay here." Crease opened the door to the cold air and closed it behind him in anger. The room was silent until Booley spoke up.

"That man would punch his mama for a dollar and a milkshake," he said from a darkened corner of the room. His thumb was wedged in between the pages of his book, keeping his place. Mr. Cooper chuckled at Booley's comment.

"Whatcha readin' Booley?" Cooper asked.

"Merchant of Venice."

"Shakespeare?"

"Yeah," Booley confirmed. Doc Thomas was checking over Mrs.

Evans and peeled off her night gown while using the blanket to cover her areas the other men in the room shouldn't be privy to.

"How is that woman alive?" Booley asked in complete shock.

"My theory is the cold water and air slowed down her heart rate. It's pretty interesting actually," Doc said as he tossed Mrs. Evans' torn nightgown on the ground near the fireplace.

"Shylock, Antonio, Portia? Is that right?" Cooper asked Booley.

"S'right," he replied.

"Read it a long time ago. I remember it."

"Is she going to be all right?" I asked.

"I don't know," Doc replied. "We'll see I guess." After a long absence, Sheriff Crease opened the door.

"Mayor is on his way," Crease said as he cupped his hands and blew warm air into the formed pocket. "They told me on the phone that Mrs. Evans was in a car accident last night on the Tenpenny Bridge. She must have fallen into Penny Creek and been carried by the current. One of my deputies said he found the car this morning," Crease said as he fished a small note pad from his back pocket. He flipped it open and read from his chicken scratch. "Her car slammed into the railing of the Tenpenny Bridge and drove into Penny Creek. It's not a far fall from the bridge, only a few feet. The car submerged half way, nose first," Crease said as he flipped the note pad closed.

"Geez, that current must have carried her about a mile or so huh?" Doc said, very surprised that she didn't drown.

"About two thirds of a mile," I said.

"Her son was taken to Ford Memorial last night and said he will be fine," Crease added. Ford Memorial was actually John Graves Ford Memorial Hospital, but everyone around town called it by its shorter name.

"Her son was in the accident too? Goodness," Cooper said touching the hairs of his caterpillar moustache.

We waited by the fire and I kept throwing logs into the fireplace to keep the heat going. Up until that point, I hadn't seen the mayor in person, but I knew what he looked like from the front page of the local newspaper. At that time, there were rumors going around town that the mayor was going to leave Georgetown and move to Louisiana. Apparently, there was a staff position open to work under Governor Leche and Mayor Evans had thrown his hat in the ring. Booley had a passion for reading the newspaper and listening to the news on the radio. He was always up to date with current events, and it was Booley who later told me that the governor of Louisiana "was as corrupt as a bunny with two peckers"-another one of his sayings.

Mayor Evans drove up to Booley's house and through the small front window I could see the shiny chrome fender and the circular headlights of his 1938 Buick Sedan. I heard the car door shut, then watched the tarnished, brass doorknob spin before Mayor Evans charged through the front door prompting Sheriff Crease to walk over and take his coat and hat. It seemed to me that the mayor had full expectations of Crease walking over to him as if he were a hired servant, taking his coat and hat from him just like a butler.

"Hello Mayor," Doc said as he stood up. Doc's greeting was received and recognized with a nod from the mayor. I had casually glanced toward Mr. Cooper and could see the look in his eyes and the way the wrinkles pressed into his face with disapproval. It was obvious that he didn't care much for the mayor.

Mayor Evans walked over by the fireplace and stared at his wife on the couch as he removed his gloves by pulling on the individual fingers. He was dressed in a three-piece suit and his shoes looked polished and expensive. Just by the way he dressed, one could tell that he was a wealthy man. The people around town knew that his family made their money from bootlegging, but it was never talked about except in sewing circles and soft spoken gossip at town picnics. The room was pretty quiet and Doc seemed as if he was waiting to be spoken to, so I started the conversation.

"Hi, Mayor," I said. "I found her a little over an hour ago in the creek." He looked at me from the corners of his eyes, never turning his head. He looked older than he was since his sandy blonde hair had receded leaving little coverage on top.

"You did, huh?" was his response. "Let's get her into my car."

"Oh no! Mayor!" Doc said. "She can't be moved. She needs to stay here or she could die. I wouldn't even send the ambulance over. She needs to lie perfectly still and kept warm." The Mayor looked at Doc with a puzzled face or maybe he didn't believe Doc, I'm not sure. "She is in a very fragile state. She may not even make it through the day. If we take her out into the cold, she wouldn't survive for sure."

"So, should I come back tomorrow?" The Mayor asked. This man, who I barely knew seemed to treat his comatose wife like a distant relative that no one liked. He looked at her on the couch, never getting within range of touching her.

"Really depends on if she is awake or not. Even then, I would like to see how she's doing before we move her and even if she is able to be moved, we should take her to Ford Memorial." The Mayor exhaled and took out his timepiece as if he was severely inconvenienced. He glanced at it and returned it to his vest pocket.

"Fine. I will return tomorrow. Sheriff can I see you outside?"

Mayor Evans walked out the front door followed by Sheriff Crease who was still holding his coat and hat.

Mr. Cooper moved closer to Mrs. Evans to get a good look. "She's a pretty girl. Her color seems to be coming back a little or it could be the orange glow of the fire, I can't tell," Cooper said. He turned his head and looked at Doc while he reached his wrinkled hand out and grabbed his Dobbs Dutton hat that was on the table next to him. With his kind eyes and a look of sincerity, he said in a tired, aged voice "I hope you won't need me." He put on his hat and headed for the front door. "Call me if you do."

"See ya, Coop!" Doc said.

"Nice seein' you again, Mr. Cooper," I whispered.

"You too Chapel," he said quietly with a wink before he closed the door. Doc needed gauze and peroxide to bandage up Mrs. Evans' head and had requested a hot water bottle to place near her feet. Booley went with me to the main house as he was still afraid of being around a half dead white girl.

The main house was located at the front of the property and could be seen from the two lane road leading into town. The house was built about six months before I was born and was considered a pretty big house in those days. After mom died, Dad needed a lot of space, and I don't think I could have grown up with him if I didn't have another floor to retreat to when he was around.

The kitchen had too many cupboards or at least we didn't have enough pots and pans to fill them, but we did use two cupboards to store the extra firewood for the fireplace to keep the logs dry. The dining room did have a table and chairs, but wasn't ever used unless my dad or I had stacks of paperwork to fill out, which was only once or twice a month. The living room had a large fireplace with a big rug in front of it and a rocking chair which Dad sat in all the time and was known as "his chair" which I never sat in it unless he was out of town.

Near the door to the patio was a radio that was the size of a liquor cabinet. It was a Stromberg-Carlson Model 68, 10-tube, 3-band radio and as heavy as a piano. Dad and I went to John B. Penn & Co. and purchased the behemoth on a Saturday the previous summer. Booley would listen to the news and ballgames. Sometimes, Dad would join us if the Yankees were playing. The bedrooms were upstairs with a very small one downstairs which my aunt used for eight years. Dad never went in my room and I never went in his.

On the second floor was a bathroom that served the entire house. Dad had it built with two sinks side by side. I guess the idea was to allow him and my mom to be able to get ready in the mornings at the same time. After I was born, no two people had ever used those sinks at the same time. The best part about the main house was the indoor plumbing and I was fortunate that I grew up with it, so I didn't know any different. Even though there wasn't a female residing in our home, we were forced to keep the toilet lid down as Banner would sneak in the bathroom and drink the cold water from the toilet bowl. Redbone Coonhounds have long, thick, bright pink tongues and if the bathroom window was left open and Dad was outside in his garden, he could hear the ferocious lapping of water by Banner's long tongue.

"Get outta there Banner! Get!" He would yell in the direction of the opened window often holding a garden trowel and wiping sweat from his forehead.

The gauze and peroxide was kept in a cupboard in the kitchen. I gathered what Doc asked for while Booley went into the living room where Dad and Banner were listening to a radio show and dozing off every so often. (The main part of Dad's retirement plan.)

"We found a woman in the creek," I heard Booley say. I slipped the gauze into my coat pocket as I listened.

"I saw Cooper's hearse," Dad responded.

"She ain't dead, she's just frozen. Doc is thawin' her out now at my place," Booley said as I found the water bottle.

When anyone talked to Dad, his questions were to the point and direct. When he and Booley played checkers on the back porch, I don't think they said more than three words to each other.

After delivering the needed supplies to Doc, we left him to watch over Mrs. Evans throughout the night. The next morning, I got up and fixed some coffee. Booley stayed the night at the main house and was still asleep on the couch when there was a knock at the front door. I thought it was going to be a neighbor asking to use our phone until I saw Mayor Evans standing on the front porch with a black woman.

"Morning, Mr. Chapel," Mayor Evans said as soon as I opened the door. This time he was dressed in a three piece suit with French cuffs and a gold colored tie.

"Mornin' Mayor."

"Doc says Mrs. Evans shouldn't be moved. If it's no trouble, I would like Harriet here to stay with my wife. Say hello, Harriet."

"Hello, Mr. Chapel," she said as she hung her head and looked at me from the top of her eyes. She looked to be wearing a uniform of some kind under her tattered winter coat. The hair on top of her head was pinned up and looked like a large bowl which made her head look abnormal compared to the size of her small, skinny frame.

"No trouble. Nice to meet you, Harriet."

"I have paid Doctor Thomas to come by and check on Mrs. Evans. When she is awake I will have her off your property as soon as possible." He reached into his coat pocket and took out several folded bills. "I trust that this money here will see to any inconvenience you have encountered." I took the money and held it in my hands.

"Would you like to come in?" I asked after realizing I hadn't offered yet.

"No sir. I am going to see Harriet to the house then I am leaving for Baton Rouge, Louisiana. Won't be back for five weeks." Up until that point, the rumors about the mayor going to work for the governor of Louisiana were only rumors.

"Look, we aren't inconvenienced. You don't need to pay us, Mayor," I said as he and Harriet stepped off the front porch. I started walking toward him.

"Keep the money Chapel. Seems that you're the only one in town who isn't asking for it," he said laughing. He continued to walk away and I looked down as I opened my hand. I walked back inside the house and closed the door behind me. After unfolding the money, I counted two twenty dollar bills.

4

Outpost was a thoroughbred colt owned by a man named Verris Wade. Transcon Railroad was started by Mr. Wade in the early 1900s and grew to be the main transportation for shipping oil in the United States. He possessed an unwavering personality and couldn't get enough of winning business deals, a game of poker or a round of golf. While his interests were broad there was one that stood out among the others, the sport of thoroughbred racing. Outpost was sired by a horse named Vagrant Spender who held records at three race tracks and had the highest stud fee at that time. At the time I took Mr. Wade's horse under a training agreement, he was rumored to be working with Howard Hughes to boost radio receivers and transmitters in contemporary aircraft and railcars.

If you're wondering how I was able to acquire one of the highest profile clients in the region, I have to tell you that it wasn't my doing. Not one horse my father trained carried over from his roster to mine. Dad trained anywhere from eight to thirty horses at a time, and with a little luck I was able to secure three horses in June of 1938 before he retired and I took over. Even though I didn't take on any horses from my father's roster, it was his reputation that enabled me to convince owners of my ability. By the time the horses came to the farm, they were already broken and ready to be trained for their first race at Keeneland the following April. The last horse to arrive at my farm that year was Outpost.

Verris Wade had heard of my father and decided that once he purchased Outpost, he would have two men drive the horse to Chapel
Farms with a note and a check. On a Sunday evening in June, I awoke
from a nap on the couch to the sound of screeching brakes on a 1938
Studebaker K10 Fast Transport Express truck. The truck arrived in
the driveway with a horse trailer in tow and Booley and I went to
greet them.

"Name's Chuck Haley," the man said as he reached out to shake my
hand. His face was long and thin with deep crevasses around his mouth.
The crevasses expanded and contracted with every word he spoke.

"Nice truck," I said.

"Thanks," Chuck was dressed in an old pair of jeans and wore a
tattered vest over a stained, white shirt. The Texas cattleman style
hat on his head coupled with his clothes and brand new truck made
him look like a cowboy with money in his pocket. "Here," he said as
he reached out his other hand. I took the piece of note paper from
Chuck's hand and opened it. I was a little confused. I had thought
he was a horse trainer coming to bring me a horse to bury in the field,
but instead I was handed a note and a check. The note was typed
and the stationery felt like fine linen paper.

Dear Mr. Chapel,

My apologies for my assuming nature. Please take my horse,
Outpost, and train him to the best of your ability. I have
enclosed a check that should more than pay for the provisions.
I will be in touch soon. I can be reached at the phone number above.

     Sincerely,

     Verris Wade

I looked up from the note and Chuck was smiling.

"You're a lucky man," he said as he pointed to the check. I looked at the amount and was astonished. That check took care of my farm expenses for an entire year. Either Mr. Wade didn't know how much it cost to train a horse or he was being very generous. "Well, let's get him unloaded," Chuck said as he clapped his hands and rubbed them together.

We put Outpost in the twenty-stall barn that was located next to the track with the other horses. The other three thoroughbreds I was training didn't come from a prestigious bloodline like Outpost, rather they came from a mediocre gene pool of less expensive bloodlines that were purchased by a group of investors. It was rare in the thirties for a single person to own a prestigious horse such as Outpost. Normally, the expense was shared by a group of investors.

Next to Outpost's stall was Priced Opportunity, a horse purchased by a law firm and shared by four attorneys from Lexington. On the other side of Price was Beyond The Pale. He was bred at a farm outside of Louisville and was owned by a bank president and several of his wealthy acquaintances. Three investors from Ohio who routinely invested in horses owned Ranger's Cape and did me a favor by letting me train him.

So if I recall correctly, in June of 1938, eight months before I found Mrs. Evans in Penny Creek, I had Priced Opportunity, Beyond The Pale, and Ranger's Cape. The owners of the three horses gave me a chance because they knew my father and I knew them just by being part of the racing community. Outpost however, was a mystery when he arrived on the farm. In fact, I thought it was a mistake. Before the two gentlemen left my farm, I made them stay in front of the house while I made a phone call. Soon after I had dialed the number on

Mr. Wade's note, a polite woman answered.

"Mr. Wade's office."

"Hi, I am looking to speak with Mr. Wade. My name is Elliott Chapel."

"Just a moment." A minute passed and she came back on the line. "I am sorry I do not have your name on the list. Who are you?"

"Elliott Chapel."

"Who are you with?"

"I'm not with anybody. I am Elliott Chapel, and I am training Mr. Wade's horse."

"Oh! I'm sorry I will put you right though. I am terribly sorry." I immediately heard a loud *click*, then a loud voice came through the line with one word.

"Yeah!" the voice said. The way he said that one word implied that I was to make it quick.

"Mr. Wade, this is Elliott Chapel in Georgetown, Kentucky and Outpost arrived safely."

"Good to hear," was his response. An uncomfortable silence followed and I could tell he was shuffling papers as he was speaking with me.

"Mr. Wade, I am calling because I believe you meant for my father, Paul Chapel, to train your horse and you may not have heard that he retired."

"Okay."

"Well, sir, if that is what you meant then Outpost wouldn't be trained by my father, he would be trained by me."

"I see."

"I just didn't want you to be under the impress…" I started to say until I was interrupted.

"Son, are you as good as your father?"

"Uh, yes sir" I said and at that point, to be honest, I wasn't sure.

"Then carry on." A click followed his response and that ended the telephone call. I went outside and thanked the guys waiting for my return. As they drove off, I reached inside my pocket, feeling the check between my fingers. Since Booley was out of a private residence for the time being, I gave him the two twenty dollar bills from Mayor Evans.

When Mrs. Evans was on my farm, it wasn't an inconvenience to anyone except Booley since he had to stay at the main house and sleep on the couch in the living room. Harriet, the Evans' maid and Doc Thomas were compensated. I had horses to train and things to do and I sure didn't need to be inconvenienced. However, that was about to change.

5

I was returning from getting the mail at the end of the driveway when Doc Thomas parked his car. He had just returned from checking on Mrs. Evans who was still in a coma in Booley's little house.

"We've got a problem," he said as he got out of his car. In 1933, Chevrolet had offered two versions of the same car. The Eagle had more horsepower than the Mercury and had a few more luxuries. The Eagle was intended for upscale car buyers while the Mercury served low-budget buyers. Doc Thomas had purchased the latter. "Harriet had to leave," he said as he closed the driver's side door.

"What?" I asked. Doc's shiny dress shoes with thin shoelaces crunched the pebbles beneath his feet as he walked toward me.

"I went in to check on Mrs. Evans, and she was gone."

"Mrs. Evans is gone?"

"No, Harriet."

"Where did she go?" I asked. Doc held up a note and handed it to me.

"She wrote that her mother had taken ill. She quit and left for Mississippi." The note was written on the back of an old, empty envelope. "She spelled Mississippi wrong," Doc added.

"What do we do?" I asked taking notice of the spelling error. Doc followed me to the kitchen in the main house and we both telephoned a few women we knew who lived in town.

After we were turned down numerous times, politely of course, I volunteered to stay the night with Doc's patient. Obviously it was not proper to for a man to sleep in the same room with a woman he wasn't married to (let alone a woman he did not know and who was in a coma) but we didn't have a choice. It was supposed to only be for one night, but it turned into three nights. However, I cannot say I didn't enjoy the break; being in the same house as my father wasn't exactly living in paradise. It felt like I was alone in Booley's little house and I would get up in the mornings and fix breakfast in Booley's little kitchen. The wood-burning stove sat opposite from the ice box and there wasn't any running water in the house. When the Nolands resided there, they dug a well and installed a hand pump just outside the front door that provided water for their household. Even though you could drink the water straight out of the well, Booley would still boil a gallon and put it in a pitcher.

I bent down in Booley's dark kitchen and reached out for the handle on the ice box. I opened the door and removed a few slices of my favorite breakfast food. Bacon. The best part was not worrying about running into Dad who would often disapprove of how crispy I cooked the bacon. He would express his distaste for my culinary preference, somehow without saying a word.

While I stayed at Booley's house, I cooked crispy bacon on the wood-burning stove and read *The Georgetown Times* at the table without anyone nearby, except for Mrs. Evans of course. *The Georgetown Times* was a small newspaper, usually filled with articles that reported on social events, the city's budget and the occasional obituary. The newsprint had a distinct smell and when you opened the paper, you could smell the printer's ink wafting in front of your face. The first night, I slept pretty well for not sleeping in my own bed and I would get up a few times in the night to check on Mrs. Evans before I threw more logs onto the fire. I would walk slowly toward the sofa and peek over at the battered and bruised Mrs. Evans. The fire glowed and popped giving off heat and light inside Booley's small house. When I nudged the fiery logs with the iron poker, I would look back over my shoulder at her resting, expecting to see her open her eyes at the sounds coming from the fireplace. I would purposely make sounds with the fireplace poker to see if I could wake her. She never moved. I stood there thinking I could clap my hands or make a hoot noise to cause her to wake from her deep sleep. Instead I opted to make one more noise by dropping a fire log directly onto the hardwood floor. *THUMP!* The loud sounds didn't stir Mrs. Evans who remained as still as a statue.

The next morning, Mrs. Thomas, Doc's wife came over to watch Mrs. Evans while I worked at the track with the horses during the day. I remember having to cut firewood into smaller pieces so that Mrs. Thomas' flimsy woman hands could pick up the firewood and fling the lighter pieces onto the flaming stack. Once three o'clock in the afternoon rolled around, I would make my way back to Booley's house. Mrs. Thomas would go back home expecting to take over the next morning. On the second night, I held a mirror in front of Mrs. Evans' face thinking that she might have passed. I was extremely fearful that she might die during my watch and I would somehow be blamed for her death. The mirror fogged up as she breathed and I went back to bed, glad she was still alive.

On the third morning of my stay, Mrs. Thomas came over as she had the previous two days, but this time with knitting needles, a bag of yarn, and a book.

"Good day to you Mr. Chapel," she said on my way out. I was always annoyed by the way she spoke to me. She said "good day" to me in a snooty, belittling tone. Mrs. Thomas was standing in the doorway and I turned my head to her as I stepped off the front porch.

"You too, Mrs. Thomas. You might want to pick your feet up. I saw two mice running around this morning." She didn't know I was joking and I refused to tell her otherwise. Her proper attitude always got under my skin and I enjoyed causing her a little grief. I kept my head down trying to conceal my smile as I walked away.

"Good lord! Mice?" she said, still keeping her proper attitude, as she set down her things just outside the front door. I kept walking toward the track, and I could hear her small feet take a few steps on the wooden porch. She raised her voice to make sure I heard her.

"Are you certain? Mr. Chapel?" she said in a very haughty manner. I turned around and yelled out over my shoulder,

"Just keep an eye out!"

"Inside or outside, Mr. Chapel?"

I continued walking and ignored her. I smiled all the way to the track thinking about her standing up on a chair looking around the room. I couldn't wait to tell Booley.

Booley was called the "assistant trainer" which really meant "barn manager." All grooms and exercise riders listened to the assistant trainer because he was their boss. In the early thirties, Dad got a call from the *The Georgetown Times* saying they had a family in their office looking for work. It wasn't uncommon back then for the paper to call around town before placing an ad and being that we lived in a small town, everybody knew everybody else's business. The Bennett family lived in Great Crossing, Kentucky and were experienced grooms. I suppose they weren't getting the hours or pay to make ends meet which is how they came to be at our farm. They worked from five in the morning to about noon every day but Monday.

There were five members of the Bennett family and they generally operated under Booley's direction although they never needed to be told twice what needed to be done. Jim and Sarah Bennett were in their mid-forties and were hired as grooms to clean out the stalls, adhere to the feeding schedule, groom the horses and occasionally help in the event of a birth when there was one. Their two children were very young and were given a compulsory education by their mother instead of being taught at a school. Kenny and Cara Bennett were around nine years old then and did more around the barn than I did at that age. Jim Bennett's brother, Palmer, was a short, skinny fella. Although he was too heavy to be a jockey, he was light enough to be an exercise rider. The members of the Bennett family, Booley, and I made a pretty good team and our daily routine was down to a science. To their credit, I think not one member of the Bennett family minded that a black man was their superior, a testament to the kindness and equality that they always seemed to carry with them.

When I arrived at the track after the second night of sleeping in Booley's house, Ranger's Cape was getting a bath from both Jim and Sarah. Sometimes Sarah's hair was braided in two pigtails, but on that particular day she had one long braid. She would bring the braid out in front of her mouth and hold onto it with her teeth when she bent over to place the sponge in the soapy bucket. Sarah would often keep her pigtails secure in the same manner. It wasn't often, but sometimes Sarah would ride alongside Palmer if we were breezing the horses two abreast or single file. She was about 120 pounds and made a good back-up exercise rider. I was grateful she was experienced enough to take the horses out and breeze them a few quarter miles with a speed of twenty-seven seconds, give or take. I knew that when I acquired even one more horse, I would need to hire another exercise rider.

The sun was rising over the horizon and the steam rolled off of Ranger as he was being sponged with a mixture of warm water and soap. He was sold at auction with the promise of being a distance runner since he had the proper conformation as a yearling. He also had his problems too, but more on that later.

"Mr. Chapel, Ranger's about set for the day. Outpost will need a cool down, and Pale is ready to go," Jim said, grunting as he bent over and took hold of a wooden bucket. He gripped the top and bottom before tipping the contents onto the ground around his boots. He righted himself and placed his right hand on the small of his back as he stretched.

Jim Bennett and I frequently wore cowboy hats, especially around the track. A couple of years ago I was talking to Jim at the county fair and we decided to try the shooting gallery. As we both stood side by side with pellet guns, a photographer took our picture from behind us. It ended up in *The Georgetown Times* with the caption *A couple of cowboys take aim at the shooting gallery.* Sarah Bennett cut it out and hung it in the barn where it stayed for years.

Jim set the bucket aside and dried his hands off with a towel before he removed his cowboy hat. He wiped the sweat off his forehead with the flannel sleeve of his left arm and put his hat back on and motioned toward the barn.

"We need a couple of bales down from the loft before we leave," Jim said.

"I got it," I said as I started toward the entrance of the barn. I looked over at Kenny Bennett, the youngest Bennett child.

"Did you hot walk Outpost earlier this morning?" I asked just making conversation.

"No sir, my mom did." I watched as Kenny used a soap conditioner to clean a saddle while his sister Cara rinsed out a bucket. For being kids, they were hard workers and could keep up with the pace of their mom and dad. They would play around the barn and chase each other every once in a while, but that was expected.

After I threw down several bales of straw from the barn loft, I walked over to the track and rested my arms on the rail. Outpost was trotting around the track and I carefully watched his gait. He was seventeen hands high and his coat was pure black. His muscular structure made him look menacing and ominous as if he belonged to a fierce knight in a medieval army and had seen many battles. In truth, he was a two year old who had yet to run a maiden race and I could only hope that his powerful frame would perform on the track. I am very familiar with horses that were sired by great thoroughbreds and sometimes you get less than favorable results—of course you hope for a great horse, but experience tells you not to count on it. Outpost certainly looked to be a great horse early on in his training.

In the same way that Outpost's coat was completely black, Beyond The Pale's was white. A white thoroughbred is very rare and whenever I heard of one, it was always located on the east coast or in Great Britain, so it was really unusual to have a horse like Pale on our farm in Kentucky. He was next in line to go out on the track as Booley had just readied him with an exercise saddle. My head turned suddenly from the horses when I heard a screeching coming from behind me in the distance. When I saw Mrs. Thomas walking hurriedly toward the track, I jogged in her direction to meet her half way.

"Call my husband!" I heard her yell. "Mrs. Evans is awake!"

6

"Central on the line."

"Doctor Thomas, please."

I told Doc the good news and I immediately rode my horse, Catcher, back to Booley's house. I slowly opened the heavy wooden front door and stepped inside, taking off my hat. Mrs. Thomas was standing up next to the fireplace like she had just thrown a log onto the existing flaming stack. Mrs. Evans was sitting up on one end of the couch holding her hand in front of her mouth as she coughed. The rattle in her lungs didn't sound good. Once the coughing sub-dued, her eyes looked right at me while clutching the ends of a quilted blanket that was wrapped around her bruised body. Her hair was shoulder length and stringy as it had not been washed for several days.

"Do you know where her son is?" Mrs. Thomas asked as she walked away from the fireplace.

"Joe Evans. His name is Joe Evans," Mrs. Evans said before her cough arose with force. Each force of air caused the rattling sound to emit from inside her lungs.

"The Sheriff said that your son was at Ford Memorial. I don't know if he is still there or not, but Sheriff said he was okay." Hearing the news, relief set in, and she relaxed her tense body trying to pacify her cough. Her eyes looked tired, but it seemed she was warm and somewhat comfortable.

"Doc is on his way," I said to the both of them. I took a few steps toward the couch and tried to seem as friendly as possible. "My name is Elliott Chapel." The way she was wrapped up and sitting with her body pushed into one corner of the couch made it look like she was afraid. She had a bandage on the top of her head with gauze that wrapped around and connected underneath her chin, holding it in place. "Booley and I were riding near the creek. We found you..." Mrs. Thomas held up her hand to stop me.

"No need to bring that up right now," she said. Mrs. Thomas was almost to the point of being obsessed over being proper. Doc was careless and could go on for days wearing the same clothes, but Mrs. Thomas wouldn't have it as long as she was alive. Fresh and clean pressed pants and a shirt free of wrinkles.

"Oh, okay," I responded now not knowing what to say. I took a few steps back into a darkened corner and sat there until Doc arrived, feeling foolish as if I shouldn't have even been there. Without warning, her cough would surface and the moments of uncomfortable silence were shattered by the coughing fits that seemed to erupt out of her chest. When Doc walked in, his eyes fixed on Mrs. Evans and he took off his brown Fedora hat and set his black medical bag down before removing his coat. I had only seen Doc tend to a few people over the years, but I will always remember his eyes and the way he looked upon his patients. It was as if he was caring for someone in his own family and that caring look in his eyes is the way you would want a physician to look upon you should you be the one needing a doctor's attention.

"She woke up about an hour ago," Mrs. Thomas said.

"Hi, Ellie. My name is Doctor Thomas. Do you remember me?" he asked. Ellie nodded her head. "Do you know your name?"

"Ellie Evans," she answered with a puzzled look on her face as she pulled the quilt closer to her neck. Sensing that Ellie thought he was crazy, Doc explained why he asked her the questions.

"Oh, I only ask to make sure you don't have any memory loss," Doc said with a smile to ease any concern she might have. "This fella here, Elliott Chapel, found you in the creek several days ago. You nearly died from hypothermia." Mrs. Evans tried to say something only to have her cough erupt accompanied with that terrible deep rattling sound in her lungs. Doc looked at her with concern and opened his black medical bag.

"Doctor Thomas? Where is my son?" Ellie said as she put her hand on his, a signal that she required his full attention.

"He is fine. A little banged up, but he is just fine."

"Did he go to the hospital?"

"He did. I examined him, bandaged him up and sent him home," Doc explained. Ellie breathed a sigh of relief. "Let's go ahead and look you over," he said as he fished out his stethoscope from his medical bag.

"Okay. I need to check you over and I need to listen to you breathe in and out." The physical examination was thorough enough that I had to leave the room. Once I was invited back in, I noticed that she was now in a dress. It was loose fitting and the frock obviously came from Mrs. Thomas' closet. I guess she brought it with her with the full intention of giving it to Mrs. Evans.

"Do you know what happened?" Doc asked questions while he

thumbed through a medical text book. She took her eyes off of him and stared toward the fireplace. I just stood there with my hat in my right hand still feeling unnecessary and irrelevant.

"Yes," she said as she repositioned herself. She drew her legs up underneath the dress and wrapped her arms around them. Mrs. Thomas repositioned the blanket around Mrs. Evans' shoulders.

At that point, Ellie Evans was thirty years old and had been married to her husband for nine years. Wayne C. Evans had been an attorney who was on a political track with hopes of being elected governor someday. When things weren't going his way, Ellie became an object on which to take out his frustrations. Fresh bruises and red marks on her body weren't uncommon and neither was her style of dressing so that her embarrassing secret remained that way. Of course, I didn't know that when she was brought to Booley's house.

Mrs. Evans' cuts and bruises on her face were difficult to look at with the worst one being at the corner of her mouth. It was still an open wound and looked to be the most painful as she kept trying to touch it with the tips of her fingers.

"I'm sorry to trouble you with my problems. You've been so nice," she said as if trying to move the conversation elsewhere.

"Ellie, I have treated you before. I remember. I know it must be difficult for you, but I think it would be best if you tell us what happened," Doc said in a very compassionate manner. I watched the tears well up on Mrs. Evans' eyelids. Her tears collected there until they could no longer hold their position and fell over and onto her bruised, puffy cheeks. Doc knew first hand of her abusive relationship; he had treated her before when Wayne C. Evans struck her in the face with an open hand, sending her to the floor with a cut above her right eye.

Mrs. Evans sobbed into her hands. She touched her face lightly as it obviously hurt to put any pressure on her wounds. "Can you tell me what happened?" Doc asked. The wound on the corner of her mouth opened up slightly and a small amount of blood began to seep out of the wound. Doc reached his hand into his medical bag and fished out a bandage cloth and handed it to her after dabbing the blood off her chin. "Place this on the corner of your mouth until it stops bleeding." Once she had composed herself and the bleeding subsided, she told us her story as the fire cracked and popped.

"Wayne had come home after a trip to Frankfort and had been drinking. He came upstairs and asked me where I had been and I told him I hadn't been anywhere. He kept yelling and carrying on and I couldn't understand him. I tried to get him to calm down and he threw me into a marble vanity and I hit my head. Blood started to stream down my face and the pain was getting to be too much. Then our son Joe walked in and Wayne pushed him out of the room and shut the door. Joe tripped over the carpet and fell onto the hallway floor." Tears were flowing down Mrs. Evans cheek as she spoke, looking embarrassed and defeated. "I knew we had to get out of there. I was tired of it and I was tired of him hitting me. In the middle of the night..." A coughing fit started. It took some time before she could speak again. "In the middle of the night, I took Joe and put him in the car and left. We left for good. The next thing I knew, I woke up here and I don't know what happened." Mrs. Evans wiped the streaming tears away with the backside of her wrist.

"With a head injury like that, it seems that you blacked out while driving toward Tenpenny Bridge," Doc explained. Mrs. Evans appeared to be humiliated. She slowly lifted her left hand and delicately touched the top of her head, feeling the wound beneath the bandage. Her facial expression quickly evolved into a grimace of pain.

"Where is my son? Is he home or is he still at the hospital?" she asked as she brought her hand away from her injury. The blanket around her shoulders had slid off a bit and she tugged on the ends pulling it over her shoulders, completely covering Mrs. Thomas' donated frock. "Can I see him," she added.

"I'll go pick him up for you, Mrs. Evans." I had been leaning against the wall and quickly stood upright. I was hoping to be of some use to the situation.

"Please, don't call me that," she said in frustration.

"Yes ma'am," I responded as I put on my hat.

"Call me Ellie."

7

In my entire life, I have only seen one albino coyote. In 1938, Dad started a garden about thirty paces from the back porch. He planted and successfully produced tomatoes, corn, peas, cucumbers, green beans, carrots and lettuce. The coyote appeared just as the tomatoes were ripe as if his animal instincts told him to wait until the perfect time. His white fur wasn't perfectly white as the juice from the tomatoes would run down his chin and onto his chest—his fur also carried some of the matted leaves and dirt from his nighttime bedding. I once got a look at his pink eyes when they fixed on me as I was on my way to the back porch. He looked at me as if I might be a predator, but I just stood there and let him jog away.

The previous September, Dad sat on the back porch with Banner and his rifle. He had left a few tomatoes on the vine as bait hoping to put an end to the thief that caused him so much trouble. A few times, I saw the coyote in the garden and turned my head toward the back porch expecting to see Dad holding his rifle while drawing a bead on the albino thief. Instead, my father would be asleep on the old couch with his rifle resting on the ground next to Banner. I now wonder if the coyote would wait until his predator's eyes were closed before making his move. Dad was a terrible shot when he was inebriated and luckily for the albino coyote, the old man was never without a bottle of whiskey. When I was a boy, I saw Dad shoot and kill many animals from as far away as seventy-five yards out, but he was sober then. Whenever Booley would see my drunken father holding his rifle and watching for the coyote he would inevitably say, "That albino is as safe as a lion in the pride."

As I walked towards my truck, on my way to Mayor Evans' house to enquire about Joe Evans—a boy I had not yet met—and wondering what I'd say to him, I was about to open my truck door when something in the garden caught my eye. I saw the albino coyote as he was sniffing around the desolate soil and I stood quietly, watching his movements. When I eventually opened the door to the truck, a harsh grinding noise emitted from the rusty hinges. The coyote quickly looked up in my direction before trotting toward the woods on the right side of our farm. No doubt he was scoping out his delicious food source for the coming summer. I hopped in my truck and started the engine, prepared to meet the son of Mrs. Ellie Evans.

Joe was nine years old (around the same age as the Bennett kids) in 1939 and attended Garth Elementary. When I first met him, unbeknownst to me, he was having trouble with a group of boys at school. His father had made him out to be an easy target since he tortured his son with malicious language and the occasional push or shove. His self-esteem was low enough for other boys in school to see that he was helpless and timid in the same way a pack of lions might view an injured gazelle.

When I arrived at the Mayor's home, I marveled at the beautiful landscape complete with trimmed trees and carefully manicured bushes and shrubs. The house itself wasn't a mansion, but it was a decent size that appeared to have three levels. The bushes and shrubs around the front door were manicured in pleasant round shapes and complimented the four large columns on the porch that were as white as the shutters. The door was painted bright red with a polished brass knocker placed at eye level. I pulled back on the heavy door knocker and slammed it into the brass backing which caused a resonating thud every time I knocked. A moment later, an elderly black man in a white button up shirt and a black vest answered the door.

"Hello, I'm Elliott Chapel. I am looking for Joe Evans."

"Yes sir. He is here. Are you the owner of the farm Mrs. Evans is staying at?" He asked as he looked at my filthy jeans and cowboy boots.

"I am. She is awake."

"Oh. Is she coming here?"

"I don't know. She is asking for her son."

"I see. Well, I suppose it's all right." He opened the door wider as if to invite me in. "He's upstairs." I looked down at the white carpet, then at my filthy boots.

"I don't think I should," I said as I gestured toward my feet. The man just nodded and left the door open as he went upstairs. I waited on the front porch, peering inside the house at the gaudy wallpaper and massive crystal chandelier wondering if the good taxpayers of Georgetown paid for this gaudy, ornate home. I quit looking around once Joe started to walk down the stairs and into the foyer. The first thing I noticed about Joe was the cowlick on the back, top portion of his head which was quite noticeable from my vantage point. His hair was the color of dirty straw and looked as if he had combed it himself, the way a nine year old boy would do. I stayed on the front porch and spoke to him from the open door.

"Hi Joe. My name is Elliott Chapel. I am going to take you to see your mom." He was wearing pants that were too long for him, but he seemed to manage as the ends were rolled up into cuffs. His shoulders hung on his scrawny frame as did his button up shirt and jacket made from a nice, thick cloth. His forehead was bruised from the accident and a bandage was taped to the side of his face. I couldn't see any blood seeping though the cloth, but he did look a little banged up.

"Is my mom okay?" he asked. His eyes looked up at me and his lips moved more than they had to when he spoke.

"I think so. She's asking for you." There was an underlying tension between us as if we both knew that his father was a monster, but neither of us broke that tension. It stayed there, hovering between us as I drove him back to the farm.

"Is this your ranch?" he asked as he stared out the window. I was driving on the gravel path back to Booley's little house.

"Yeah. It's a farm. We train horses here."

"Where are they?"

"The horses are in the barn right now. When they are outside, they are in that field over there," I said as I pointed. "They usually walk around and pick at the grass."

"How many do you have?"

"Right now we only have four." I parked the truck and Joe got out on his own by sliding off the seat and planting his Buster Brown shoes on the soft grass. He turned around and used his body weight to close the passenger side door to the truck. He seemed very interested in his surroundings as we walked to the front door of Booley's house. Joe wandered toward me as his eyes danced around taking in the landscape. Once he walked through the front door, his mother called to him.

"Joseph!"

"Mom!" he cried out as he ran to her, his cowlick strands of hair bouncing with every step forward. She was still sitting on the couch with a blanket over her legs. They embraced for what seemed like five minutes until she calmed down enough to try and stand up. Doc rushed to her side as did Mrs. Thomas.

"Should I not stand up?" Ellie asked.

"Actually it's best if you do start to move around. I just don't want you to lose your balance," Doc said and helped her slowly stand up. "The more you move around the better. Helps circulation," he added. She eventually stood up straight and made her way to the kitchen table. Joe sat close beside her. Ellie took a deep breath and Doc backed away. The stark light from the kitchen window revealed the emotions on the faces of a mother and son in trouble. Mrs. Evans' stringy, unwashed shoulder length hair kept getting in her face anytime she looked downward. After using her hand to keep back the loose strands for some time, she had had enough.

"Is there a rubber band or a piece of ribbon around here?" Ellie asked. Mrs. Thomas walked over to her bag of knitting needles and yarn balls. She fished out a red strand of yarn that looked to be of a sufficient length and handed it to Mrs. Evans who tied up her disheveled hair into a ponytail.

"My wife and I need to be leaving," Doc said as he walked over, picking up his coat and medical bag. "I need to be at the hospital and I have another house call this afternoon. I will be back this evening with a bottle of cough medicine and to check on your bandage, yours too, Joe." Mrs. Thomas had put on a white button up sweater with pink buttons before turning toward Ellie.

"Please keep the clothes. They don't fit me anymore," Mrs. Thomas said in a kind voice.

"Thank you," Mrs. Evans said. Doc turned to me and shook my hand.

"Is it possible to allow her to stay here for a few more days?"

"Oh no, we can find somewhere to stay," Ellie said.

"No, it is fine. Really," I insisted. We have more than enough room, in fact we have an extra bedroom up at the main house," I explained. Doc patted me on the back and looked at Mrs. Evans.

"Try to move around and stay warm," he said with a wink.

"Thank you so much for helping me. Please send the bill to the Mayor's office." Doc nodded his head and smiled as he and his wife left.

"You're welcome," he said just as he closed the door. Mrs. Evans was looking down at the dress Mrs. Thomas gave her, I didn't think it was her style, but it was all she had for now.

"Do you have any family you and Joe should call and let them know you're okay?" I asked. "We have a phone at the main house."

"No. My grandmother died a few years ago. She was all I had. I am not sure what we will do, but I am sure we will think of something." Now I really felt out of place. I thought that I shouldn't be there and needed to leave as this was a family matter between Ellie and Joe.

"Mrs. Evans, I mean Ellie, you can stay on our farm as long as you like. This is Booley's place and it gets pretty cold at night unless you keep adding logs to the fireplace and it only has an outhouse. We have indoor plumbing at the main house and it would be more comfortable for you both. On the first floor, we have an empty bedroom and we would be happy to have you and Joe stay."

"Oh, I don't know. I don't want to put you out none."

"You are more than welcome to stay until you figure out what to do."

"Oh, I don't want to impose. I appreciate the offer."

"Are you going to go stay at your house until the mayor gets back?" I asked as I took a few steps and leaned my weight against the wall in the kitchen. Ellie was thinking about her options as she reached back, making sure the red yarn would hold her hair up. Her facial expression revealed that she didn't like the idea of continuing to stay there even before she said it out loud.

"No. I don't think so. I think I want to try and remove us from that life. Going back there isn't a good idea," Ellie answered as she seemed satisfied with the red yarn and put her elbows on the small kitchen table top. Her hands rested on her mouth and her eyes gazed out the dirty window pane. She exhaled, as if she wasn't sure that she had any options.

"Where else do you have to go?" I asked. She sat silent for some time without coming up with an answer.

Later that evening, Joe and I picked up a few of their things from the Mayor's gaudy house. While we were there, the phone rang and the elderly black man wearing the white button up shirt and black vest called me into the hallway and handed me the phone before walking into the kitchen. It was Ellie calling from my farm.

"Mr. Chapel, I hope you don't mind me using your telephone."

"Not at all," I said. "Please call me Elliott."

"Certainly. Elliott, I've been thinking of a way to kind of earn my keep around here and I would like to cook breakfast tomorrow morning. I figure it would help for me to move around like Doc said and I'd be doing something productive. I was hoping it would be okay if I had Douglas pack a box from my pantry in the kitchen and have you bring it with you." I peeked around the corner of the hallway and looked in the kitchen. The elderly man was already at work packing a box for Mrs. Evans.

"Of course. But we do have eggs and bacon at the house," I said. There was a short pause on the other end of the line before she responded.

"I think I can do a little bit better than bacon and eggs," she said as if she was smiling on the other end of the line and about ready to laugh.

After Joe packed a few of his things along with what his mother requested, I took an open top cardboard box from Douglas's arms and went back to the farm. With the intention of moving Joe and Ellie into the small bedroom downstairs, I opened the door to the dusty room. No one had stayed in there since my aunt passed and we had since been using that room for storage and nothing else. It was only fifteen feet from the front door and didn't have any curtains which made it very bright in the morning. A small dresser with a mirror stood against one wall and on the other side was a small bed. Storage boxes were stacked four to five high, filled with old *LIFE* Magazines, accounting records from years past and a massive steamer trunk full of Mom's clothes that Dad refused to part with. While it wasn't a lot, it did take twenty minutes to get it all moved out. When we got everything situated, they looked quite comfortable in their small room.

Knock. Knock. Knock. I walked to the front door and opened it to Doc Thomas standing on the porch holding his black medical bag. Once he came in, he listened to Ellie's lungs once more with his stethoscope and removed Joe's bandages. Doc cleaned up Joe's minor cuts with alcohol and gauze without applying another bandage.

"Joe, your wounds shouldn't bleed anymore and you'll be just fine," Doc said with a smile.

"Thanks!" Joe replied. Doc then took out the cough medicine in a green bottle with a white label. Before he left, he spoke with her about the dosage and saw himself out the front door. I had been talking with Booley out on the back porch. Booley had yet to meet Ellie and didn't want to introduce himself during all the commotion she was going through. He had stayed out of the way and was ready to get back to his little house. I came inside and found Ellie picking up the cardboard box with the items that she asked me to bring her.

"I will just put these away for tomorrow. If I can't find enough room in the refrigerator, I will set some items on the back porch. Should be cold enough," she said and started toward the kitchen.

"Oh. Here, let me help," I said as I walked over to take the box out of her arms. "Aren't you sore? You probably shouldn't be picking up anything heavy anyway." She released the box and I now had the full weight of it in my arms.

"It's no big deal really. It actually feels good to move around."

"You know, Doc says you're lucky to be alive. I would think it would be better for you to rest."

"Doc did say I should be moving around and I don't think I could refrain from doing so anyway. I am always up and about."

I had brought the box in the kitchen and set it on the counter near the refrigerator. I didn't know what else to say and I started feeling awkward so I headed out to the kitchen.

"Feel free to use the bathroom," I said. "It is upstairs and to the left." I had walked out of sight when she called me by my last name. She walked out of the kitchen and looked at me with a thankful expression upon her bandaged face.

"Mr. Chapel?"

"Please, call me Elliott."

"Yes, I forgot," she said with a near apologetic, but sincere smile. The wound on the corner of her lip was pushed to the limit. "I just wanted to thank you again. You are very kind." She lightly rubbed the bruises on her arms and I couldn't help but think of the man who laid hands on such a pretty and courteous woman.

"You are most welcome," I said as I started toward the second floor with each board slightly creaking underneath my feet. She walked back to the kitchen and I kept wondering how in the world did she get mixed up with a man like Mayor Evans. As soon as I stepped into the hallway, I could see light coming from under Dad's bedroom door. I gave a courtesy knock and turned the doorknob, pushing gently on the squeaky, hinged door. He was sitting on the edge of his bed half asleep with one strap of his overalls undone and his boots off of his feet, lying side by side on the unfinished hardwood floor.

"Dad, we have houseguests in the small bedroom downstairs. It's the woman I found in the creek four days ago and her little boy, thought you should know." He grunted before going back to undressing by removing the other strap of his overalls. I closed his door and started walking toward my room, not realizing that my inability to distinguish between Dad's alcoholic haze and lethargy would nearly get Joe killed.

8

I awoke to a child's scream, an old barking dog and a grumpy old man's questioning coming from the hallway outside my bedroom. I jumped out of bed, planting my bare feet on the cold hardwood floor and ran out into the hall. There was my dad standing somewhat off kilter while holding his rifle and squinting his left eye closed. His right eye glared hazily down the length of the barrel, aiming directly at Joe's left eyeball. Banner was half awake as he stood by my father with his aged eyes half open and his tail lazily sweeping from side to side. You couldn't ever confuse Banner for being a guard dog, especially since he thought that the midnight encounter was fun. Joe probably didn't even think anything of Banner as his eyes were fixed on the barrel of Dad's gun while his arms and back were hugging the wall behind him in fear.

"You're trespassin' in your damn jammies!" Dad growled while cocking the hammer back on the rifle. No doubt alcohol was traveling through his bloodstream.

"Dad, quit it! What the hell are you thinking?" I shouted as I ran over pushing the barrel of the gun toward the ceiling. Dad's eyes were rolling around in his head as if he was having a hard time focusing.

"This kid is in our house," he grumbled with his eyes half closed. Obviously Joe was on his way to the bathroom when the old codger saw a small figure walking around in the dark.

"This is Joe Evans. He is our guest. I told you that already." I could hear Ellie coming up the stairs.

"I don't want no guests!" Dad shouted.

I looked down for a second and caught a glimpse of a puddle of urine forming underneath Joe's feet.

"They are *my* guests, Dad!" I yelled. Ellie came into view at the top of the staircase. Dad quickly aimed his gun toward her. "Damn it! Will you stop pointing that thing?" I shouted. With some difficulty, I grabbed his Remington M37 Rangemaster from his old, worn hands that were gripped firmly around the gun. Even in his old age and alcohol induced haze, he was a very strong man. From the corner of my eye, I saw Ellie, on tired and badly bruised legs, rush over to Joe making sure to get between her son and the threat of the old man.

"Who the hell are you?" Dad said as he looked at Ellie.

"I'm Ellie Evans," she said as she grabbed Joe's arm and moved even further away from Dad. "This is my son," she answered. I pushed Dad back into his room with force, something I had never done in my entire life.

"Get back in your room you ol' buzzard. Go back to sleep." I sounded harsh at the time, but that was how he spoke to me. It didn't seem to put a dent in him. I kept the rifle with the intention of keeping it in my room. Dad walked to his bed while Banner followed and plopped down on his bed of old quilts as if it was just another average night in the Chapel household.

"Damn trespassers," I heard him slur before I closed the door. Actually, I may have slammed it.

"I'm sorry. I am so sorry," I said doing my best to keep the gun behind me and out of view of Joe. Ellie grabbed for tissues from a pocket in her nightgown and quickly slapped them onto her mouth as her death rattle cough erupted. She placed her other hand on the staircase railing to maintain her balance while she forcefully coughed into the tissue. Once it subsided, she was able to speak again. The sound of fluid rattling in her lungs still sounded bad. Made me think Doc should have given her the cough medicine sooner.

"Should we leave?" Ellie asked. She put her hand on her chest with an expression of pain as it must have really hurt to cough.

"Good lord, no! I should have told you about my dad. He's just a grumpy, old man and drinks like a sailor. It'll be fine."

After a brief explanation and a quick clean up of urine on the hardwood floor, Ellie took Joe to their bedroom. Before she closed the door, she turned to me.

"Mr. Chapel?"

"Please, call me Elliott."

"Sorry. Elliott? If we are a bother, please don't hesitate to tell us. We certainly don't want to impose or nuthin'."

"It's no problem. Really," I said. "My father is just an old drunkard. I'll talk to him tomorrow when he's sober." She smiled and thanked me. I whispered through the door to Joe, "Sorry about that, Joe."

"It's okay, Mr. Chapel," I heard him say. I went back upstairs and it took forever until I was able to go to sleep. I finally drifted off and even slept a little past my normal waking hour due to my midnight wrangling of a drunken codger. It wasn't until morning that my father would meet our houseguests for the second time.

Now, I wasn't there to see it, but Ellie described it to me after it happened. Breakfast at our house usually consisted of bacon, eggs and coffee. That was it. I don't believe I ever had anything else for breakfast, unless I was at a friend's house. Back when my aunt lived with us she tried to cook a few times, but she couldn't boil water much less manage eggs and bacon. Dad was usually the one that cooked breakfast, and he would set out a portion for me from time to time. Like I said, I wasn't there to see it, but Ellie later told me that after she had made breakfast, Dad walked into the kitchen and stopped. He looked at Joe who was sitting at the small kitchen table with a half bite of food in his mouth. Stunned and rightfully frightened at the sight of my father, Joe held the fork still, frozen between his chin and plate. His eyes were focused on the old man, forgetting to close his mouth and chew.

"Trespasser," Dad said as he looked at Joe with eyes like a gunfighter just before drawing on his opponent. Joe didn't move. Ellie stared at my father who slowly turned his head and looked at a plate on the counter. On the plate were seven pieces of French toast stacked high with warm maple syrup flooding the top floor of the French toast tower. The syrup dripped down the sides as a pat of butter sat on top dissolving into the thick, brown syrup.

"Are you hungry?" Ellie asked, trying to be friendly. No response from the old man. Just his eyes moved as he stood motionless, scanning the counter. He looked at another plate with sausage links and hash browns. Ellie described it as if the old man had walked into a cave full of gold and silver. Next to the plates on the counter was a bowl that held my father's favorite breakfast dish, grits. I believe my mom used to cook them which is why I think he loved them so much. Ellie explained to me that he walked across the room toward the counter. His foul, frowning face had disappeared and was replaced by a look of enlightenment. He had started to reach his wrinkled and spotted hands for an empty plate on the counter before stopping himself. He looked at her as if to ask "Is it okay?" without saying a word. She just looked at my father, nodded her head and he began to fix his plate. First a piece of French toast with syrup and butter, then sausage links and hash browns with one section of his plate left for a heavy fixing of grits. After Dad sat down, Joe began to chew again, realizing he didn't have to run for the door.

I remember the smell of breakfast that morning. I saw my father's plate which was pretty much clean by the time I made it downstairs. I took in the buffet of food on the counter with my eyes and my sense of smell. The most remarkable thing about that particular day was the fact that I was sitting at the breakfast table with my father. Ellie had sat down as well. We were like a family – gathered and eating at the table. It may not seem like a big deal, but it took a stranger to come inside our house before I finally got to eat breakfast with my dad. I secretly thanked her in my head as I took a bite with my dad sitting on the other side of the table. Ellie carried on a conversation with Joe about school. Dad was wiping his mouth and finishing his coffee while I looked at him with breakfast table resentment. I wished I'd had that growing up; eating with him and carrying on a conver-sation about school or whatever. At the very least, Ellie's culinary ef-forts eased the old man's concerns about my house guests.

From the very beginning, Ellie had made life on the farm brighter. When I walked into the kitchen that morning, it was very warm from the heat of the oven and the burners on the stove. However, it was something more than that. Her eyes, the way she smiled and the way she enjoyed the morning the way I had never seen anyone enjoy it before. Instead of being inconvenienced with houseguests, Ellie made her stay more than welcome as far as my father was concerned, at least for the time being.

9

Early the next morning, I walked out the back of the main house and started toward the track on the backside of my property. I walked past Dad's garden and the willow tree just to the right where Banner slept during the summer. It takes a little while to walk to the track from the main house, but I always enjoyed the break of morning and the orange clouds that the dawn painted across the sky. Once at the track, I watched Palmer trot Priced Opportunity, and from the corner of my eye noticed Ellie walking toward me. I remember this day well because that was the first day I saw Ellie's hair in a ponytail. Well, a real ponytail and not the mess of hair she tied up behind her head just to get it out of the way back at Booley's little house. She was still wearing a bandage on her head and somehow she had made it look more like a headband. When she walked toward me, I could see her ponytail bouncing around.

"Hey. Is there anything I can do to help out? I mean, I should be earning my keep." Her nose and cheeks were red as she had just returned from walking Joe to school, which wasn't far from our farm.

"Believe me, that breakfast you made this morning was more than earning your keep," I said with a big smile.

She smiled back as she shielded her eyes from the sun. Her ponytail made her appear more attractive, I thought. I did notice that she had used the same strand of red yarn given to her by Mrs. Thomas.

"Can't I do something else?" she insisted.

"Shouldn't you be inside?" I asked. "It's cold out and your cough still sounds terrible."

"Doc said I need to move around as much as I can. The cold doesn't bother me and my cough will be fine," she insisted as she stretched her jacket around her petite figure to increase the warmth. "I think staying outside for an hour or so won't hurt."

"I don't know. You could get pneumonia."

"Well, I can stay out for an hour and then go inside. I should be okay."

At that moment Booley rode toward us on Eros and tipped his hat toward Ellie as if he was a cowboy on the silver screen. "Did you get all thawed out?" he asked her.

"I sure did," she answered nearly laughing. That led into a cough which prompted her to produce a tissue from her pocket. I glanced over at her conveying my look of disapproval that she was outside.

"This is Booley. You stayed at his house while you were recovering," I said once she stopped coughing.

"Well, thank you. I hope I didn't put you out."

"You did, ma'am. You owe me one," Booley replied. He was only half joking.

"I wanna breeze Ranger's Cape and Beyond The Pale single file and alternate. I want dirt in their face. " I said. "I'm not so worried with Pale so much so let Sarah ride 'em. Ranger wants to duck out and I need Palmer to convince him."

"Yeah, that's fine," Booley replied. "I'll have Price and Pale hot walked. I have Jim riding lead all day if that's all right."

"Yeah, that's fine," I answered.

Sarah Bennett took off her coat and grabbed a helmet, goggles and a crop before heading to the track. Little Cara Bennett waved at her mom from the doorway of the barn while Kenny sorted horseshoes in a wooden trunk, making sure that they were sorted by size. Whenever their mother galloped or breezed a horse, the Bennett kids would usually hang out on the fence and watch. Palmer began galloping Ranger behind Pale. As Sarah took Pale to a full breeze, Palmer would keep up, directly behind her. The dirt kicked up by Pale started hitting Ranger in the face. The farm was in full swing, for us anyway.

"What's hot walking? I am not familiar with that term," Ellie asked as she brushed a few strands of loose hair behind her ear while watching the thoroughbreds breeze around the track.

"It means cooling them off or warming them up."

"Oh, okay."

"I think it's only a term used with thoroughbreds."

"Do you have races out here?" Ellie asked as she pointed towards the track.

"No, this is just a training track. My dad built it."

"It's pretty amazing. I have lived in Scott County for awhile and never knew this was here," she said taking in the landscape as she glanced around.

"Yeah, no one can see it from the main road," I replied. Her hands were resting on the track fence watching Palmer galloping Priced Opportunity.

"Is it always this busy in the mornings?"

"Yeah, we train 6 days out of the week. The Bennett family works

Tuesday through Sunday."

"What about their kids? Do they go to school?" She was full of questions.

"No. Their mother teaches them in the afternoons."

"I see," Ellie said. Jim Bennett managed Catcher's reins and navigated him in my direction. Catcher was a working horse on my farm, and would accompany other horses on the track and even run beside the thoroughbreds during their workouts as a companion. Being a trail horse, Catcher never raced on the track, but he would gallop with them from time to time depending on the circumstances. In Jim's left hand was my clipboard which had the daily feed schedule, training routines and worksheets.

"You have gate exercises written down for today."

"Ah, yes. Okay thanks. I'll go get the gate ready," I said. I looked at Ellie deciding I could use her help. "How's that cough of yours? You sure you want to work outside?"

"It takes more than a cough to bring me down." Her smile was incredible, even with the healing abrasion on the corner of her mouth.

"Well, follow me." I walked Ellie out onto the track over to the other side where a small shed was built that housed a starting gate.

Dad bought the gate about five years prior as he was having a problem training his horses to get out of a starting gate. The only time a trainer can get his horses accustomed to a gate is when they are at the race track such as Keeneland or Churchill Downs and even then the area around the gate can get congested with ten to twenty thoroughbreds at a time. Dad rationalized that he could get his horses easily accustomed to the gate if he had one on his farm. In 1934, he contacted a company that made starting gates for Churchill Downs and had them make a custom two-stall gate. When it arrived, it was pretty impressive as it was brand new and shiny. Within six days of its arrival, Dad and Booley built the shed to house it as Dad always treated his things with great care.

When Ellie and I rolled it out onto the track, I could tell she was impressed. As I pulled the large metal structure while she pushed, I could see that ponytail of hers sweeping back and forth with brief glimpses of the red yarn that was tied in a bow. For whatever reason, it's the little things that I remember about her.

"Wow! This is pretty neat!" she said as she looked it over. After five years, the steel and paint still looked brand new. "Is this for a two horse race?" her question caused me to laugh a bit.

"No. It's for training horses to get out of the starting gate."

"Really? I never thought about that. I guess I just thought they would just go in there and come out when the gates opened." We wheeled it into position and I could see Booley getting the horses ready to walk over. I bent over and reached for a locking mechanism, pushing the lever into place that kept the large, metal gate from straying.

"The starting gate is the most unnatural part of a thoroughbred's training," I said standing straight up. "Many of them hate it or at least they seem to," I explained.

"Really?"

"The more time a horse has practicing in and out of the starting gate, the better."

"I never thought about it, I guess. So what can I do?"

"Well, this gate works on a spring system and I will lock it down here, like this," I said as I showed her how I forced the doors closed using both hands. She could hear the click sound as they locked. "When I give you the go-ahead, pull this rope and make sure you stand very still before you do. Try not to cough when they are in the slot as we don't want any sudden noises right now."

"Okay," she said as she got into position clear of the horses path using both hands to grip the rope.

Booley brought Priced Opportunity over to the gate with Palmer mounted in the riding saddle. "Is there a bell or anything? Like they do at the track?" Ellie asked.

"Nope. The gates just spring open," I said as I took the reins from Booley. I carefully led the horse into the slot. Priced Opportunity had done it several times before so he was familiar with the process.

"Easy now. Real easy," Booley said gently to Opportunity. Once the horse was in, Booley closed the rear doors.

"You good, Palmer?" I asked.

"Yep," he replied. I nodded at Ellie and she pulled the cord. Palmer smacked Priced Opportunity's hind quarters with the riding crop getting him to move as fast as he could out of the gate. They took off down the track and Jim began walking Beyond The Pale to the starting gate. When Palmer had made it around the track, he jumped off Price's saddle and mounted Beyond the Pale. Jim took Priced Opportunity back toward the barn. This time Ellie's assistance wouldn't be needed.

"Just drop the rope to the ground. We aren't taking him all the way just yet," I said.

"Okay," Ellie replied. She watched as we left the gate wide open and allowed Beyond The Pale to walk through the gate a few times. Although the horse hesitated, Booley continued to talk to him as we walked him into the slot.

"Slowly. Slow and easy," he said in a soft tone of voice. Pale refused several times until Palmer used a little persistence by pulling on the reins and nudging him with his riding crop. Finally we got him in the slot and let him stay for a few moments before backing him out.

"Why do you just let him sit there?" Ellie asked.

"They don't know what to expect and we have to get them used to it, kind of like swimming in cold water. You don't just jump in, you let yourself get accustomed to the temperature."

"That makes sense," she said.

"Just walking them in without the loud sounds of the doors being closed or sprung open lets them know there is nothing to fear. Beyond The Pale absolutely hates the gate. I mean hates it."

We loaded Outpost with no problem and released the spring on the gate while Palmer used the riding crop on Outpost's hindquarters. Then Ranger's Cape went through in the same manner. I could tell Ellie was soaking everything in trying to learn something new. She was quiet and listened as Booley, Palmer, and I discussed certain issues. After a brief conversation about starting side by side gate coaching, I had Jim mount Ranger's Cape and walk him into the stall next to Palmer and Outpost. We released the gates and they both tore down the track, kicking up dirt as their hooves slapped the track surface. I explained to Ellie why we trained the horses in certain ways and how we overcame the difficulties of getting a horse to become accustomed to the gate. She asked questions and I answered them while watching her interest in thoroughbreds increase as the day progressed.

Once we were finished for the day and we were all around the barn, I hollered out as I always did just before we wrapped up for the day.

"Bridles up!"

"Coming your way!" Jim immediately replied as he took the exercise saddle off Beyond The Pale.

"Two bridles and counting!" Sarah yelled out from inside the barn. Ellie had taken notice of the immediate responses as if they knew that I was going to yell out.

"Bridles up? What's that?" Ellie asked.

"Uhhh…well, it's kind of," I could barely tell her without laughing as it sounded so ridiculous. "It's kind of a superstitious task around here," I said as Sarah walked toward me carrying two bridles in her hand. "Since I was a boy, Dad made me hang up the bridles at the end of every training session. Then several years ago the horses started losing. I mean, not one of them placed. Booley, being very superstitious, pointed out that I hadn't been hanging up the bridles as I always had." Sarah handed me two bridles and walked away smiling as she listened to me explain the story to Ellie. "So Booley told me to hang them up and strangely the horses started placing and winning again. Dad thought it was dim-witted, but everyone else around the barn thought better of it. Now, I always hang up the bridles."

"I never knew how superstitions started."

"Sounds silly, I know. But last October I was sick and Jim hung them up."

"Yeah?" Ellie asked. "What happened?"

"Dead last. Every single one of them," I answered. "Well, I am exaggerating a little, but not one of them placed." Ellie laughed and once again tucked a few loose strands of hair behind her right ear.

"That's no joke! You better hang them up every time!" she said laughing.

"I do!" I replied with a smile. "We are done here and you've been out in the cold long enough. You better get to the house and warm up," I added although I tried to sound lighthearted about it. She rolled her eyes and playfully saluted me saying, "Yes sir" before heading back to the main house.

I think it was her eyes that first caught me off guard that day, like I was seeing a woman for the first time. It's that feeling you get where all you want to do is be around that girl and make her smile. I had dated a few women in town, but I'd never met anyone like Ellie. At that point in time, I didn't know how long she would stay with us, but I did know that I didn't want her to leave.

10

After a trip to Guthrie's General Store, Ellie cooked green beans, corn, mashed potatoes and cornbread for dinner. No meat this time around and we didn't need it. Booley had missed breakfast, and Ellie had made sure that he was invited to dinner since she owed him one. Ellie reached her hands out and Joe took her left hand and I immediately took her right. Ellie was instigating a dinner time prayer and Booley looked at us with a puzzled expression as I had forgotten. Ellie wanted to pray before dinner and I instinctively grabbed her hand, for the most part I leapt at the chance to hold her hand without thinking. Dad's eyes fell on Ellie as he realized what she was trying to initiate at the table.

"We don't pray in this house," he said. His tone sounded a little gruff, but managed to sound somewhat considerate. Booley looked satisfied that he hadn't taken part in the prayer as he knew what the consequences would be.

"I'm sorry. Do you not believe in God?" Ellie asked. I let go of her hand.

"Nobody prays to him in my house. I don't allow it," he said, this time sounding a little more harsh. Ellie looked at me and I shook my head "no" as if to warn her. I supposed she couldn't abide by that.

"May Joe and I pray?"

"Fine. Go outside and do it. Not under my roof and not on my property. In fact, you go outside and stand on the road in front of the mailbox, off my property. You're my guest and nobody prays to that son of a bitch here!" Dad angrily used his spoon to eat a small mound of green beans from his plate. Ellie looked as if she wanted to get up and leave. I placed my hand on top of hers and looked at her speaking with a slight whisper.

"Sorry, I should have told you. No big deal, just not at the table," I explained. With Dad's demeanor being nothing new to Booley, he began eating as if it was a sunny day and enjoying the sunshine, perhaps at a picnic table. Ellie and Joe however, had to calm down after hearing the callous and seemingly cruel tone of voice my father had used when speaking about God. Ellie and Joe had spent many years under the harsh tones of an abusive man in their lives and they certainly didn't need another. Banner had quickly taken to lying underneath the table in the kitchen when Ellie cooked, hoping for a piece of food to fall to the floor. To help break the tension, I let Joe feed Banner from the table. Just as Joe finished handing Banner a small chunk of golden fluffy cornbread, Ellie caught a glimpse of headlights turning into the driveway.

"Someone is here," Ellie said leaning to one side of her chair as she looked out the window. I could see the headlights and a I could barely make out a horse trailer behind the vehicle that parked near the front porch. I immediately turned to Booley.

"Do we have a hole in the field?" I asked. Booley was busy chewing. Looking down at his plate, he had mixed his mashed potatoes and corn together. The kernels of corn stuck to the moist mashed potatoes as Booley sopped them up with a fluffy piece of cornbread.

Before his creation crumbled, Booley popped all three items into his mouth at once. Without thinking about our guests at the table, he answered with a mouthful.

"Near the oak tree. Right side," he said nodding and absentmindedly shoving the food in his mouth to everyone who was paying attention. Thinking nothing of his rudeness, he went back to the food on his plate.

The person that drove into our driveway at seven o'clock that night was Mrs. Sunny McDaniel. She had driven from Ohio towing a horse trailer and in that trailer was a dead horse. Its name was Paper Pilot and he used to be a big name in the world of thoroughbred horse racing. After a decent career and retiring to stud for many years, he died of an infection. I remember finishing what was on my plate in a hurry before I ran out and greeted Mrs. McDaniel. The headlights on her truck were hitting me in the face making her barely visible from where I was standing.

"That you, Chapel?" she asked from the darkness.

"Yeah, who you got in there?" I asked referring to the horse trailer. Her truck was old but it was a good truck. A 1925 Model TT that was known to be very durable and easy to fix. I remember the doors were lightweight and Mrs. McDaniel could use the tips of her fingers to sling it close.

"Pilot," she said.

"Sorry to hear about 'em. He was a great horse," I said looking at the horse trailer. Sunny was a widow as her husband was killed in World War I by poison gas while raiding an enemy camp. In June of 1917, Mrs. McDaniel received word of her loss and was forced to take on what her husband had left behind to earn a living. I recall seeing Mrs. McDaniel at the track when I was a kid. When she drove up in our driveway that night, Mrs. McDaniel was nearly sixty years old. She was a pretty woman, but at sixty years of age she was worn and tired.

"Infection got 'em. No medicine would do it," she added.

Paper Pilot's tail was hanging out the back and must have been flapping in the wind all the way from Ohio.

"I have a hole ready to go on the back side near an old oak tree. Let me get in my truck."

I heard the kitchen door open and close. I turned my head and saw Ellie walking toward us wearing a sweater. Her arms were folded and her eyes looked curious. "What's going on?" she asked.

"Horse burial," I answered.

"Oh," she said as she looked at Sunny. They introduced themselves and even shook hands, not something that was common in the thirties between women.

"I'll follow you," Sunny said with sadness in her eyes. She started walking back to the driver's side of her truck when her eye caught Paper Pilot's tail hanging out of the back.

"You're going to bury her horse?" Ellie asked. I was watching Sunny from the corner of my eye as she walked behind the trailer and carefully tucked Pilot's tail back in the trailer.

"Yep. Wanna tag along?" I asked. I knew she was still upset from the verbal lashing my father dished out. I suppose she didn't want to be in there alone should Booley get up and leave.

"I guess. Can Joe come?"

"Sure. He can hold the lantern."

When we left the house I was sitting in the driver's seat with Joe sitting between me and Ellie. Joe's cowlick kept bouncing up and down like a needle in a sewing machine as we drove along the uneven terrain.

Booley usually came with me and helped out, but I was sure I had it covered. The field of dead horses was located about three quarters of a mile from the house and it took some time to get there as we had to drive slowly.

"Who is she?" Ellie asked.

"The woman in the truck? That's Mrs. McDaniel. She's a trainer in Ohio and her horse died. Great horse, too."

"Why did she bring the horse here?"

"Well it's kind of a long story but, a long time ago, my father started a tradition on accident. We have a big field on the back, left side of the farm and it's far away from Penny Creek. Dad allowed several people to bury their horses there," I said as I steered the truck on the uneven ground. "They weren't just average horses. They were Kentucky Derby winners and Preakness winners and one even won the Triple Crown."

"Yeah?" Ellie said trying to hold on to her seat. The road was very bumpy and she sat with one hand on the dash and the other on the seat between her and Joe. I kept looking in the rearview mirror to make sure Mrs. McDaniel was following okay over the uneven ground. I would always creep along at five miles an hour so no one would wrack their truck axles and need repairs.

"Then other people wanted their horses to be buried with the great ones. It is a sentimental thing. These animals raced together their whole lives, why not bury them together."

"I see," she said with an understanding look about her.

"These horses are not just important in terms of racing, but important to the family. They raised them from birth. They are a source of income and the family even travels from track to track with them. They bond with them over time. When they die, they want the best for their family member. I guess most people like the idea of their horse next to the legends."

"How many are buried in the field?" Joe asked. Ellie looked proud that he spoke up and asked a question.

"Oh I don't know, maybe thirty or so," I said with a purely estimated number. Ellie looked as if she was thinking hard about the field. Almost as if she was trying to make a decision before she finally said,

"I think it's nice. I can see how meaningful it is."

"Well, not to mention that we make money off of it," I added. Ellie was silent. "Well, it's not a lot. It's only twenty dollars, but it's for our time digging the hole and a few materials. It takes us a couple hours," I explained thinking that she thought ill of charging money.

"Oh no, I don't think bad of that, sure twenty dollars is understandable," she said nodding her head. Joe sat still holding on to the Burgess Red Twin-Six Lantern watching intently as we arrived at the gate for the field. I got out of the truck and opened the gate.

"Is this field just for the dead horses?" Ellie asked as I got back in and closed the door shut.

"No, sometimes we use it as an exercise field. It's nice and flat," I explained. "We won't ride horses in the field if we already dug a hole though, wouldn't want a horse to fall in."

When we arrived at the burial site for Paper Pilot, I got out and stood by the hole in the ground leaving Ellie and Joe in the truck for the time being. Using hand signals, I helped Mrs. McDaniel back her truck into position. The process of getting a horse into a large hole in the ground isn't pretty and is sometimes disconcerting which is why I thought Ellie and Joe should remain in the cab of my truck. Whenever we dug a grave in the field, we set up a pulley system next to the hole that was framed using oak and maple. We staked the frame into the ground and attached the pulleys which helped us move and lower a horse into a grave. I won't go into the details, but after twenty-five minutes, Paper Pilot was on his side in the hole. Once a deceased thoroughbred was situated in the grave and an incision was made in the horse's abdomen, I would take a bag off the back of the truck and cover the horse with a powder concoction that was required by local law. If I remember correctly, it was a mixture of salt and calcium oxide. After I signaled them, Joe and Ellie had gotten out of the truck and stood nearby while Sunny was fetching something from her truck. They both watched intently while Joe kept the lantern pointed in the right direction so Sunny could see what she was doing.

"I got 'em," she said as she wrapped her arms around a large mass of fabric. Some owners covered up their horse with a tarp or a sheet of plastic to separate the dirt from their beloved horse, but Mrs. Mc-Daniel used three old quilts to cover up Paper Pilot. That was the first time I had ever seen an owner use cloth the cover their horse. Some owners never even covered the horse up and just let the dirt cover the body one shovel full at a time.

Sunny helped me shovel enough dirt on Pilot until he was completely covered. The following day I would get the tractor out from the five-stable barn, attach the digger and fill in the rest of the hole. After Paper Pilot was covered up, we all drove over to the southeast corner of the field which was a dead end. On the way there, I took out my Tenney made, bone-handle whittler pocket knife that Dad purchased from a Mattingly-Haise & Company catalog at Guthrie's. Once I took it out of my pocket, Joe's eyes stared at it with a question.

"What's the knife for, Mr. Chapel?" Joe asked. I glanced in my rearview mirror making sure I wasn't driving too fast for Mrs. McDaniel who was still following us in her truck.

"I'll tell you what, you both come out with me when we get to the fence and I will show you. Keep in mind that we are about to witness a very emotional time for Mrs. McDaniel and we need to be reverent and quiet for her, okay? I will whisper to you what this is all about."

"Okay," Joe whispered not knowing it wasn't yet necessary to keep his voice low. We made it to the southeast corner and before we got out of the truck, Ellie's cough erupted. She covered her mouth with the sleeve of her sweater.

"Mom, you okay?" Joe asked. Ellie nodded her head just before her coughing ceased. She cleared her throat.

"I'm fine." She looked at me, "I won't cough, I promise."

Mrs. McDaniel stayed in her truck momentarily as we walked over to the fence. I took the lantern from Joe and aimed the beam at the wooden planks. The posts and boards were painted black which made the names highly visible when carved with a knife, as if the names were written with a tan colored pencil. With the light running across the plank fence, we could see names carved into the wood. *Wintergreen, Old Rosebud, War Cloud, Chance Shot* and *Speed Chronicle* were some of the names we could see. There looked to be about thirty legends of the racetrack carved into the weathered plank fence.

"These are the names of the horses," I whispered.

"What horses?" Joe whispered back. Mrs. McDaniel was still sitting in her truck.

"The horses that are buried here in this field," I responded. I held the knife loosely in my hand as I brought it in front of the lantern. "Mrs. McDaniel will use this knife to carve in Paper Pilot's name."

As soon as I finished speaking, Sunny McDaniel opened the door to her truck and got out. She walked over toward us with her arms crossed and her head lowered, keeping her eyes on the ground. As she got closer, she uncrossed her arms and brought her hand toward her rosy cheeked face, wiping the tears from under her eyes. It was the moment that she had to put her horse's name on the Chapel fence, a task no owner wanted to endure. She took the knife from my hands and walked over to the fence. I kept the beam of light on the board in front of her. After she unfolded the blade from the bone handle, she carved the name into the wood and promptly folded the blade back into the handle. She took a step back looking at Paper Pilot's name she just carved while Joe, Ellie and I stood silent behind her. Mrs. McDaniel was a tough woman, the kind of farm girl that could wrestle a steer to the ground with her bare hands and then spit out the juice from a chunk of chewing tobacco stuffed in her right cheek. I don't think that she actually did either of these things, but she looked and acted as if she could have, even at her age. The tough woman in her left momentarily as she stood there with tears running down her cheek. Her horse, her friend and family member had died. Ellie, Joe and I stood there quietly until Mrs. McDaniel thanked us, handed me my knife and walked back to her truck.

"Tell your father I said hello," Mrs. McDaniel said wiping her tears with her sleeve.

"Sure will."

"Thanks, again," she said as she got in the truck. When we got back to the house, Booley came out saying goodnight to both Ellie and Joe.

"Turning in for the night?" I asked.

"Surest thing you know!" Booley said. "Mrs. Evans, thank you for the lovely dinner. Best food I have eaten since I was a child."

"Thank you, Booley, and you're welcome," Ellie said with a smile. Booley leaned in closer to Ellie and spoke softly.

"You cook dinner at my house and you can pray at the table. Don't ya pay no attention to that mean ol' cuss, ya hear," he said with a smile.

"I will keep that in mind," Ellie replied. She and Joe walked into the kitchen closing the door behind them.

"You know what makes a trainer great?" Booley asked.

"What?"

"One good horse," Booley replied.

"Yep."

"And, of course, you know what makes a trainer less than desirable."

"What?" I asked.

"One bad horse."

"What brings this up?"

"Oh, I been thinkin' about Outpost. Been thinkin' about him a lot lately," Booley said.

"What are you thinkin' about?"

"Well, I can see it in his eyes. I can see it in his gait and you can just feel it when he runs by you."

"And you think he has what it takes?" I asked.

"He's got it, the question is, can he keep it?"

"That's where we come in."

"No sir, that's where you come in. No bad horse is going to ruin my greatness," Booley said laughing. We talked briefly about jockeys who were in the area, while he lit a rolled cigarette, a habit that only showed itself after dinner. As we spoke, I could see Ellie through the window walking into the kitchen after she put Joe to bed. She began cleaning up and it looked as if Dad had left and had gone in the other room.

"Yep, we're all one horse away," Booley said.

"Where did that one come from?" I asked.

"A very smart man."

"Yeah, Booley? Is that smart man you?" Booley stepped off the back porch and took a long draw on his cigarette, enjoying it the way a rich man would enjoy an expensive cigar.

"Your father," Booley replied as smoke rolled out of his mouth and nose at the same time. He turned around and started toward his little house. At first I thought he was joking, but something made me think he was serious. I watched him walk away into the darkness with his hands in his pockets strolling along without a care in the world.

"Just one horse?" I said out loud although Booley seemed to ignore me. Anxious to talk to Ellie, I opened the door and walked in the kitchen.

"You know, I never thought about how horses were buried," Ellie said as she washed a dinner plate. I closed the door behind me.

"Yeah, I guess I've been around them my whole life, I just don't know any different," I said as I sat down at the kitchen table. The yellow, blue and purple shades of bruises on her face were still evident, but didn't look as bad as they once did.

"I also never thought about how important horses are to their owners. They're like family. Not like a used truck or something."

"Yeah," I replied. I really didn't know what to say although I had hoped that I could keep the conversation going. It turned out that Ellie had a few questions on her mind.

"Can I ask you a question? I mean, it's kind of a personal question, and I don't want you to be offended," she said as she dried a dinner plate with a white dishtowel. She had put on an apron (I still don't know where she found it unless Douglas packed it for her) and tied her hair up into a ponytail that swished side to side caused by the motions she made while drying the plate in her hand. She seemed comfortable and at ease looking the way she did and I liked it, even with the bruises. It seemed to me that she didn't need to be made up and dressed in fancy fabrics to be comfortable around people. She was close to my age, but somehow, she seemed much younger. Maybe it was the ponytail.

"Sure, I don't mind," I said as I readjusted my posture to a more comfortable position.

"You grew up here right? Have you ever left this farm?"

"Sure. Dad and me have traveled all over taking horses to race at different tracks." I took my hat off and hung it on my boot which was resting on my knee. I rifled my hair trying to make it look more pleasant.

"No, I mean, lived anywhere else," she said as she picked up another plate and began drying it.

"I've lived here my whole life. Thirty-five years except for college. Even then I came home quite often."

"Did you date anyone around here?" she asked.

I felt a lump rise out of my chest and settle in my throat when she asked that question. I was hoping that I knew where it was going even though she was a married woman.

"I dated," I cleared my throat, and took my hat off my boot and put it back on my head. "I dated several girls from around here." I put both feet on the floor and leaned toward the kitchen table, folding my hands and setting them in front of me.

"None of them appeal to you?"

"Not really. Why?" I moved my hands off the kitchen table as I couldn't get comfortable. Finally I just sat still. I knew I was fidgeting too much.

"Oh I don't know. You're just a successful, hard working man, and I would think you would have been married by now."

I didn't know what to say to that. I could still feel the walnut in my throat, and I started shaking a little. I kept staring at her ponytail swishing behind her head and getting distracted momentarily. I was thinking too long and she seemed to think I was offended.

"I am sorry. It's not my place," she said shaking her head.

"No, it's fine. Really. I guess I always thought that I would find the right person someday." She finished drying the last plate and turned around. I couldn't tell if I looked casual or not. I felt gawky and awkward.

"I married too early in life. I didn't know what I was doing." Ellie gently pushed herself away from the counter and casually sat down as if she had lived in my house her whole life. My palms were sweating, and it felt like it was a hundred degrees in that kitchen. God bless, I thought, I hope I'm not sweating. Ellie continued, "I made a mistake by marrying early. I didn't know what I was getting into." She propped up her head with her elbow resting on the table top and lazily drew imaginary circles on the wooden surface with her index finger.

"What are you going to do now?" I asked.

"I don't know yet. I've been thinking about it, and I can't come up with a reasonable answer."

"I am glad you're here," I said without thinking. I tend to do that a lot. Ellie smiled and stopped moving her finger in circles.

"I'm glad I'm here, too," she said as she looked at me.

We talked some more, mostly about my father. She asked about his hatred for God and I gave her the short version of my mom's death. At one point we even talked about Booley. Joe came up in the conversation a few times, and she explained that he had been having problems at school with a group of boys beating up on him. She talked about it like it was a problem, but until the next day, I didn't know how big of a problem it was.

11

The next day, I was walking toward the main house from the track when I saw Ellie walking with Joe, using her laced handkerchief to cover his nose and I could see that there was blood on her shirt. Strands of her hair had broken free from her red yarn ponytail and waved in the wind as she made her way to the porch. I ran to her before she got to the front door.

"His nose is bleeding pretty bad," she said as she bent over looking at his nose with the look of motherly concern. She gently removed the cloth from his face, inspecting the weak stream of blood from both nostrils. Once in the kitchen, Ellie began to clean him up as he stood in front of the sink. I kept his head back with his eyes staring at the ceiling.

"What happened?" I asked.

"Boys from school beat him up. I got to him just as they started to walk away." Joe had tears in his eyes, and blood was flowing down over his mouth and onto the underside of his chin.

"Hang on. Keep staring at the ceiling, Joe," I said as I walked to the cupboard that held our medical supplies. I looked around until I found a bottle of Humphrey's #9 headache medicine.

We walked Joe into the living room while keeping his nose pointed toward the ceiling, being cautious that he didn't trip and make things worse. Dad was sitting in his chair listening to the radio with Banner by his side. As soon as he saw that the commotion was going to last a while, Dad walked out onto the back porch holding his bottle of whiskey. Banner got up and followed him looking as if he was about to lay back down with each step. The door closed and the old man and his dog were gone.

"So what happened?" she asked her son. "I don't know," was his answer to every question she asked. With tears in his eyes, he turned his head toward the cushions of the couch. I kept the towel on his nose and pinched it to help stop the flow of blood while Ellie continued with the questions to no avail. After the flow of blood eased up and eventually stopped all together, Ellie and I walked back to the kitchen and spoke softly so Joe couldn't hear.

"You mentioned he was having problems at school, what is his teacher doing about it?" I asked. The loose strands of hair that had come loose from her ponytail dangled in front of her face. She brought her hand up to her forehead and swept the strands to the side of her head, tucking them behind her ear.

"Nothing. Most of the time Joe gets caught by these boys after school. The boys live near the courthouse and they haven't been able to get to Joe since he has been staying here on your farm."

"Can't the school do anything?"

"Not if they don't see it." Frustrated and angered, she continued. "I don't know, I am thinking about going over to the boy's houses and talking to their parents," she added. I immediately disapproved.

"I wouldn't do that."

"Why not?"

"Trust me, it would make it worse. I wouldn't do it if I were you."

I said. That night, Joe and Ellie went to bed early and I stayed up late, filling out progress reports on my client's horses and putting them in mailing envelopes.

The next afternoon Joe's shoulders were slouched, and his head hung low. I thought that he had gotten into another fight, but Ellie explained that Joe's teacher told her he had been sulking all day. Apparently he hadn't said a word to anyone at school and showed little interest in anything. At dinner, Joe rested his elbow on the table and held his head up with his hand, staring at the soup in his bowl.

"Can I be excused?" Joe said. Ellie seemed at a loss.

"Sure," she replied. Joe walked out of the kitchen, over to their little room and closed the door. Ellie stared vacantly at her bowl as she stirred the vegetables with her spoon. "I have repeatedly told his father about the boys at school and he says it's just boys being boys and he will grow out of it." Dad and Booley were focused on slurping spoonfuls of vegetable soup as if tonight were their last meal. Ellie had used the left over cornbread by crumbling up the pieces in the soup. Booley looked as if he was considering putting the spoon away and just drinking straight from the bowl. If he was alone in his little house, I bet he would have.

"Have you spoken with the teacher or the principal?" I asked. "They should be able to do something. They can't just ignore this."

"No," she said in a frustrated tone. "I thought about teaching him at home instead of sending him off to school." Dad's spoon hit the soup bowl from which he was eating. The metal utensil rattled around the ceramic edges before settling down. My eyes moved from his clattering bowl to his eyes which were glaring at Ellie as if rays of light were about to shoot out of his eyes.

"Listen here," Dad growled. "A man doesn't solve a problem by ignoring a problem. You face it head on. If you want that trespasser to grow up to be a weak little kid, you keep treating him like one." Dad stood up and put his bowl in the kitchen sink and walked out onto the back porch. Banner crawled out from underneath the table and followed. Dad took a cigar out of his shirt pocket and closed the door after making sure Banner's tail was clear. Only a few days before, my father was prepared to shoot Joe in his left eyeball, now he was dishing out parenting advice. Ellie leaned back in her chair and crossed her arms.

"No, don't let the old man get to you. He's a grumpy old coot. Just forget what he says. I do," I said.

"Well, I guess I don't disagree with him. Not completely," Ellie said. I was used to my father's terse attitude, Ellie wasn't. The rest of the night she considered what Dad had said, at least she seemed to be thinking about it. I certainly didn't disagree with Dad, but I would have said it much nicer than he did.

The next morning at the track, Ellie once again proved to be proficient at helping out. She even helped hot walk a couple of the horses around the barn. I didn't really like having her work for me in this manner, especially since she was still coughing with a death rattle in her lungs, but I did get to be around her which I did like.

I remember thinking that she was a married woman, but perhaps one day that marriage would end as it seemed to have been failing at that point. This is not something I should have wished; however it would be for the best. I knew in my heart that I could take care of Ellie better than Mayor Evans. She deserved better. Even now as I write this I can envision her pouring a bag of feed into a barrel, her ponytail tied with red yarn swishing back and forth with her movements. I am certain that the little things about Ellie went unnoticed by Mayor Evans, but it was those little things that made Ellie as precious as the day was long.

When we wrapped up for the day, it was just before lunchtime and Ellie had mentioned that she was going to head over to Guthrie's. Thinking that I was clever, I made an excuse to go with her in order to be with her. I think I had told her that I needed shaving cream or something. I climbed into the cab of the truck and started down the road with Ellie sitting beside me. As I drove, I was hit in the face with a question out of the blue. It was a question that started a fire in my chest and rose inside my body, flame broiling my head.

"What girls did you date?" Ellie asked as she stared out the windshield with a grin on her face. She grinned, but didn't smile too much as the wound on the corner of her mouth was healing and looking much better.

"What?" I asked. That was when the flame ignited underneath my rib cage. I cracked the window in the cab.

"You said you dated a few girls in town, and I might know them. Who did you date?" she asked. There was a smirk on her face that was playful and somehow inviting.

"Well, uh, I courted Mrs. Foden for a while," I said as I rolled the window down a bit further. Ellie's face furrowed, and her eyes glared at mine. She raised her hand and slapped me on the arm as if I insulted her mother. She didn't hit me hard as it was an enervated slap. I couldn't help but smile as she tried her best to hide her playful grin behind her expression that was trying hard to appear insulted.

"Mrs. Foden is married! Has been for years!"

I laughed as I spoke. "She wasn't Mrs. Foden when I dated her. It was before she was married." I could tell that she was only half-joking. I suppose back then, I didn't know what flirting was, but I am sure that was what she was doing.

"Oh, well okay. I guess. Who else?"

"Kitty Kingston."

"Mmmm…I don't know her."

"You might know her as Joan Kit Webber."

"Joanie Webber? Her name is Kitty?"

"That's what we called her in school. Nickname."

"She is in my social chapter."

"Oh, great!"

"I'm gonna find out the dirt on you," she said as she extended her index finger and poked me in the arm.

"You'll find plenty with Kitty. We used to be engaged." Ellie's eyes enlarged as she drew in a big breath.

"Mr. Chapel! You are mysterious. A mysterious cowboy!" She said teasingly. I smiled, enjoying the banter back and forth. I parked in front of Guthrie's General Store and opened the driver's side door as Ellie continued to prod me.

"You're not safe, Chapel. The dirt I'm gonna get on you! You're very unlucky," she said as she got out of the passenger side. "Joanie and me are thick as thieves. She'll spill everything." Ellie seemed more alive and comfortable around me and it was because of this, I would catch myself thinking about her—even when she wasn't around.

"I'm sure Joanie will have a lot to say. I'm worried, very worried," I said with a smile.

"You better be."

Guthrie's General Store was owned by the Guthrie family that lived in Georgetown. They also owned a very successful feed store operation that funded their business venture of opening their own grocery store. Jerry Guthrie left Georgetown for several years and came back carrying a Bible with his name embossed in gold lettering on the front leather cover. He received the fancy Bible upon graduating seminary and used it every Sunday at the local Baptist church. He became the full time pastor after my father punched Brother Cochran during a home visit after my mother passed away.

In the same way that everyone knows that Sheriff Crease shot the Howard dog, everyone in town knows my dad punched Brother Cochran and screamed that he "didn't want to have anything to do with you two sons of bitches." Of course he was referring to both Brother Cochran and God. Either way, brother Cochran explained to the church that he thought it was time that he move on (he was as old as the hills anyway). After many years of preachers that came and went, Brother Guthrie took the pulpit and was there for as long as I can remember.

When Ellie and I walked into Guthrie's, the familiar smell of fresh baked bread floated in front of me. Much later in life, I would smell the aroma of fresh baked bread and immediately be taken back to Guthrie's in the 1930s. It wasn't a big store—more of a long rectangular space with just enough room for a display case, cash register, and a small lunch counter with five bar stools. Three aisles of shelved goods reached toward the back of the rectangular space and the hardwood floor swelled and contracted throughout the varying temperatures of the seasons. The squeaking beneath our feet went unnoticed as there was plenty to distract us from the creaks and cracks as we walked.

Seven penny jars of candy sat next to the colossal gold-lined cash register on a long display case that housed meats and cheeses. Beside the display case was a lunch counter which served breakfast, and of course, lunch. Dinner was served only on Friday and Saturday nights. The counter itself was made of solid oak and was very smooth—none of that particle board and Formica business that I see so much of today. There were only five barstools and they never added any more that I remember, as their customer base was limited to travelers and the residents of Georgetown. When you ordered a sandwich to take with you, it was wrapped in wax paper. If you were lucky enough to be at Guthrie's when they had Coca-Cola in stock, you could purchase a sandwich and a Coke for 35 cents.

I always think back to the thirties when I would buy a sandwich and a Coke from Guthrie's. I would eat while I drove back to the farm. The cold Coke bottle would rest between my legs, and I would take a bite and take a sip while the warm summer air would flow into the cab of my truck. It's a small thing, but I hold onto that memory as if it were an important, life-changing event. A small memory with little impact on my life as a whole, but I think you understand why something so insignificant can mean so much to a person. I would give anything now just to revisit one of those moments that I casually took for granted.

Ellie had shuffled into Guthrie's walking directly to the shelf that held a bag of flour.

"Need any bacon, Mr. Chapel?" Herb Guthrie asked. He was Jerry's brother.

"No, not today," I said casually pointing to Ellie. Herb stood at the counter with a sign above his head that was nailed to the wall which read *Credit makes good customers. Cash makes great customers.*

"Need anything, Mrs. Evans?" Herb shouted. He was wiping his hands on his apron as he smiled in her direction. Ellie's hand could be seen waving over the shelves, signaling that she was fine. "I got it Herb," she said. I was supposed to be there for shaving cream, however, I had forgotten about the white lie I had told so I could be with Ellie. I just stood there and Herb looked at me with a perplexed look on his face.

"Do you need anything, Mr. Chapel?"

"Oh no, I'm with Ellie. She needs some cooking supplies, and I gave her a ride."

"Is she still staying on your farm? Her accident was a while ago, wasn't it?" Herb whispered. Privacy has never been a luxury in small towns and I have heard Booley say many times, "Georgetown is like a giant sewing circle".

"Yes, sir. She is staying on our farm," I answered. Herb's face was still puzzled and looked like he had more questions, but Ellie came to the counter just in time. Her arms were full of items and managed them from her arms and hands to the top of the display case. Herb rang up the items on the register as he looked at both Ellie and me as if he was studying our faces.

"I got it," I said to Ellie as I slid the twenty dollar bill from Mrs. McDaniel's horse burial across the top of the display case toward Herb. Once I got my change back, Herb began to ask a question which I purposely interrupted with a "thank you" and a statement about coming back later for bacon. Herb just nodded his head, seemingly in frustration that he didn't know why Ellie was still at the farm.

On the way back, Ellie jabbed me again with questions about Joanie Webber and our short engagement. I didn't give her much information as there wasn't much to tell. I would occasionally take my eyes off the road and look over at her and a few times, she caught me looking at her the way I shouldn't have looked at a married woman. I couldn't tell, but it seemed to me that she looked back the way a married woman shouldn't. We spoke about different things and at a half mile away from the farm, one of her coughing fits surfaced and I thought I was going to have to pull over or turn the truck around and head for the hospital. Once the coughing subsided, she patted her chest and muttered, "I'm fine. Goodness this is unpleasant."

When we drove up to the house, there was a truck in the driveway with a horse trailer attached to it. The trailer was old and rust was collecting around the welded joints of the steel structure. The paint was flaking off in small, uneven chips and the tires looked like they needed to be replaced two years ago. The truck that was pulling the trailer however, looked fairly new and I could tell it was a 1938 Ford pick-up which had the newer cab design and bed. Inside the rusty horse trailer was a famous horse by the name of Eastern Express. The owners intended to bury him on our farm even though at that moment the horse was still alive.

12

It wasn't always owners that brought dead horses to the farm. Sometimes it was the trainers that drove up in our driveway and not everyone was as sentimental about it as others. We had just returned from Guthrie's and Ellie and I were in a good mood, but that was about to change. The horse in the rusty, old trailer wasn't a Derby winner, Preakness winner or a Belmont winner, but had won many races. Eastern Express came to the farm with a fractured leg and was still able to walk quite well considering his injury.

This was nothing new as we had a few owners and trainers that wanted to go about it in this manner as it made the trip easier on them. It was a very simple process of walking the horse to the edge of the hole and placing a rifle to its head and pulling the trigger. Once the trigger was pulled, two people stood on one side and pushed the horse toward the hole and it would fall in. I know it sounds like a terrible thing to do, but in the sport of thoroughbred horse racing, shooting a horse wasn't an uncommon thing and it didn't require Booley and me to set up the framed pulley system. Nowadays, they use an injection that makes the horse go to sleep before the medicine shuts down the animal's organs. It's obviously a more humane method that we weren't able to take advantage of in the thirties.

There were two trainers, one was an older guy, and no doubt the younger fella was the trainer's assistant. Both were dressed in tattered cowboy hats and denim jeans with holes that exposed their knee caps. Ellie and I got out of the truck, and I greeted them with a smile. I didn't know them, but the horse was easily recognizable as his name was printed on the back of the deteriorating trailer.

"There's an angry, old man inside that told us to wait out here. We've been waiting for about a half hour, and he hasn't come out yet. Do you live here?" the older man asked.

"Yeah, that angry, old man is my father."

"I'm sorry. I didn't know."

"Don't be. He's mean to everyone," I explained.

"Sounds like my pa. All he does is drink and cuss," the younger fella added. The horse trainer patted his hand on the metal exterior of the horse trailer.

"This is Eastern Express. Ever heard of 'em?"

"Of course," I said.

"Well, he's got a fractured ankle. Needs to go soon, I would think."

"You'll have to give us until tomorrow morning. We don't have a hole dug yet," I explained, "Takes me almost two hours to dig with the tractor." Ellie caught on quickly to the conversation and took several steps toward the trainer with a grimaced look on her face.

"Wait a minute. You're going to kill this horse?" Ellie asked. I should have seen this coming.

"Yes," the trainer said. "His ankle is fractured."

"Is the horse in pain?" Ellie asked.

"Yes ma'am,"

"Can't you do something else?" she questioned.

"Thoroughbreds only purpose is racing," the older man explained.

"It will take a lot of time and money to get the horse to where it is pain free, even then he can't race," Ellie didn't like the answer. She seemed appalled and excused herself taking two bags of groceries inside.

"She okay?" the trainer asked.

"Yeah," I said. "You can stable him in the large barn on the back of our property," I said pointing toward the dirt path. "If you come back around eight-thirty or so tomorrow morning, we'll get it taken care of."

"Okay. See ya then," the older man said as they both got in the truck. There was one more bag of groceries and I took it inside and walked into the kitchen. Ellie didn't look happy as she put away the groceries and I helped clean up the sink and stove from the night before. I looked out the window and saw the truck pulling the horse trailer, making its way down the dirt path, kicking up dust as it moved forward. Once the trailer disappeared over the hill, out of nowhere I heard the loud crack of a rifle coming from the back porch.

Ellie and I ran outside and saw Dad standing on the wooden floorboards of the porch holding his Remington M37 Rangemaster with smoke swirling out of the end of the barrel.

"Son of a bitch!" he said. Ellie and I looked out to where he was shooting and saw the white coyote running into the woods on the right side of the farm.

"Miss him Dad?"

"Yeeeeah," he grunted.

"What is it?" Ellie asked.

"A cy-ote" I replied.

"I thought so, but it was white."

"They call it an albino," I said.

"Does it bother the horses?" she asked.

"No, just eats the vegetables out of Dad's garden, especially the tomatoes. Pisses him off. Not sure what the little fella is doing around here now. It's not warm enough for tomatoes."

"Son of a bitch!" Dad said again. Booley rode toward the house on Eros.

"It was Dad shooting at the white cy-ote," I yelled out to him.

"I figured, but I need you to come to the barn. Ranger is bleeding."

When horses are exposed to pollution (could be black smoke from a steam engine on a train), the capillaries in their lungs can sometimes burst after exercise. Thoroughbred race horses are bred for speed and in turn, that speed causes their blood pressure to rise from strenuous exercise or during a race. The walls of the vessels break and release blood into the airways which appears in the form of a bloody nose. For humans, a bloody nose (like in Joe's case) isn't a big deal; however for a race horse, it can end their career on the track.

When I arrived at the barn, I looked Ranger's Cape over and put my ear on his side as if I was listening through a door to hear a secret conversation. Instead of a conversation, I could hear faint gurgling sounds of blood in his lungs. As soon as I got back to the house, I called Dr. Langston Wallach.

Everybody called him Dr. Wall since he preferred that to people getting his last name wrong. He was older than my father and walked with a side to side waddle. The fedora hat on his head was always crooked which was attributed to his side to side waddle that seemed to increase as old age set in. His voice was raspy, and the wrinkles around his eyes were very animated as he spoke. He lived in Lexington and would only come to Georgetown if it was important. It wasn't uncommon for him to just give advice over the phone.

Once he arrived in the driveway, I went out to greet him as did Booley.

"Dr. Wall. Thanks so much for coming," I said as I walked toward his car.

"Damn, doc," Booley started in, "Time hasn't been treating you well," I watched Dr. Wall waddle toward us.

"Booley, I see that time has also been cruel to you as well. You look like a dried up ol' raisin with powdered sugar on your head." Booley just shook his head with a smile. Dr. Wall and Booley had known each other for as long as I had been alive.

"Is your father still above ground?" Dr. Wall asked me.

"Yes."

"Ahh, too bad," Dr. Wall said as if he meant it, although all three of us laughed. "Well, where's your horse?"

After a trip up to the barn in the truck, Dr. Wall used the instruments in his veterinarian case to detect the extent of Ranger's bleeding. This wasn't the first time we had a bleeder on our farm as Dr. Wall had been here a few years ago for the same problem with a horse on my father's roster. While we were talking, Ellie came into the barn and walked over to Ranger's Cape. She studied him out of concern, but didn't interrupt us as we spoke about his health. I watched her from the corner of my eye as Dr. Wall explained the brown vial of medicine he was holding. Ellie stroked Ranger's mane and crest, comforting him and putting him at ease. I kept my eye on Ellie as she eventually walked out of Ranger's stall and into the stall holding Eastern Express. After a few more jokes about their age, Booley and

Dr. Wall said their good-byes, and I thanked Dr. Wall as we started to walk out of the barn.

"Dr. Wall?" Ellie said. She couldn't be seen, but we could all hear her voice.

"Yes?" Dr. Wall said as he shuffled around and looked in the direction of where the voice was coming from. Ellie then poked her head out of the stable.

"Could you come here a moment?" Ellie asked. Dr. Wall did as asked and walked into the stall containing Eastern Express. Booley and I followed.

"Dr. Wall, could you please examine this horse's front left ankle. I am curious to know if it can be healed."

"I guess I could take a look at it since I am here," he grunted as he bent his tired, worn body and kneeled down. He used his hand to feel the back of Eastern's leg. His hand moved all the way down to the ankle, applying pressure ever so gently in certain areas. Eastern grunted as he pulled his leg back away from Dr. Wall. The ankle was meticulously studied and his examination was very thorough while using great care and noticeable respect for Eastern. When he was finished, he straightened up holding his black medical case and looked Ellie in her eyes.

"Seems to have a fractured ankle. When did this horse acquire this injury?" Dr. Wall asked. Ellie looked at me.

"I am not sure," I said.

"As I cannot tell when the injury occurred, I cannot be certain of recovery. This horse is in pain. Have you considered putting it down?"

"That's why this horse is here," I said as I nodded in the direction of the field of dead horses.

"I see."

"What would it take to try to heal this horse?" Ellie asked.

"Well, of course it could never race again. You know that."

"Of course," Ellie replied.

"Well, you could try. It wouldn't be cheap. I would recommend that you put the horse down. Even if you heal it, this animal wouldn't be doing much other than eating feed and milling about all day long." Dr. Wall said. Ellie looked down at Eastern Express' ankle. She obviously didn't like the answer. "Okay?" Dr. Wall added with a smile and a nod as if to seal his suggestion. He turned around as Ellie caressed Eastern's neck. Booley and I walked Dr. Wall to his car, and I paid him what I owed in cash. Ellie stayed in the barn for a while and I didn't see her until dinner time. I could tell Ellie wasn't very happy about Eastern's plight, but it was commonplace on our farm.

That night, Dad was already at the table before Ellie was finished cooking. I was reading LIFE Magazine in the family room on the couch and Joe was tuning the radio. I watched Joe and observed his mannerisms as he turned the knobs and moved the dial past the stations that came in clear. As soon as he reached the end of the dial, he would go back and begin turning the knobs in the other direction with no intent of finding a clear station. Static and crackling sounds emitted from the speakers more than music or a news report. He seemed to be despondent until a sudden noise of pots and pans clanging in the kitchen caused Joe to turn his head. I didn't want him to know I was observing him, so I quickly tilted my head down toward my magazine. In the February issue that year, there was a story on the actor Errol Flynn and Franklin D. Roosevelt attending a horse show together. Seemed like an odd pairing to me. I was looking at a photo of the two notable figures when Ellie announced that dinner was ready. I walked into the kitchen followed by Joe who continued to look rundown and depressed.

As soon as I stepped into the kitchen, I was greeted by the aroma of grilled cheese and baked potato soup. My dad already had his spoon in his hand when she set the bowl in front of him. Booley came through the door just before I sat down.

"Great eaters and great sleepers are incapable of anything else that is great, and for right now, I'm fine with that," Booley said to anyone listening. The silence commenced except for the clinking of the spoons to the bowls and slurping beverages from our glasses. Booley had gone into town before we ate to pick up a box of horseshoes we had ordered from a farrier in Indiana. On the way back to the farm, he had purchased a bottle of Coca-cola and was drinking it at the table. Joe's eyes were on the Coke bottle every time Booley took a sip. His eyes showed a glimmer that looked to bring him out of his depressed attitude and I thought I could help.

"Joe, do you like Coca-Cola?" I asked. Joe nodded his head. "I have one in the fridge if you'd like it."

"Joe can't have Coca-Cola," Ellie said. "It makes him so that he can't sleep at night." I looked at Ellie, and she seemed to be pretty stern on her rule. I sensed a frustrated tone in her voice as if she had no idea how to bring Joe out of his dismal state, although it seemed to me that a Coca-Cola might help. I went back to my potato soup and grilled cheese sandwich knowing I should stay out of the matter.

I later found out that Ellie couldn't sleep that night since her husband was due back in town in a few days. Wide-awake, she walked out on the back porch after wrapping a quilt around herself to keep warm. She later told me that she had sat down on the old couch and was thinking of how she was going to handle her divorce when she looked up and saw that Eastern Express had gotten out of the barn and was eating leaves and bark off of the willow tree. I wonder now if the trainers had even bothered to feed the horse since the next day was going to be its last. Ellie later explained to me that she went into the kitchen and grabbed an apple and walked over to the fence. Eventually the horse approached Ellie, and she extended her arm out toward him. The horse began to nibble on the apple and did so before gently taking the whole apple from her hand. She stroked his mane and scratched around his ears. At some point in the early morning, Ellie fell asleep in her little room and I woke up before dawn and started the coffee.

I took a mug with me and sipped on it as I got the tractor out of the five-stable barn and attached the digger. I puttered up the dirt path and drove the tractor into the field of dead horses and started digging. After an hour or so, Booley walked from his little house and made his way next to the tractor. The colder weather made the ground firm and somewhat difficult to get the digger into the earth, but I managed.

Anytime Booley would help me dig a grave he would often say for his own amusement, "Getting money is like digging a grave with a needle." Sometimes I wish I had written down his expressions and sayings as I have forgotten many of them in my old age. Once the hole was of sufficient depth, I took the tractor back to the five-stable barn and Booley rode on the back, standing on a cross joint. Once I put the tractor away and closed the barn doors, we looked over at the willow tree and saw Eastern Express.

"How did he get out?" Booley asked.

"I don't know," I said scratching my head. "That's odd. I'll take him back."

"When they comin'?" Booley asked.

"Around eight or eight-thirty," I answered as I walked toward Eastern. I walked him all the way back to the barn next to the track and looked for signs of weakness in the gate that kept Eastern in the stall. Nothing seemed out of place so I latched the door and started back toward the main house. At eight fifteen, the two trainers had arrived and made their way to the barn and loaded Eastern Express into the trailer. Booley and I watched as the truck arrived in the field of dead horses and I was already on my third cup of coffee. They parked the trailer and the two trainers unloaded Eastern and guided him as close to the hole as possible while Booley and I stood next to him, ready to help push him into the hole. The young trainer loaded a round into his rifle and cocked the trigger back. With a hint of hesitation and a look of wanting to get it over quickly, he raised his rifle and placed the barrel next to the temple of Eastern's head.

13

The sound of a honking car horn came from behind us. The roaring of an engine could be heard between the repeated honking of the horn. The young assistant trainer who was holding the gun to Eastern Express's head, carefully put the rifle to his side and released the hammer.

"Now, what in the hell is that?" the young man asked.

"I don't know. Must be an emergency," his superior responded. When the truck came to a stop, Ellie jumped out of the truck after applying the hand brake. With the engine still running, she jogged toward us holding money out in front of her.

"Don't do it! Stop!" she said as she was running out of breath. "I want to buy your horse." Ellie had a determined look on her face as she extended her hand, holding a wad of money. She began coughing and covering her mouth with her other hand. The look on the trainers' faces was of pure bewilderment. They both looked at each other from the corners of their eyes, never moving their heads. Their eyes returned to Ellie who was still holding out her money, whatever the amount was, I don't remember.

That morning, the trainer and his assistant left, leaving the horse behind and letting Ellie keep her money. I am sure they were still shaking their heads as they drove down the highway. In the field of dead horses was a hole that was meant for Eastern Express, but wasn't filled until much later and with a different horse. Dr. Wall was called back to Chapel Farms, but this time it was for Ellie's horse.

"With a simple fracture, just apply the pine tar and iodine," Dr. Wall explained as he held a big jar of the concoction he was referring to. "No more trotting for this horse, walking only. Gentle exercise after three months of treatment, once a day if possible. Keep in mind that when you apply this, you do it only to dampen the skin. Don't just slather it all over," he said as he made crazy hand motions. Ellie paid him with her own money, and I gave her one of the stalls in the five stall barn since it was closer to the house. I did have to move the tractor and its digging attachment to the far end of the barn, but there was more than enough room for Eastern.

Dr. Wall seemed perturbed that she would spend money on keeping the horse alive, but he didn't complain out loud. "I don't see this horse living more than three or four years, but good luck," was the last thing he said before he drove off. Ellie and Joe would go out and feed him, using the methods and medicine prescribed by Dr. Wall to help ease the pain and help heal the fracture.

It was around this time that Mayor Evans returned from Louisiana, (when all hell broke loose) but there is one more thing I have to tell you before we get to that. It has to do with an old coot and an albino coyote.

14

We were only into the fourth day of March and Dad was already reading his *Farmer's Almanac*. He was checking the temperature each day and kept looking outside for signs of buds on the trees. In case you're unaware, the *Farmer's Almanac* was eerily accurate. It made use of an old, but effective weather pattern formula that took a variety of factors into consideration. Those weather patterns were heavily relied upon by my father and he was waiting for the perfect time to plant seeds and get things started even though it was March. Supposedly, he read an article in the almanac that suggested planting tomatoes indoors in pots. I believe he said he would keep the tomatoes inside at night and leave them out in the sun during the day. All I knew is that it was a lot of work just to eat tomatoes, but it certainly gave the ol' man something to do. I was pretty sure that Dad was hoping his garden would produce enough vegetables so that Ellie could use them in her recipes at some point. He did love his garden, and I think that if he were to eat a dinner prepared by Ellie with his vegetables, he might actually smile. Maybe.

At five in the morning, our routine began at the track and once the horses had completed a heavy workout, they were either given a full bath or just a rinse. As the warm soapy mixture was poured onto their hide, the waft of the steam rolled off their bodies and dissolved into the cool morning air. Jim and Sarah were given strict guidelines that great care was to be taken as to the temperature of the water. I insisted that the water be what I called "just above lukewarm" and once they dried the horse off, they covered the thoroughbred with a turnout blanket.

Ellie and Joe had made a trip to the five-stable barn and fed Eastern after applying the pine tar and iodine concoction. Once Joe was at school, Ellie worked with us at the track for most of the day, cleaning out stalls and filling up hay receptacles. Later in the day we heard the crack of a rifle ring though the air; Ellie and I came running. I had thought that maybe Mayor Evans had come back early and Dad was signaling us that he was on the property—either that or he was firing at the coyote again. Sure enough, the white coyote had come back and was running toward the woods unscathed. He disappeared just past the tree line as we came into view of the back porch.

"Did you get him?" I yelled out toward the house.

"No," Dad grumbled as he cycled a shell out of the chamber of his rifle. The pinging noise of the shell bouncing on the wooden porch floor could be heard from where I was standing. Banner had picked his head up, looked around and promptly plopped his head back down and closed his eyes.

"Do you want to get him? I can help," Ellie shouted out. I turned and looked at Ellie, confused as to how exactly she could help *get* a coyote.

In her younger years, Ellie had grown up on a corn and soybean farm where coyotes, deer, and other farm pests were prevalent on their land. Ellie explained that her father would set snares made of wire and rope and once the animal was caught, it was killed in a humane manner. Ellie explained her past briefly to us as she made motions with her hands on how to set a snare and trap an animal.

"A snare trap is made from a loop of wire," she explained to my father. He seemed interested and watched her closely. "You can snare an animal relatively easy without any bait." Although she never utilized her practice on our farm, she mentioned that as a young girl, she used to run out of the house in the middle of the night and set trapped animals free unbeknownst to her family.

After a quick trip to Nunnelley's Hardware Store, my father watched Ellie as she dug a hole about the size of a big can of coffee.

"Not too deep. If it's too deep or shallow, it won't work," Ellie said as she was digging while resting on her hands and knees with a garden trowel in her right hand. Dad was half way bent over, with his hands on his thighs, watching Ellie from over her shoulder. He watched her tie one end of wire into a snare, with her thin fingers.

"Just one piece of wire?" he asked in his gruff voice.

"Yep, that's all you need. See that?" she was pulling on the snare with her bony finger and showed Dad how it would trap the animal. "Now we just tie this other end to a stake." I watched Dad take part in the project as he got on his knees and readied himself to assist in the creation of the snare. He held the stake in his left hand and gripped the hammer with his right. His loose-skinned arm brought the hammer down with noticeable force. Dad's bicep protruded through his shirt as he pounded the stake. Even in his older age, he was a tough man with a lot of strength left in his old body. Ellie stood there and watched him with a grin on her face.

"Here," she handed him the other end of the wire. He tied it to the stake and Ellie began gathering leaves and bits of grass.

"Now what?" Dad asked as if he suddenly thought that he was doing all this for nothing. Ellie didn't respond. She scattered leaves and grass over the wire and the hole. Underneath the camouflaged ground was a hole with a snare waiting quietly to trap its intended target.

"Once the coyote steps into the hole, he will try to pull away from it, tightening the snare," Ellie said. Dad looked curious, but also skeptical. He grunted and nodded his head before walking toward the back porch.

"Did he say, thank you?" Ellie asked me, with a smile and her hands on her hips.

"Yeah, that was his way of saying thank you. I guess."

Ellie smiled and looked over the snare once more before we left it alone. From time to time, I would see Dad look outside toward his garden. A few times, he and Banner would walk over to the snare, making sure it wasn't disturbed. I was just glad it gave him something to do.

After the trap was set, Doc Thomas drove up in his 1933 Chevrolet Mercury. He got out of the car carrying his medical bag wearing a shirt that was ironed and free of wrinkles with perfect pleats in his tweed pants. No doubt that Mrs. Thomas had been hard at work making sure her husband looked more than presentable. He had come to follow up with Ellie to make sure her cough was cured, and her lungs were free of infection.

"Ellie, how are you feeling?" was the first thing Doc said as he walked up to us.

"Good, Doc. That medicine has helped tremendously."

She sat on the old couch while Doc reached his hand underneath the back of her shirt and placed the end of the stethoscope on her skin.

"Geesh! That's cold," she said as she jumped.

"Sorry about that. I forget sometimes," Doc said as he quickly removed it from her skin and warmed it in his hands before continuing.

She took in deep breaths and exhaled. Dad opened the door and stepped out onto the porch holding a newly opened bottle of whiskey and two small pots with tomato sprouts protruding from the soil. Without even noticing the three of us standing next to the old couch, he walked over to where the sun was shining and put the pots on the ground. His eyes scanned the land around us looking for the coyote. Banner was following him taking one step at a time as his back left leg was numb from sleeping on it too long. As soon as Dad saw us gathered around the old couch, he turned around with a grumble coming from his clenched teeth.

"Hello, Mr. Chapel," Doc said. Dad went back inside without saying a word. Banner wasn't quick enough though. By the time Banner discovered Dad was going back inside, Dad had already closed the door. Banner stood there and looked at the chipped paint on the wooden door while his tail continued to sweep slowly from side to side. I guess when Dad realized his faithful companion wasn't with him, he opened the door and watched Banner limp back into the house. Once his rear end had cleared the frame, the door promptly closed. Doc went back to his examination.

"I have to tell ya that you are in great health considering what you have been through."

"Really?"

"Yeah, I mean it's remarkable. Your lungs are pretty much free and clear, just remarkable," Doc said with a smile. "Take a look at this," he brought a medical textbook with him that gave details about hypothermia and hypoxia. He used words like "acclimatization" and explained what "polycythemia" was. I didn't understand it all, but I was glad Doc Thomas did. We stayed out on the back porch for some time just talking and listening to what Doc had to say, even though he had a knack for talking your ear off.

Just after Doc left, the phone rang and it was the Mayor's housekeeper. Ellie was given the message that she ought to pick up Joe from school. When she returned from the short walk, she took him into their little room and laid him down on their bed. There wasn't any blood this time, but he was injured. A punch to the stomach and repeated blows to his shoulder was the attack Joe received from the same group of boys at school. Apparently, Ellie consulted with his teacher and the principal since he was beaten up on school grounds. She was shocked to hear them say they can't do anything if they didn't see it happen. This time depression had set in and made him sick. His stomach was turning; a stubborn headache didn't seem to leave no matter how much Humphrey's #9 Ellie gave him and the most shocking part was what Ellie said at the dinner table.

That night we ate beef stew and cole slaw with corn muffins. Dad, once again in rare form, was actively eating like it was his last meal on death row. Booley had been eating with us every time Ellie cooked which was understandable. Her skills were on a culinary level that I couldn't fathom, and neither could any of us that sat around the table. That particular night Joe stayed in his room and didn't come out for dinner.

"Where's the lil' man tonight?" Booley asked.

"He got in a fight again," Ellie said with a troubled voice. Her eyes looked to be filled with concern and frustration.

"Is he still having a tough time?" I asked.

"He is sick to his stomach. He doesn't want to eat, and I think he is worrying himself to death."

"Worrying himself to death?" Booley responded before biting into a piece of a buttered corn muffin. "What you goin' do about it?" he asked with a mouthful of food.

"I don't know," Ellie said as she absent-mindedly dropped her fork onto her plate. She was at her limit, and the stress was evident the way she rubbed her eyes. Booley reached across the table and took another piece of corn muffin from a basket sitting in the middle of the table. He broke the piece in two and spoke while he waited for the right time to take a bite.

"You're movin' to Baton Rouge with your husband aren't you?" Booley asked. "Joe will have a new school to attend. New school, new friends," Booley said as he took a bite from the corn muffin. I wanted to reach across the table and push the rest of the corn muffin in his mouth to get him to shut up. I called him an asshole in my head, and said it with my eyes. I had to let it go since he was unaware of how I felt about her. I about dropped my fork when Ellie answered.

"My husband isn't the most ideal man to be around considering his temper; however, I feel I must go with him if Joe will fare better in another school." My heart jumped. No, it stopped, at least for a full second. All this time I had thought that Ellie was trying to get Joe away from his father. I had thought she had decided on a divorce. I couldn't believe what I was hearing.

"The Mayor has a temper? He doesn't take it out on you, does he Miss Ellie?" Booley asked not knowing her story. I never told him as I didn't feel right spreading other people's problems as gossip. Ellie looked down at her plate and stared at her food. She looked like she was embarrassed. Before any of us could say anything, Dad said,

"Get the trespasser out here,"

All three of us turned our heads. Dad was finished eating, his napkin was on the table, and both hands were resting on either side of his bowl.

"He's sleeping," Ellie said with a respectful, but timid tone in her voice.

"You get him out here or I will, God-damn it."

Ellie was wary of him, especially since he was asking to see her son using the Lord's name in vain. Now if you remember, when Dad was pointing his rifle at Joe's left eyeball, I forcefully made him get into his room and shut his door. I could do that then because he was hammered and half awake. If I told him to back off now, I would suffer under his wrath. If Joe was his guest in his house and he wanted to see him, then I had no say in the matter. Ellie stood up, keeping her eyes on my father. She eventually broke her gaze and walked to the little room and opened the door. Booley shoveled a spoonful of beef stew and scratched the itch above his eye in a casual manner. Dad never seemed to rattle Booley. Ever. After a few whispers back and forth, Joe came out rubbing his eyes with his hair twisted in disarray from lying down. The light coming from the kitchen made him squint as his eyes hadn't yet adjusted. Ellie stood next to her son and patted down his cowlick.

"Trespasser," Dad said. Joe quit rubbing his eyes and looked at my father. "Go in the living room. On the table is a box. In that box are several cigars. Bring me one of them," Dad instructed. Joe immediately left the room. The look in Dad's eyes was one of authority, the kind of authority you would fear. I was at the other end of that gruff voice my entire life. "Pick up that box." "Shut the damn gate." "Damn it to hell!"

Ellie looked at my dad with cautious eyes as she sat back down at the table. She turned her head toward me. I just went back to my last bite trying to stay out of it. I knew my father was harsh, but he wouldn't hurt anyone.

"You wanted me to wake him up to get you a cigar?" Ellie asked my father. He stared at her for a moment, but didn't say a word. When Joe returned he had one single cigar in his hand. Ellie, with a protective look, watched Joe interact with my father.

"Get your coat and come with me. We're going out to the back porch," Dad said as he stood up and took a few steps toward the door.

Ellie objected.

"I don't think so!" Ellie jumped up out of her seat. Dad slowly extended his arm and reached out his hand before extending his index finger, pointing right at Ellie.

"Sit down, Cook!" Dad opened the door and stood under the frame looking at Joe. "You comin'?" Joe looked at Ellie; Ellie looked at me before sitting down. I stood up.

"Dad…" I started to say in Ellie and Joe's defense. Instead of talking, he just stared. He didn't shout or cuss, he just looked right at me with those eyes that said everything. I just sat down. Dad looked at Ellie,

"I ain't gonna hurt the boy. Come on, Trespasser!" Joe cautiously walked over to the chair next to the refrigerator and grabbed his coat and put it on. He walked suspiciously onto the back porch behind Banner before Dad closed the door.

"What is he doing?" Ellie asked.

"I don't know," I replied. Then the door opened and Dad poked his head in the kitchen.

"Leave us be." ...the door closed with an unambiguous *Slam*.

Ellie had a look of concern on her face, as did I.

15

Palmer Bennett, Jim's brother, weighed about 140 pounds or so which made him the perfect weight for an exercise rider. His thin frame and muscular arms were in perfect proportion for riding. I rested my arms on top of the track fence and watched him work Outpost by jogging him at first and slowly progressing to an easy gallop. Palmer knew the horses better than I did, which was his job and I relied on him to the point of allowing him to tell me what we should do with certain horses based on their behavior. Palmer lived the good life getting to ride horses all day and not having to deal with clients, paperwork or the financial side of the business.

When we put Outpost in the barn for the day, I went to the main house to fill out a stack of paperwork waiting for me on the dining room table. Not the most glamorous side of my job, but it was a very necessary part. As there is a downside to every job, paperwork for a horse trainer is the least desirable. My job carried with it a responsibility to the clients who own the horses I trained. Part of that responsibility is mailing out progress reports every month to the owners of the horses.

For example, here is Outpost's training log for February, 1939 showing the date, distance and time:

3	3 Furlongs,	40
7	3 Furlong,	38 3/5
10	4 Furlongs,	51
13	5 Furlongs,	1:08 4/5
16	3 Furlongs,	39
19	5 Furlongs,	1:09
22	6 Furlongs,	1:23 4/5
25	3 Furlongs,	37 2/5
28	6 Furlongs,	1:16 4/5

Worked a bit fast for the stage preparation he was in. One cup blinker was used for seven days. Helped focus and became easier to control. High marks from exercise rider.

I kept notes on every horse and was very methodical about sending out the report. For some reason Dad seemed to enjoy writing the reports. He would sit at the dining room table and drink coffee and take his time. I suppose it was relaxing for him, but not me. I preferred to be at the track.

After I completed my paperwork, I saw Ellie once again walking Joe home from school. I peered through the front window and noticed that instead of appearing beaten and disheveled, it looked like Joe was in trouble with his mother as if he had done something wrong.

As soon as she took Joe into their little room, Ellie made him sit on the bed and stay in the room by himself. She closed the door as her left hand immediately went to her forehead and her right hand went to the side of her hip. Perplexed and in deep thought, she exhaled as I approached her. She explained to me that Joe got into another fight.

"How bad did he get hurt?" I asked.

"He broke a kid's nose and knocked out another boy's tooth!" Ellie said before walking to the kitchen. I followed her and watched as she reached into the white cupboard and grabbed a green drinking glass.

"Joe did? He punched another kid?" I asked somewhat confused.

"I was told by his teacher that Joe's class was at lunch and he walked up to one of the kids in the lunch line and slugged a boy in the face." She held the green glass under the tap. I was trying to imagine Joe punching one of the other kids. "Another boy tried to stop him, and Joe punched him and knocked out his front tooth," she said as the water had reached the top of the glass and was spilling over the edges. All of a sudden it hit me. I knew what had happened.

When I was a kid, I experienced getting picked on by classmates just as Joe was being picked on and my father had gotten tired of hearing about it. He knelt down to my level and showed me how to hold my fists. He then showed me the weak points of the face and where to strike. Not only to strike, but to strike hard and accurately. Once a punch was executed, he taught me to follow it up with more punches to vital areas. These specific areas were to be attacked until the opponent submitted by falling to the ground.

When my father had taken Joe out onto the porch that night, he had sat on the old couch and puffed on his cigar quietly until he was finished. No doubt that Joe was pissing his pants while this old, terrifying man puffed billows of smoke into the air—not knowing what the old coot wanted. I am guessing that my dad asked Joe about the boys at school; how big they were or at least how tall they were. Then came the lesson about cartilage and vital areas. Graphic details were not spared as my dad explained how to break the cartilage in an opponent's nose and described the intense pain his opponent would experience. (This wasn't necessary since Joe knew firsthand what it felt like.) Then the instructions followed on how to hold your fist and strike without breaking your thumb while rotating your torso through the punch. Alignment was key as I am sure he instructed Joe how to align his knuckles with his wrist. I imagine that Dad said something like,

"Wherever there are a lot of kids, the lunchroom or recess, walk up to these sons-of-bitches and knock their God-damn block off! You don't stop until you have their blood on your fists, got it?"

It all made sense at that moment when Ellie said that he broke a boy's nose and knocked another kid's tooth out. It was the sudden strike to the end of the nose that laid out the first kid. Then another face full of knuckles for the second kid only he didn't go down, nor did his nose break. Joe followed it up with an uppercut to the chin, thus knocking out a tooth. I am sure after the uppercut, the second kid went down.

"It was my dad," I said breaking my gaze from the kitchen floor as I thought about Dad and Joe on the back porch.

"What? Your Dad?"

"Last night, when he took Joe out onto the porch. He taught Joe how to fight."

"Your Dad?"

"I am sure of it. He taught me the same thing when I was about Joe's age," I said nearly laughing. Ellie didn't find it so funny. She stormed off toward her little room and grabbed Joe by the hand before storming toward the back porch with Joe's hand firmly gripped in her own. Her skirt rippled in the air as her swift movements took her around the corner and into the living room. She headed directly for the door to the back porch. I followed her trying to talk her out of confronting my father.

"Look, it's not going to do any good," I said. "He was trying to help." Ellie reached for the doorknob and promptly turned it, opening the door. She stepped onto the wooden planked porch, pulling Joe's hand behind her.

"Mr. Chapel, I would rather you not interfere with my son thank you very much and I…"

Before Ellie made her entrance, Dad had been asleep on the old couch with his old, black wool coat wrapped around him. In his left hand was a near empty bottle of whiskey with the top off. Banner was lying on the doormat, as it was warmer than the floorboards.

"Hold it!" he yelled.

"What the hell are you yammerin' about, Cook!" he yelled again. Banner picked his head up and promptly laid it back down once he realized he didn't have to get up. The yelling took Ellie by surprise as his voice was thunderous.

"You do not have the right to intrude on our lives by teaching my son anything violent!" Ellie said trying her best to stand her ground. Then Dad stood up. Banner did as well thinking they were going inside.

"Listen here, Cook! You are intruding on *my* life. This is *my* house, and you are under *my* roof. I didn't ask you to be here or the trespasser." Ellie wasn't used to his temper or loud mouth. I knew it would surface as soon as she went out onto the porch. I just stood behind her.

"Now, your boy was bleeding all over my couch and something needed to be done. You don't want him running for his life. He needs to be a man."

"Not at nine years old he doesn't."

"Especially at nine...that's where it counts!" Dad yelled. His voice was raspy and it sounded as if he needed to clear his throat. "You can't have everyone thinking of him as a scrawny weed that anyone can just push over!" Ellie stood silent. Joe just watched. Dad eventually felt as if he was understood and sat down before he took the last swig of his whiskey. From where I was standing, I could see that there was a small amount left in the bottle. A common occurrence so that he could let Banner lap up the last bit of whiskey.

"Leave the boy. Stay here, Trespasser," Dad said as he set the almost empty bottle on the wooden plank floor boards and removed a brand new bottle from his black wool coat. He unscrewed the top of the bottle and repositioned himself to the edge of the old couch.

"I am not leaving Joe here with you!" Ellie shouted. Dad grabbed Ellie's wrist with his iron grip. He got her attention and mine as well. I was just about to interfere when Dad looked up at Ellie from his seated position.

"You're my guest. You do as I say," he said. He released his tight grip from around her wrist and stared at her as if he *was* her father. The demanding tone, and the certain wrath that would come down upon her should she not comply was evident. Although he seemed malicious and callous, I could tell he was trying to help. If he were to hurt Ellie or Joe, Dad would have found himself under the heel of my boot, but he wasn't the kind of man to hurt anyone. In general, he wanted to be left alone. Frustrated and defeated, Ellie walked into the house leaving Joe. She knew Dad wouldn't hurt Joe, but she did want to keep him away and I completely understood why. I followed Ellie into the house and she looked as if she wanted to cry. I closed the door behind us leaving Joe on the back porch with my dad.

"No. You stay there and watch Joe," Ellie yelled at me as she spoke. "I don't trust him," she said with tears in her eyes before walking into her room and closing the door. I exhaled and heard talking outside. I peeked out through the window and saw Joe holding Dad's brand new bottle of whiskey with a grimace on his face that would imply he was about to take in a mouth full of castor oil. I looked at Dad who was talking to him, but I couldn't make out what he was saying. Then, Joe took a sip from the bottle and immediately spit it out. Dad held out his hand and took the bottle from Joe.

"You're a man now, Trespasser," I faintly heard Dad say through the door. Joe was wiping his mouth and coughing.

"Damn it, Dad," I muttered, but no one heard me. For one thing I wasn't happy about Dad interfering with Joe and Ellie, but at the same time, it seemed that he was taking an interest in something. I was glad to see him open up a little, even if it was to teach a kid how to fight and drink whiskey.

16

Since I had a brand new roster of horses and the fact that they didn't start racing until April, I was able to stick around the farm. If I had been training horses for several years and built up a roster of 15 to 30 horses, I would have been travelling all over the southern states taking horses to race at different tracks. It was March when Ellie set the trap for Dad, and it was the same month that Joe became a prize fighter. If it were March of 1938 or 1940, I would have been in Miami at Tropical Park or even in Havana. When I mention to people that I used to take my horses to the track in Havana, Cuba, people seem to react the same way. They look at me with questioning eyes and some even have a concerned look.

Of course back then, Cuba wasn't the country it is at the time of this writing. I am not interested in giving you a history lesson, but I do want to explain to you that Cuba was the most beautiful place I had ever seen. The beaches were so perfect that you could not envision a more beautiful ocean landscape. The sky seemed a deeper shade of blue, and the air was somehow constantly moving over your body in the form of a perfect breeze. I loved Cuba and the people there. When Dad and I would take our horses to Oriental Park Racetrack, I would always play cards with other horse trainers and jockeys who spoke terrible English, but we always seemed to manage. I don't mean to get sidetracked, but if Ellie had come the year before or the year after 1939, I never would have gotten to know her the way I did.

"Timing and luck," Booley said from time to time. He was referring to our horses winning races, but timing and luck played a bigger part that year than it did on the track. I was able to stay on the farm with Ellie for quite a while, but I hate to tell you that it was all coming to an end. It was at the high point of Ellie's stay that she and Joe were taken from us. Ellie was doing really well by then as her cough had all but disappeared and her bruises had cleared up. Joe seemed to be coming out of his shell after his double knock down fight at school and seemed to be much more outspoken and lively. Ellie seemed to have accepted that Joe's back porch education from my father was more of a good thing than a bad one. Once she saw that Joe seemed happier and that his issues at school became less of a problem, she appeared to be thankful. Although she acknowledged to me that Dad helped in the matter, Ellie purposely never showed gratitude toward my father for his assistance, nor did he require it.

The night when Ellie and Joe were forced to leave, Dad actually laughed at something that was said at the dinner table, which was the first time I had ever heard him laugh in my entire life. We were sitting around the kitchen table like a family. As I write this, I wonder why the happiest moments in our life seem to come crashing down without a moment's notice?

"One of the fellas at the feed store tol' a joke today. Anybody wanna hear it?"

Earlier that day, Booley had gone to the feed store where he would usually pick up a few jokes and bring them back to the farm. I know he had told a few to Dad and never got anywhere. If Booley was looking for a laugh, he would tell me without fail. That night, Booley had a new joke.

"Sure! I love jokes," Ellie said just before she bit into a piece of fried chicken. Ellie had prepared another incredible feast. Fried chicken, mashed potatoes and corn on the cob were on the menu that night. I couldn't remember the last time I had fried chicken, and I am sure Dad and Booley couldn't remember either.

"Let's hear it," I added.

"A doctor arrives at a house of a woman who was about to give birth. The father was away and only their five year old daughter was around to help. So the doctor lit a kerosene lamp and handed it to the five year old girl and told her to hold it so he could see what he was doing. After the baby was born and the cord was cut, the doctor smacked the baby on the behind to get it breathing." Booley is already smiling as he knows the punch line. "The little five year old girl that had watched every part of the birth said, hit that baby again! It had no business crawling up in there." Booley belted out a contagious laugh as did Ellie. I chuckled, and Joe didn't seem to quite get it. I looked at Dad who was preparing his fork with mashed potatoes. No laugh. No smile. After a moment of silence, Joe spoke up which took most of us by surprise.

"I gotta joke," Joe said. Ellie immediately looked at him.

"You do?" Ellie said.

"Yeah, I heard it at school."

"What is it?"

"How do you...no, wait...why does a squirrel swim on its back?" Joe asked. He fidgeted in his chair as he spoke. No doubt nervous as he spoke to everyone out loud.

"Why?" Booley asked.

"To keep its nuts dry," Joe answered. Not expecting the punch line, Dad laughed immediately setting down his glass of water using the back of his other hand to keep the food in his mouth. Booley rested his elbow on the table and propped his head up as laughter emanated from his mouth and nose. I was stunned by my father's laughter as I had never heard it before. The wrinkles etched into his face scrunched together in a tightly packed pattern. I could hear Ellie tell Joe that it was not a proper joke for his age.

"But I heard it at school!" Joe said over the laughter of Booley and my father. Even Ellie was having a hard time not laughing as she reprimanded her son. As soon as everyone calmed down, the phone rang and I got up from the table to answer it.

I don't know that I could describe the look on Ellie's face accurately after I answered the phone. My expression must have said it all.

17

"Mr. Chapel? This is Mayor Evans." I turned my head and looked at Ellie. We didn't receive many phone calls back then and she knew the mayor would be returning any day. Maybe it was the way I looked at Ellie that caused her facial expression to slowly freeze in the same way a drop of water would freeze as it traveled down a metal pole in mid-winter. When the mayor asked if he could speak with Ellie, I said "yes" not knowing what else to say. She excused herself from the table and walked toward me in a hesitant manner, almost as if she had to force herself to answer the phone. I handed her the receiver, and she stood with her back to everyone. When she spoke she did so very quietly. At the time, Joe was unaware of who his mother was talking to as he carried on a conversation with Booley…that is until she hung up the phone and walked to her room with tears in her eyes and sounds of sobbing emitting from her direction. It had started to rain just before we sat down to dinner and by the time Ellie had hung up the phone, the thunder and lightning accompanied sheets of rain slamming down on our farm.

When I knocked on Ellie's door and opened it, she was sitting on the edge of the bed as tears streamed down her face. She covered her face with her hands.

"What did he say?"

"It doesn't matter. He's coming," she sobbed.

"What did you say to him?" I asked. She was wiping her tears in between sniffling.

"I said no. I told him no and to go to Baton Rouge without me. He said if I don't come, he will make me sorry. He yelled-stay where you are-and hung up the phone," she explained as tears began to drip on her dress. I talked with her about the options, but she quickly explained that there weren't any. The only solution for us was to call the Sheriff, but Georgetown had elected a man who was for sale and it was Mayor Evans that had paid up. Twenty minutes later, two cars pulled up in the driveway and Mayor Evans got out of the first car. Somehow through the rain and darkness of the night, I was able to see that the car behind his was Sheriff Crease's.

Dad had already adjourned to the living room while Joe and Booley were still sitting at the kitchen table. I walked to the front door and opened it enough for the mayor to see my face. Mayor Evans had stopped short of the front porch, standing in the rain.

"Mayor," I said as I nodded.

"Is Ellie here, or is she at the house in the back?"

"She is here."

"Uh, huh. Chapel, be a good man and get my wife and kid out here." I froze. I didn't know what to do. The Mayor stood there in the rain as water collected on the brim of his black hat before spilling off of the edge.

"Chapel? Would you, please?" he asked again. I shut the door, turned around and saw Ellie standing in the doorway of her room. Tears continued to fall down both sides of her cheeks. The thunder caused her to jump, and the sheets of rain kept pelting the windows.

I once again cracked the front door open.

"Mayor, I don't think that's possible," I said. He didn't seem to mind the down force of the water beating against his hat and coat. He took a step onto the porch and looked me in the eye.

"Are you certain?" he stared at me before turning his head toward the police car. Three men got out of the vehicle, one of them being Sheriff Crease and I suppose the other two were his deputies. Through the rain and lighting, I could see that Crease was carrying a shotgun in his pudgy hands. Mayor Evans turned his head toward me with a glare of evil that I will never forget. He reached out his hand and put his black leather glove on the wooden door. Drops of water dripped off his glove and onto the door, making a damp trail on the painted surface as gravity pulled the beads of rain toward the ground. Sheriff Crease and his deputies made their way to the front porch as the Mayor pushed the door wide open. He could see Joe at the kitchen table and Ellie in tears standing in the doorway of the little bedroom.

"It would be very wise of you to get my wife and kid on this front porch, Mr. Chapel," Mayor Evans said with a quiet, but forceful tone. "This could go very badly for you."

"Leave them out of this!" Ellie shouted from out of view of the men on the front porch.

The fact that three men were standing behind the Mayor with one of them carrying a shotgun made me feel uneasy. The Mayor turned his head toward Sheriff Crease and pointed toward the kitchen.

"Get that piece of shit away from my boy would you?" Mayor Evans said. Sheriff Crease looked at Booley sitting at the kitchen table with Joe.

"Be glad to," he said as he started toward the front door.

"Okay!" Ellie said as she put her hands up with her eyes shut tight in frustration. "Okay. Fine." She wiped her tears off her face and began gathering her things. "Just don't come in here. I don't want any of you in this house," Ellie demanded. Sheriff Crease stood still and didn't move. "I'm serious! Get back!" she added and motioned Joe to come to her. Mayor Evans whispered to Crease, telling him to take a few steps back. I closed the front door half way as Ellie and Joe walked toward me, both of them had tears in their eyes.

"You have been very kind to me and Joe," Ellie whispered. "I think it's best if we leave."

"I don't want you to go. There must be a way out of this," I said quietly.

"Let us go. I will contact you if I can. This is my problem, and you shouldn't be burdened with it," Ellie said in a whisper before starting out the door.

"But I am," I gently whispered as I grabbed her hand – out of view of Mayor Evans. I looked into her eyes the way I knew she would understand. "I am burdened with it," I said with a very faint whisper.

"Let's go, Ellie!" Mayor Evans yelled. He took a step inside and grabbed Ellie's other hand, pulling her away from me. Joe followed his mother, and out into the rain they went. I watched as she and Joe were put in the Mayor's car. Lightning gave me short illuminated views of Joe's face as he looked out the back window as they drove away. I stood there, helpless.

18

The day after Ellie was taken from us was a difficult day. There was no breakfast and no laughter. The day dragged on as if it were tormenting me by slowing down time. Booley didn't show up to eat. Dad was his usual self which was expected. I thought of how he had laughed only seconds before the phone call. Questions arose in my head about Ellie if she had stayed. Would Dad have smiled or laughed again? Would he have continued to be enthusiastic about dinner, arriving at the table waiting for his food with knife and fork in hand? I was having a hard time with the fact that Ellie was controlled and not free to do as she pleased. I didn't like reminding myself that she was only a guest, not a permanent addition to the household and it felt as if I was in mourning although no one had died.

The Bennett family was one member short as Sarah had taken ill from a severe cold. The Bennett kids were working a little harder than they usually did to make up for it.

"So?" Booley asked as I arrived at the barn with my jacket on and my hands in my pockets.

"So what?"

"What are you going to do?"

"I haven't figured that out yet," I said as I rolled my eyes. I knew what he meant when he asked the question.

"What do you want?" Booley asked.

"Peace and quiet," I said trying to end the conversation. Ranger was going out next so I walked over to the saddle rack and picked up his exercise saddle. Ranger had been through many days of rest and medication. We had been taking him around the barn for minimal exercise and I was hoping that today Palmer could get him to a gallop.

"You could go over there with your Colt forty-five and challenge him to a duel."

"You really need to quit listening to the radio," I said as I placed the saddle on Ranger's back.

"You gonna run him?"

"Yeah, let Palmer take him around the track, and we'll check him after a couple laps."

"Can I ask you one more question"? Booley asked. I was done with the questions, but I hoped Booley would let me be after one more.

"Yeah, I guess."

"If Mrs. Evans wasn't married, would you court her?"

"Booley, damn it."

"Well you said I could ask you another question."

"I know, but I didn't know you...just stop it. Cut it out."

"Don't know why you wouldn't. She's like a speckled pup in a red wagon."

I took Ranger's Cape out of the barn hoping to escape his incessant questions. Booley followed behind and kept his mouth shut. I gave Palmer a leg up helping him get situated in the saddle and watched as he took Ranger around the track. Not fast, but enough to get his heart rate up and his lungs moving in and out. He took the second turn and somehow Ellie's ponytail popped into my head. I imagined her hot walking the horses around the barn and filling up the feed barrels with the red strand of yarn securing her ponytail. I was fine before she came to the farm. It wasn't until she came and left that I felt hollow and pointless. The void inside me must have been there all along and I just didn't know it.

Palmer slowed Ranger down and patted his neck, talking to him in a soothing voice. Booley and I immediately walked over and checked Ranger's mouth and nose for signs of blood.

"Looks good," Booley said as he peered inside Ranger's mouth.

"Yep," I replied.

"Are you just going to let her go? Are you going to just live the rest of your life and not do anything?"

"Booley, stop it!" He didn't say another word. I knew he was just trying to get to me.

"Cool him off," I said to Palmer. Jim was riding Catcher and was trotting over in my direction. "Jim, can you hot walk Outpost? I'll get Pale and prep him."

"Yes, sir," Jim replied as he tugged on the reins and headed for the barn. Booley was walking toward the barn with his back to me. I couldn't see his face, but I know he was smiling. He only said his little comment to get me riled up. Later on after a mealy lunch, we were cleaning out the stalls in the barn.

"Booley, how come you never got married?" I asked as I cleaned out the bedding in a stall with a rake.

"Did once." Booley was bringing a wheelbarrow of straw into the barn to fill up the stalls he'd cleaned out.

"You're kidding?"

"Nope, she was an awful and loathsome woman with big buck teeth. She used to holler at me as if I was the devil his self."

"Sounds like a nice lady."

"She was before we got married. Life was so miserable that I felt like a statue and she was a pigeon." Booley's sense of humor seemed to be present even in his most distressing hour.

"What did you do?" I asked.

"Went to the judge and got a dee'vorce."

"Couldn't stand it, huh? Are you lonely?"

"I reckon, but I figure it's better to be a little lonely than a whole lot miserable," he said, another one of his sayings.

"Did you ever want to get remarried?" I asked.

"Yeah, I suppose. It was your father who convinced me to be picky," he said. I stopped raking the stall and looked at him.

"Dad? What did he say?"

"Nuthin'. People in town tol' me that he used to be a kind and joyful man, until his wife passed."

"What do you mean?" I asked. Booley had been spreading straw in one of the stalls. He stopped and looked down the aisle at me to answer.

"Your dad found the one person that mattered and didn't settle for less. I settled for less by marrying buck tooth. I always wondered if I had waited, would I have found the one too," Booley answered and then went back to spreading the straw. "I guess I could have remarried, except that I wouldn't do it unless she was perfect. Not perfect, but perfect for me," he added. I stood there thinking about what he said. A plethora of thoughts flooded my mind—my mom and dad,

Ellie Evans and the few girls that I dated. I was never in a hurry to get married and luckily I wasn't married when I met Ellie. I figured that if I could come up with a plan to get her away from Mayor Evans, then I would have a chance. I wouldn't have to settle. I did know one thing to be true, Mayor Evans was Ellie's buck tooth.

When the day ended, I walked to the five-stable barn near the main house and opened the door to Eastern's stall. He walked right out and looked energetic and alive. I bent down and felt the back of his ankle where Dr. Wall examined him. Eastern grunted a little and his tail fanned from side to side. His ankle was still sore, but seemed to be healing and putting full weight on his leg. Eastern had escaped death and seemed to be doing okay, and I could sense that he knew he was rescued. I could have been just thinking too much into it, but he seemed grateful as he wrapped his thick, wet lips around the strands of hay and chewed thoroughly before going back for more, while I applied the pine tar and iodine to his leg before putting him back in the stall.

At dinner time, the kitchen was empty, but it also seemed as if the paint on the walls had faded. The kitchen table looked bare and life-less. We fixed what we could—wasn't much though. Dad ate in his chair in the living room and listened to the radio with Banner resting beside him. Booley was already at his little house fixing his own din-ner and reading in peace. I sat alone in the kitchen, thinking about Ellie and I thought about what I could do to get her and Joe out from under Mayor Evans. I knew I had to do something, but I had no idea where to start. The next couple of days made me sick to my stomach and I had a difficult time concentrating on anything as my thoughts were fixated on Ellie and Joe.

Several days later we began our usual routine and I began to feel useless. Palmer would ask me a question when he was situated in his riding saddle and he would have to repeat his question as my mind was elsewhere. Thoughts of Ellie and Joe were infiltrating my mind without me realizing it. Palmer had already hot walked Outpost and approached me, sitting comfortably in his riding saddle.

"How many furlongs today, Mr. Chapel?" Palmer repeated.

"Gallop twelve," I kept thinking of the suitcase Ellie held in her hand and the way Mayor Evans spoke with a harsh tone and that black, leather glove gripping the side of the door. My mind wouldn't let go of the image of Joe peeking out the back window as they drove away. The rest of the week passed without hearing from Ellie, and the shades of each passing day became grayer than the one before it.

About ten days after Ellie had left our farm, I was walking from the barn to the main house when I saw Dad with his rifle in his left hand. He had just stepped off the back porch toward an ensnared albino coyote. The coyote was fidgeting, trying to release the snare from his paw to no avail. Banner had woken up and sat on the edge of the porch looking too afraid to go near the animal. I remember Ellie saying "Once the coyote stepped into the hole, he will try to pull away from it, thus tightening the snare," which was happening exactly as she described it.

As Dad walked closer to the coyote, I hid over by the willow tree watching the event take place. The only noise I could hear was my father's footsteps and the tugging and struggling of the white coyote. Faint whimpering noises emanated from the doomed animal as if it knew what was going to happen.

At that time, Dad was still working on his early tomato concept, planting his favorite fruit in a pot and was taking it outside during the day and bringing it in at night. The coyote, with its curious nature was inspecting the budding tomatoes and was ensnared in the process. Dad got within five feet of the coyote, and it stopped struggling. It just stood there, silent, staring toward the ground as the barrel of the rifle was raised. Dad aimed at its head and stood there for what seemed like a full minute as if they were posing while an artist painted them on a canvas. Dad was motionless as was the coyote. The furry creature seemed to be awaiting his death.

The trigger was never pulled. The barrel of the rifle was lowered, and my father reached into his pocket and pulled out a knife. He cut the snare, freeing the animal. Dad stood up and watched as the albino coyote jogged away with a small limp, no doubt the wire had cut into his ankle. Once the coyote leapt into the woods, Dad looked around to see if anyone witnessed his action other than Banner. I quickly moved out of view by hiding directly behind the willow tree. The last thing I saw was his hand folding the blade of his pocket knife before walking to the back porch, leaning his rifle against the wall and going inside.

Once I was done for the day, I went inside and started up the stairs to take a shower when I heard the phone ring. In those days we didn't have answering machines, but we did have the central telephone office. The women who placed the calls would sometimes take messages based on their importance. When a physician needed to get in touch with someone you could bet that the women in the central office would make sure that the message was delivered. When I answered the phone the familiar melodious, soft voice came through.

"Is this Elliott Chapel?"

"Yes."

"This is Central. Doctor Thomas has been trying to reach you."

No doubt the woman on the other end had been calling once every hour on the hour as that was usually how they went about reaching someone. Dad either ignored the ringing or slept through the repeated phone calls.

"Okay. Can you put him though?" I asked.

"Right away, sir." *Click. Ring. Ring.*

"Hello," Doc said.

"Hey, Doc."

"Chapel, you had better come to the hospital. No way am I going to tell you this over the phone," he said. The eavesdropping ladies at the telephone office must have been disappointed, although it was only a rumor that they listened in on their customer's conversations.

"I will be there shortly," I said.

I jumped in the truck and sped over to Ford Memorial and found Doc in the lobby. He was on his way out.

"Follow me," he said. As we were walking he held out his hand showing me what looked like a vial of clear liquid.

"What's that?" I asked as we walked outside.

"An ampoule of morphine," he replied.

"What's it for?"

We made it into the parking lot and Doc stopped. He looked at me over the top of his rimless glasses.

"It's for Ellie. Her husband hit her so hard I think he may have fractured her zygomatic arch." Doc tapped his face in front of his ear. "The side of her cheek bone. She needs stitches too." We continued walking and reached his car. "I am taking care of her at the Mayor's house. I was called in, and I thought I was going to be checking up on her from her accident back in February." Doc seemed to be out of breath, and he was trying to catch it as he spoke. "The mayor told me she fell. I asked him to get me a wet towel and ice. After he left the room I asked Ellie if he hit her and she nodded. Elliott, I don't know what to do. I feel like if I call the police, it's just like calling the Mayor and telling him to arrest himself. You and I both know that the Sheriff is in his back pocket! He's over there right now at the Mayor's house at some ridiculous dinner party!"

Doc was obviously upset. I was stunned and pissed off to high heaven at the news of Ellie being assaulted. I couldn't even speak I was so infuriated. When I was able to put words together that made sense I said, "I'm going with you."

"What are you going to do?" Doc asked.

"I have no idea."

We pulled up in the driveway and I became nervous, but I was still pissed off. There were four cars in the driveway and the Sheriff's car was parked on the manicured grass. I got out of Doc's Mercury and headed toward the front door.

"Stay out here," I said to Doc. I opened the front door without knocking and walked into the foyer leaving the door wide open. This time I didn't care if my boots were filthy and soiled their white carpet. I could hear the sound of the dinner party in the dining room which was to my right. On the left was a gaudy living room with a green upholstered couch. I assumed that Ellie and Joe were upstairs and my intention was to speak with the mayor, make my point, and then take them out of there for good.

I headed towards the noise of the dinner party, the ruckus growing louder with each step. When I approached the entrance to the room, I took a deep breath and walked into view of the Mayor and his guests. Damn, I was nervous. At the head of the table was the Mayor himself.

He was surrounded by people I didn't know except the Sheriff, of course. I looked my intended target right in the eye. You have to admit, it took a lot of gumption to just walk into his house. Maybe it was my father's personality coming out, perhaps I had just had enough. When the Mayor saw me, he immediately stopped talking as did his guests. All eyes were on me.

"Mayor, could I speak with you a moment?" I asked. I expected him to look at me with an angered face and begin yelling at me. Instead he was quite jovial. He was holding a wine glass as if he had just picked it up. In his other hand was a cigarette wedged between his ring and middle finger. Upon seeing me step into view, the glass remained between the table and his mouth while his cigarette sent thin, wavering streams of white smoke up into the air. He smiled as he spoke, "Why, Mr. Chapel, I didn't remember sending you an invitation."

"I don't need one," I said.

"Ladies and gentlemen, I have an unexpected guest who requires my attention. Would you please excuse me?" he set his wine glass down on the table having never taken a sip. "Chapel, in the kitchen," he gestured still holding his cigarette. I looked at the guests in the room trying to ignore Sheriff Crease.

"Excuse me," I said to the party guests as I made my way to the swinging, white door and entered the kitchen. The room was quite large and covered with white tile. The same black man in the white button up shirt and a black vest was washing pots and pans under running water. I took my eyes off him and focused on the mayor.

"Now, Mr. Chapel, I hope you know that you are inconveniencing me a great deal. Now, what do you want?" His jovial attitude had turned to a malevolence, and his face looked like it did when he was standing on my front porch. He brought the cigarette to his mouth and inhaled two lungs worth of smoke while he fidgeted with his neck tie.

"I know you hit Ellie," I said. I didn't say it as if I was stepping on glass, I spoke as if I was ready to fight. "Let her stay on my farm. You'll never have to see her again." Then Sheriff Crease opened the swinging kitchen door and walked toward me. He hooked his thumbs on his worn belt and stared at me like he was ready to prove his worth as a Sheriff. Mayor Evans briefly tilted his head back as he exhaled, sending a white cloud toward the ceiling. He righted his head and stared at me with focused, daunting eyes. "I have money," I continued. "I can pay whatever you want." The Mayor never broke his threatening gaze as his face reddened while he loosened his neck tie. He took three steps forward, as if he was going to hit me.

"Crease," he said calmly through clenched teeth as he kept his eyes on me, "Get this uninvited piece of shit out of my house." I could feel his breath as he spoke.

"Glad to," Crease said.

"Look, I'm telling you..." I started to say. The Mayor stepped out of the way, and my arm was quickly twisted behind my back. Mayor Evans flicked his cigarette into the kitchen sink and disappeared behind the white, swinging door as Sheriff Crease raised my arm upward in a painful position, forcing me out the back door. My feet clumsily plotted forward as my body hit the screen door, flinging it open. At the edge of the porch, Sheriff released my arm and pushed me forward off the concrete steps. Not being able to catch my balance, my feet couldn't catch up and I fell forward onto the ground. The right side of my face slid to a stop on the loose dirt as if it were playing baseball and stealing second. The only thing that illuminated the backyard was the back porch light and I could see a small amount of blood on my fingers after I briefly touched my face.

"Time to move on, Chapel."

My clothes were filthy and my heart was beating fast. I got back up and came at him ready to knock his face into next week. My hands balled up into fists, and I reached back ready to break all of the cartilage in his nose. He withdrew his gun and cocked the hammer. I stopped in my tracks.

"I would love to pull this trigger. All I need is a reason. Go ahead, Chapel, give me a reason. Just come at me. I'm ready. Believe me I'm just waitin' for you to come at me so I can pull this trigger and put a bullet in your brain." I took a step back. "Please, Chapel, I want to. I really want to pull this trigger. Please." I took several more steps back, and the Sheriff eventually holstered his gun. "That's a shame," I heard him say under his breath as I started around the side of the house toward the front. Crease yelled out, "Consider this a warning, Chapel. You come near this house again, and I will put a bullet in your head. That is a promise! You hear me, Chapel?"

Doc saw me walking toward the driveway from the side of the house. He could see that I was bleeding.

"What happened?" he asked.

"Doesn't matter. I am going home. Just go in there and take care of Ellie." I started walking down the road with the intention of walking all the way home. There's nothing worse than being forced into a situation where you feel completely helpless and unfortunately for Ellie, it seemed that I was forced to be of no help at all.

19

Several days after Dad set the albino coyote free and I walked into the Mayor's house with a death wish, I helped the Bennett family get everything put away at the track. I was feeling foolish and defeated from being tossed out of the Mayor's house and threatened with a gun. I knew I had to do something to help Ellie, but I didn't know what I could accomplish on my own. Kentucky didn't have State Police back then, but we did have the Highway Patrol. I called them and vaguely explained the situation, but they just referred me to the county Sheriff. I kept thinking about what I could do in order to help Ellie and Joe which kept getting in the way of my daily job responsibilities. I did my best to focus on my job while occasionally thinking about Ellie.

I had gathered the bridles and took them into the barn to hang them up. I remember walking toward the back wall where a set of nails were hammered into a wooden beam and on those nails is where I hung the bridles. I could hear Booley saying goodbye to the Bennett family as they started their truck and began to drive away. I took one of the four bridles in my left hand and before I hung it up, a piece of paper caught my eye. It had been pressed hard enough against the nail so that it punctured the paper. The paper was hastily hung and if a light breeze were to have floated over the paper, it would have simply spun around the nail in circles. Upon examining it more closely, I could see that it was a handwritten note from Ellie. I reached out and pulled the note off the nail and read the following:

> *Elliott –*
> *Meet me by the oak tree on the college campus at 11pm.*
> *Ellie*

The rest of the day was complete torture as I was forced to wait out the remaining hours until I would see her at the oak tree. The meeting place in which Ellie designated was located on the campus of Georgetown College behind Giddings Hall. It wasn't the biggest tree I'd ever seen, but it was the biggest in Georgetown. Everyone in Scott County knew "The Oak Tree" and I didn't have to think twice when I left the farm that night in anticipation of seeing her. Guided by my dim headlights and the moonlit avenues, I drove the truck to West Main Street and parked it on the side of the road and got out.

In the early 1900s, four large buildings formed Georgetown's campus which provided for a student body of four hundred. Sometime around 1939, the college was in danger of being shut down. After World War one and the Great Depression, things didn't look good and competition from the University of Kentucky didn't help. At the time of this writing, the university somehow, still stands.

The moon was full, providing more than enough light for me to see where I was going. I shoved my hands into my coat pockets and took careful steps as I approached her predetermined meeting place. Once I got within view of the giant oak, I could see Ellie standing up, leaning against the trunk. The slight chill in the air made her breath slightly visible. The picture of her lying in the cold waters of Penny Creek flashed into my mind—when it seemed she wasn't breathing.

As I approached the oak tree, Ellie turned her head. She pushed herself away from the trunk and walked toward me. She had a bandage on the right side of her face and I still had marks on my face from my injury. I was nervous and elated at the same time and the excitement surged through my body when she opened her arms and embraced me. I wasn't prepared for it. This was our first embrace, the one I would always remember most...as I could feel her body heat through her knit sweater. Her face was still badly bruised and I immediately wished I had killed the mayor the last time I saw him.

"I knew you would find the note since you always hang up the bridles."

"How are you? How's your face?" I asked looking at the bandage. I was so mad just looking at the gauze on the side of her cheek. I wanted to tell her to wait and I would go over to the mayor's house and drown him in his own bathtub. "Are you all right?" I asked as she parted from me and pulled her sweater tighter around her torso.

"I'm okay. Doc has been fussing over me for days."

"I was at your house."

"I know. Evelyn Fields told me about you coming into the dining room." Ellie was smiling. I hoped it was because she was excited to see me. Her eyes glanced over to the scabbed flesh where my face had been grounded into the dirt. "What happened to you?"

"Nothing. It's no big deal. Are you sure you're okay? Doc said you might have a fractured cheek bone."

"I needed stitches, but really I am fine. Are you sure you're all right?"

"Yeah, Crease roughed me up a little. There was nothing I could do since he had his gun pointed at me."

"Elliott, I'm sorry."

"Don't be. It's no big deal," I assured her.

"Well, I'm just glad you found the note," she said changing the subject.

"When did you leave it?"

"About this time last night," she said as she looked up at the moon.

"I am glad you did. I wanted to see you again."

"Really?"

"Of course," I said. I wanted to tell her that I couldn't stop thinking about her, but I held those thoughts back.

"Joe misses the farm, and he wants to see our horse. How is Eastern by the way?"

"Just fine. I have routinely been putting the pine tar and iodine on his ankle and he's now putting full weight on it."

"Wow. That is good to hear!" she said. I couldn't help but look at the bandage on her cheek.

"Ellie, are you sure you're okay?"

"Please, yes. I'm fine."

"That's not necessarily what I meant. What if he hits you again?"

"Elliott, I don't know. Can we just drop it?"

I didn't want to. I wanted to try to figure a way for her to get out of the situation she was in. "I don't think I can," I said. Ellie's eyes looked away from mine and stared at the ground. She crossed her arms and seemed to think about what could be done. After a moment of silence, she decided to change the subject.

"So, do you all miss me around the farm?"

"I know Booley and I do. Dad doesn't say anything of course, but I can tell he misses your cooking."

"I would give anything to be back there, I would cook every day."

"Really?"

"Yes. In a heartbeat."

"Ellie?"

"Yes?"

"Why don't you?" I asked trying to return the conversation back to finding a way for her to leave. I was so happy to hear her say that she wanted to be back at the farm. She uncrossed her arms and put her hands on her hips.

"It's difficult to explain."

"Why?" I asked. She turned away from me and started kicking the ground with her right foot. "You know you can leave him?" I added.

"I can't."

"Why?"

"Could you stop asking why?" she said. I could see a hint of tears in her eyes from the moonlight that illuminated her face and that perfect ponytail, still tied with the red yarn.

She kept her back to me as she spoke, still poking at the dirt with her right foot. "Did you know that voters tend to favor a family man over a divorced candidate?"

"What?" I blurted out in astonishment.

"The Governor of Louisiana has given Wayne a job on his staff with the intention of setting him up to run for office some day. Governor Leche told him that family is important to people down there and he can't get elected unless he campaigns with his family."

"So he is using you?"

"That's why I can't leave. He won't let me."

"Why don't you just leave with Joe?" I asked. "Look, if he abuses you and Joe, it should be easy for you to get away. Any judge will be able to see that." She wiped her nose and her tears with her sleeve. I didn't want to make her cry, but at the same time I needed information. Since she wanted out, I thought I could have helped in some way even though I knew I would have to face the business end of Sheriff Crease's gun.

"He told me that if I left he would take Joe and I would never see him again." Heartbreaking sounds of distress emitted from Ellie as she lost control. I reached out and embraced her for the second time, only not under the circumstances I had hoped for.

"I'm sorry. I don't want you to get hurt."

"It's not you. It's not your fault," she added as she sniffled and wiped her tears. I held her head in my hands being careful of the bandage and looking at her telling her everything was going to be okay even though I didn't know for sure myself. I had hoped that I could come up with something.

Before we parted ways, I offered to give her a ride which she declined. She embraced me one more time before she left for her house, and I walked to my truck.

20

I was sitting at the kitchen table looking over the 1939 Spring Condition Book for Keeneland when I heard the knock. The "Condition Book", is a small, thin booklet every horse trainer uses to decide what races the horses they are training should enter. Keeneland's 1939 spring issue had a bright orange cover and I had written my name on the cover in the top corner. Using a pencil, I had just written down Outpost's name in the margin next to a maiden race when I heard a knock coming from the front of the house. I opened the door, and there on the front porch was Ellie and Joe with a suitcase resting between them. The blood pumped through my veins at full speed thinking she had left her husband and they were going to stay forever.

"Hey," Ellie said.

"Come in. What's going on?" I asked. Ellie didn't come in. She opted to stay on the front porch.

"Joe, can you leave Mr. Chapel and me alone for a moment?"

"Okay," he said and walked inside toward the living room where Dad was asleep in his chair with Banner by his side. Ellie spoke just above a whisper, and I half way closed the front door behind me as I took a step out onto the front porch. Her bandage looked new as if it had recently been changed.

"I have to go to Baton Rouge with my husband. Joe has school and I am supposed to take him to Mrs. Raines' house, but I wanted to know if you would take him for a week or so. You don't have to, it's just that I know he would like it here better than an old lady's house."

"Of course, Joe can stay here," I said. Ellie immediately smiled. She asked to see Joe before she left, and I got him back out onto the front porch.

"Now you be good and listen to everything Mr. Chapel tells you. You know how I have told you over and over that a farm can be very dangerous, so you have to be careful," Ellie said as Joe listened intently. "I love you, and I will see you soon," Ellie said as she hugged her son.

"I love you, too," Joe replied. Ellie stood up and crossed her arms. Joe walked back inside and shifted his feet quietly toward Dad.

"Thank you for taking him. He needs this. Try not to take him out around town. I don't want anyone to know that he is staying with you, especially his father."

"No problem," I said as it really was no big deal. I felt that I could keep him out of view from Sheriff Crease without any real effort. She stood on the front porch and looked off into the distance while she took a deep breath. She looked sad and as if she was about to cry. She uncrossed her arms and placed both of her hands on the small of her back.

"Don't say anything else. I will cry. Joe can't see me cry."

"Why? What is going on?" I asked.

"I miss you. I miss you so very much," Ellie whispered before she stepped off the front porch. I could see it in her eyes that she was distressed. I could see everything in her eyes. Those soft blue eyes were easy to look at. I loved her exuberant attitude with her infectious laugh. I loved her and it was making me sick that she was being forced away from me. She said she would be back, and as she turned around I watched that ponytail swish from side to side before she got in the car and drove away. I walked inside and closed the door behind me thinking of the day when I would see Ellie for the last time.

At the very least, I knew I would see Ellie one more time as she would have to pick up Joe. The thought of her leaving town for good was a hard one to accept and at that point I still hadn't come to terms with the fact that she was leaving. I reached my hand to my face touching the scab on my cheek caused by being thrown off the mayors back porch. My face had slid on the loose dirt, helping my body come to a stop. I thought of Sheriff Crease pointing his gun at my forehead and it made me think what would have happened if he pulled the trigger and killed me? A cover up? It wouldn't have been reported as a murder and certainly no repercussions would have befallen on the Sheriff as Mayor Evans would have made sure his purchased gun was called a hero. I knew what I was up against. I knew whatever I came up with; it had to be a smart and well thought out plan.

Standing at the bottom of the staircase, I took my hand away from my scabbed face and turned my head just in time to see Joe tip toeing towards Dad and Banner in the living room. Dad was asleep until Joe's careful steps caused a floorboard to creak. Banner was too deaf to hear it, but my father did. The right eye of the sleeping monster slowly opened and looked at Joe with a one-eyed stare that would frighten any nine year old boy, but not Joe. He stood still with his hands to his side.

"Trespasser," Dad said in a tired, old grumble.

"Hi," Joe whispered. The monster's eye slowly closed and the ancient beast slowly drifted back to sleep. Joe bent down and petted Banner who opened his eyes and slowly wagged his tail.

"Joe, let's go outside," I whispered loud enough so that he could hear me. It was only about nine in the morning and Booley and I had planned on meeting about then so I took Joe with me. The Bennett family would be arriving at the track early the next day to help get the horses to Keeneland and we had to get a few things together before they arrived.

The races started in several weeks and the training that occurred on the farm would continue on Keeneland's track. Joe was put to work with Booley and me as we prepared the feed for transportation. I was glad to see him open up a little, especially when Booley asked him questions about school.

"Delivered any knockouts lately?" Booley asked as he stacked a bag of feed on top of another bag. Joe was moving bales of straw by scooting them together. His cowlick frolicked about on top of his head, swaying and bouncing back and forth as he moved. Beads of sweat were already forming on his forehead—as if he'd never worked outside before. Maybe he hadn't up until that point, but he didn't complain.

"No sir. I haven't had any trouble since I laid out those two kids in the lunchroom." Booley laughed and smacked his knee.

"Better to fight than die like a dog. Right, Joe?" Booley said, offering up another one of his sayings.

"I'll say," Joe added as he wiped his sweaty forehead.

The Bennett family arrived the next day before dawn with their trailer, ready to load up and get the horses to Keeneland. Kenney and Cara Bennett took to running around the barn, chasing each other while Palmer and their mom and dad worked diligently. Booley and I attached our horse trailer to my truck and loaded Outpost and Price. Pale and Ranger boarded the Bennett's two stall horse trailer.

I had previously applied for a barn at Keeneland and was approved to stable our horses for the spring meet. When Keeneland opened in 1936, Dad had twenty-two horses stabled there. My four horses seemed like a small time operation, and I had to keep reminding myself that I was just starting out. Priced Opportunity, Beyond the Pale, Ranger's Cape and Outpost all boarded the trailers and traveled beautifully. Since it was spring and my truck barely fit three people in the cab, Booley rode in the back, enjoying the sun and the cool air. Joe rode up front with me without having to be squeezed in between two adults. He rested his elbow on the side of the door with the window down looking out over the fields of horses as we rode by the farms on the way to Keeneland.

The drive to Keeneland from our farm looked like a moving painting. As I drove down a two-lane road, we passed by civil war era fences made of loose rocks. Perfect green pastures and horses scattered across the rolling landscape were painted by the rising sun. The occasional barn that accompanied the miles of fencing coupled with the sunrise would employ any landscape artist for years.

"Have you ever been to a race track before?" I asked. Joe responded without taking his eyes from the moving scenery outside.

"No sir. I have heard them race on the radio before."

"It's a big place. You might not want to wander off until you get a feel for things."

"How many horses will be there?"

"Oh, I don't know. Right now there won't be many since there's still racing going on at other tracks. We are arriving early, but by the time the races start, you won't be able to count the horses there will be so many."

"That's a lot. I can count pretty high," Joe said.

When we arrived, there were a lot of horse trailers being unloaded and some were sitting empty. The barns were only a couple of years old so they looked much nicer than the barns at other tracks. The Bennett family unloaded the horses while Booley and I set up the feed barrels and hay receptacles. Joe, Kenney and Cara helped scatter straw in the stalls before the horses were escorted inside. With help from Palmer, Booley unloaded a trunk of horseshoes and several boxes of farrier tools. When we finally got everything situated, I took Joe around the many barns before we walked to the grandstands.

"See the number by the light?" I said pointing to the top of a barn where a lamp was placed above the loft doors. Next to the lamp was a number that labeled each barn.

"Yeah,"

"We are in barn twenty-one. If you get lost you just look up and find out what barn you're at. They're all in order. See that?" I said pointing all the way down the line. "There's barn twenty and then nineteen and so on. Okay?"

The barns at Keeneland were a sight to see in the late thirties. They were very clean and every winter after the fall races they were repainted with a shimmering new coat of white paint, which was a different world compared to other race tracks at the time. After Joe was acclimated to the surroundings, I took him to the grandstands which were as empty as a ghost town. We stood in one of the aisles with rows of seats on our right and left.

"On race day there will be thousands upon thousands of people here," I said. The massive roof over our heads really was something to look at and the enormous poles supporting the giant wooden roof made it look like a colossal insect standing over us. Joe stared at the rafters taking in the monstrosity of the building. He and I sat down, and I pointed toward the track.

"There is something about watching horses in a race." Joe looked at me as I spoke. "These powerful animals, race against each other and the control the jockeys have over their horses is amazing. Each race is a series of moments and these moments have the potential to be burned into history. Each event is assembled through hard work, skill, luck and determination—not just the determination of the trainer, but the determination of the horses. They want to run, Joe. They fight for it. You can see it in their eyes and the way they garner all of their strength as they run around the final pole, pushing themselves to cross the finish line. I promise you it's magnificent." Joe's eyes left mine and scanned the landscape and let his vivid imagination fill in the blank spaces out on the track. "When we run the first race, you can sit up here and watch them tear around the final quarter pole."

"I can sit up here?" he asked.

"Of course," I said suddenly thinking that he might not be around then. I didn't want to lie to Joe, but I guess I wasn't as I didn't know when he was leaving.

"I can't wait!" Joe said. His elated expression reminded me why I wanted to train thoroughbreds in the first place. His smile and wide-eyed excitement made me think of the first time I ever saw a horse race.

Once we got back to the farm that night, Booley went back to his little house, and Joe and I ate sandwiches in the kitchen.

"You going to be okay getting up and going to school by yourself?"

"Yeah, I think I can handle it." Joe's legs were hanging off the edge of his chair swinging back and forth, kicking the air as he ate.

"What time do you normally go to bed?"

"Um…about eight-thirty or so," he replied. I looked at my watch and then opened the refrigerator and took out a Coca-Cola. I opened it and set it in front of Joe.

"Don't tell your mom, okay?"

"Thanks! I won't," he said with a smile.

When we finished eating, we listened to the radio with the sleeping monster sitting in his chair. He didn't open his eyes the entire time we were in the living room, although Banner stood up and stretched his legs before lying back down on the rug. His tail stretched out and rested beneath the back end of the rocking chair. If Dad were to rock back far enough, ol' Banner's tail would have been in the way and he would've woken up with a sharp pain emanating from his appendage.

Opening day was around the corner. The radio was buzzing about baseball, and what a wonderful year it could be. They reported on the progress of Comiskey Park as if it was going to be the greatest baseball stadium in the world. In fact I got a little tired of hearing about it after about the hundredth time. Joe ended up falling asleep just before eight-thirty, and I carried him to his little room. I thought about Ellie and what she was doing as I closed his bedroom door and walked back into the living room where I surprisingly received an update on Ellie's activities.

The voice came through the radio "Georgetown, Kentucky's very own Mayor Evans has officially accepted the position of director of boards and commissions on Governor Leche's staff. Aspirations of running for Mayor of Baton Rouge next term were hinted at during today's press conference." I listened as the Mayor spoke. It was strange for me as I had just heard his voice not long ago. Once his speech was finished, the voice reported on the Mayor's family.

"Mayor Evans, his wife, and son will be making the big move soon. No doubt that Georgetown will be losing a key figure in its local government." I walked across the living room and turned the radio off. As I walked by Banner, his eyes slowly opened and his tail wagged slowly, coming to a rest in a safer position than under Dad's chair.

21

The Georgetown Times printed a front page story with a photo of Mayor Evans standing on a stage behind a podium. Next to him was the Lieutenant Governor of Louisiana and just off to the side of the front page photo was Ellie. I could only see the left side of her body and a fake smile that was upon her face. I couldn't see the bandage, but the thought of it pissed me off. I threw it away and looked at the calendar. Three more days and they would be returning from Baton Rouge. In the back of my mind I had stored away a thought that could get Ellie and Joe out of their situation, but I didn't really have a full plan. I didn't really know how to go about it. Yet.

Booley and I reached the track at Keeneland around five-thirty in the morning. The Bennett family had already saddled Ranger's Cape.

"Let's hot walk Ranger around the barn before we get him on the track." I said.

"I'll take him now," Jim offered. Palmer was trying to get into his riding boots and Cara was helping Kenny clean and oil a spare exercise saddle. The sky was growing brighter every minute and Ranger's Cape looked eager to get out there and run. Once Jim completed several laps around the barn, I helped Palmer up in the riding saddle.

"How many today?" he asked.

"Trot and gallop eight. Break before you breeze. I want to check over his mouth and nose for blood. If he's fine I want to see what he'll do on the back stretch, but don't take him full. I want to be careful here."

"Okay," Palmer said before heading off to the track.

Over the years, I have had to explain to people exactly what it is I do in order to train a horse. I tell them that it is an uneventful, unexciting day in and day out routine. The routine involves a lot of conditioning and training to build up stamina. Much like the training of an athlete, so is the training of a horse. The training that goes on at the track is no different than training at the farm, other than the track conditions are nearly perfect and we were able to use the actual starting gate.

I watched as Palmer took Ranger's Cape around and took notice of his gait. If there were any inconsistencies I would have reason for concern, but everything looked okay. Before I would let him breeze, Booley and I checked him over for signs of blood. I placed my ear to his rib cage and listened to his lungs through his thick hide hearing the deep whoosh sounds of air being taken in and exhaled from his lungs. No gurgling. No evidence of fluid spattering around in the thoroughbred's passage ways. To me, his lungs sounded free and clear. I gave Ranger an approval smack on his hind end and looked up at Palmer.

"Take him eight furlongs, but not full. Pay close attention and if you feel him shudder or waver, back him off and bring him in," I explained.

"Will do," Palmer said before he started Ranger toward the track.

"When you come back in, let Booley check him over one more time," I hollered out. Having an exercise rider who knew his job and was fully aware of the condition of each horse was rare back then. Palmer was the best and I have yet to meet another exercise rider of his caliber.

After the first day of exercising the horses on Keeneland's track, I spent the forty-five minute drive home with Booley talking to me all the way. I remember he talked about other trainers having a hard time succeeding which made me feel really good about having a horse on my roster such as Outpost. I hadn't given him any special treatment or any more attention than I had the other horses and I had yet to see Outpost's full potential, but I could tell he was fast and wanted to run. His work ethic was good and his ability to become so accustomed to the daily training regiment was impressive. I thought about his gait and stride as I walked back to the house, imagining Outpost racing his first race.

When I walked in the front door of the main house, I heard talking in the dining room. I walked carefully without making a sound and listened in on the conversation.

"It is all relative to furlongs. What did I say a furlong was?" It was my father. Dad was talking to someone and his voice sounded more lively than usual.

"Um, one eighth of a mile," Joe said. I couldn't believe it. Dad was carrying on a conversation with Joe, but why were they in the dining room? I didn't peek my head around the corner; I just listened.

"Right. One eighth. So to make the number one or one mile, how many eighths do you need?" There was a pause. I still didn't know what was going on. "You have one eight, then two eights, then three. You would have to go to eight-eights which is one or one mile."

"Okay. So if I am trying to figure one tenth, I would need ten on top and bottom to make one."

"Correct. You got it," I heard my dad say followed by the familiar sound of whiskey sloshing around in a bottle as if he just took a drink.

"So that's fractions? Is it that easy?"

"Yeah, but don't worry. You don't need them much in life except for measuring the distance of a race at the track. What kind of horse do you not bet on in a ten furlong race?"

"Um…I don't know."

"There are horses that are fast, and some are distance runners. How far is a ten furlong race?" Dad asked. The scratch of a pencil and paper followed and then Joe replied.

"Two miles?"

"Shit no. Try again," Dad answered. More scratching on the paper and finally, Joe answered.

"A mile and two eights, or one quarter." There was a pause and finally Joe sounded confident in his answer. "One mile and a quarter. Right?"

"Right. Don't bet on a horse built on speed in a long race. You should always go with a distance runner. Start out with two dollars for every bet. You can win a lot of cabbage by knowing the distance of each race and how each horse performs under short and long races," Dad said followed by another swig of whiskey. "Don't ever bet to show. Always to win. Suckers and skeevies bet to show." I peered around the corner. "Don't be a skeevie," Dad added followed by another drink from his bottle of whiskey.

"Hey," I said. Dad and Joe looked at me at the same time. "What's going on?" I asked. Dad went back to the paper in front of him that mostly had Joe's scribble written across the page.

"Homework," Dad replied. Joe looked at me and seemed very content sitting next to Dad with his legs dangling off the seat, not quite touching the floor.

"I have a fraction test on Friday," Joe said swinging his feet.

"Oh. So Dad you're helping him?" I had to ask as it was a bit of a shock for me to see my father talking with someone, let alone helping a little boy with his homework.

"See that?" he said to Joe as he leaned in, no doubt spreading the aroma of whiskey as he spoke. "He is smarter than he looks." Dad waved his hand at me without making eye contact, gesturing for me to leave. "We're busy," he said.

He had added gambling to Joe's education between fighting and drinking, which, I am sure, Ellie would appreciate. On my way upstairs to take a shower, I could faintly hear the radio in the living room. The reporter was talking about a special mayoral election to take place after Mayor Evans' resignation. Ellie had only a few more days left and she would be back in Georgetown, but who knew for how long?

22

They call them "Outriders" now, but back in the early 1900s they were called the "Pony Patrol." Their job was to be on the track at all times during training at race tracks. Sometimes horses would get loose and need to be caught and other issues would arise such as a trainer needing an escort for one of their horses exiting the track. During a workout at Keeneland, Palmer was riding Priced Opportunity when a group of maintenance workers pushed over a heavy, large steel plate allowing the metal plate to smack the pavement. The sound rang through Priced Opportunity's ears and spooked him to the point of bucking Palmer off his back. The soft dirt track provided little comfort to Palmer as his body smacked into the ground. Priced Opportunity took off running around the track in the wrong direction. When this happened, an alarm went off that sounded much like an alarm that rings at the fire department. The alarm continually rings until the horse is caught as it is very dangerous for a horse to be running free on the track in any direction. I ran over to Palmer who was getting up off the ground.

"You okay?"

"Yeah!" Palmer said as he dusted himself off. "I was taking him around the turn when a loud noise spooked him."

The alarm continued, and I watched Priced Opportunity take off with the Pony Patrol after him. A man dressed in overalls and a straw hat waved at me to get my attention. He must have been one of the custodial guys that cleaned up around the barns.

"Mr. Chapel, you have a phone call," the man said, but I couldn't hear him over the loud alarm.

"What?" I yelled as I cupped my hand behind my ear.

"You have a phone call in the office!"

"Thanks!"

Sarah and Jim Bennett came onto the track watching the patrolmen and Priced Opportunity. I yelled over to Jim so he could hear me over the loud ringing.

"You got this? I have to take a phone call."

Jim nodded his head and I left for the manager's office. Cara and Kenny Bennett had temporarily abandoned their current chore to run over to the track to see what the commotion was about. I watched them run at full speed toward the track gate as I reached out and turned the door knob of the barn manager's office. It was more of a small shack than an office and was located next to barn seven. The manager of the barns (I have since forgotten his name) made sure that all rules and regulations were followed. All veterinarians had to check in with him before even looking at a horse as he was the one who controlled such things. When I walked in, he was just leaving.

"Phone for you, Chapel."

"Thanks," I replied. That day in March was unusually warm and the windows in the office were wide open which let in the inconvenient sound of the alarm. "Hello?" I answered as I plugged my other ear with my finger.

"Mr. Chapel, this is Jean Gibbs. I work for Mr. Wade."

"Yes! Verris Wade."

"I am to tell you that Mr. Wade will be visiting Keeneland on Tuesday the twenty-eighth."

"Oh, okay." The alarm stopped which meant Priced Opportunity had been caught. I removed my finger from my ear.

"He would like to see his horse on the track and have lunch with you."

"Great! I look forward to it."

"Bye-Bye." I left the office in a hurry and found Jim and Sarah taking Priced Opportunity back to the barn.

"Elliott!" Jim yelled as he looked in my direction. "Price has a laceration." I started jogging in their direction as Jim turned his head toward the barn. "Booley, get some rags and some water."

"What happened?" I said as I approached him.

"They caught him between the outside rail and got cut here. See?" Jim pointed to Priced Opportunities hind quarters where I saw a cut deep into the skin. Blood was emitting from the wound.

"Aw, dang it!" I said in frustration.

Once again, Dr. Wall arrived to tend to one of my horses and was greeted by Booley and a warm compliment. He arrived in his 1934 Ford DeLuxe Fordor which looked filthy as if he had been driving on dirt roads all day. Dr. Wall cut off the engine and opened his driver's side door. Booley and I were waiting for him.

"Booley, you ol' bastard, weren't you friends with Benjamin Franklin?" Dr. Wall grunted as he shifted his body around in the driver's seat to get out of his car. Dr. Wall looked for the barn manager and saw him in the distance. He waited until he was seen and then Dr. Wall raised his hand, signaling he was checking in as that was all he needed. Dr. Wall had been caring for thoroughbreds since before the manager was born.

"Yep. Didn't you sit next to Jesus in school?" Booley said with an ill-behaved smile. Dr. Wall laughed as he walked next to Booley, shuffling his tired legs toward the barn.

"Chapel, I am seeing more of you than I like. What is going on with your horses?" Dr. Wall asked as he looked at me with a smile.

"A streak a bad luck I guess," I replied.

"Well, let's see what we're dealing with."

I took Dr. Wall inside the barn and brought Priced Opportunity out in the aisle, pointing out the injury.

"Bring him out. Let me look at him in the daylight," Dr. Wall said as he began to shuffle out the barn door. After a careful examination, it was deemed that the laceration needed a bandage and daily attention.

"Keep your eye on it. Apply this ointment twice daily," he said handing me a small glass jar with a white cream inside. "No more exercise until it has a nice firm scab, should heal nicely with the ointment. It's not bad, I have seen these kinds of wounds heal in a matter of no time with daily attention. You just don't want it to open up again." Dr. Wall set his black medical bag down and reached inside, pulling out a roll of bandages. "Here's what ya do, keep the bandage on for two days then take it off. Let the air get to it. Keep to the ointment and don't let him exercise for three days, then light work for five, should be fine and scabbed in about eight."

"Thank you for your time," I said handing him a cash payment. He took it and put it in his left breast pocket of his coat without counting the money.

"Keep an eye on your horses, ya hear?" Dr. Wall said. He turned his back to me and started shuffling toward his car. "I wouldn't want to see you again unless you're next to me in line at the betting window." Booley walked along side him and I couldn't make out what they were saying but whatever it was it was making Booley laugh.

"I'll apply the first round of ointment and get him bandaged up," Jim said heading back into the barn with Priced Opportunity.

"Thanks, Jim." Trying to focus on more positive subjects, I told everyone the good news. "We have a client coming next Tuesday to see his horse," I said. Sarah looked at me with eyes as big a silver dollars.

"It's not Mr. Wade, is it?"

"It is," I answered.

"Wow! Verris Wade here at Keeneland," Jim said. Booley was on his way back from walking Dr. Wall back to his car.

"Hey Booley, guess who's coming next Tuesday?"

"Verris Wade," he replied.

"How'd you know?"

Booley reached behind him and took a newspaper out of his back pocket and tossed it at me.

"Have a look," he said. *The Lexington Herald* had printed a story on Verris Wade's trip which included a visit to Keeneland. It seemed that wherever Mr. Wade went he always got press.

When Booley and I got home that night, the house was empty. There was no sign of Joe or Dad. We checked the barns and neither of them were there. We gave up after a half hour of looking around. Booley went to his little house, and I went upstairs and took a shower. When I came down the stairs, I heard talking in the living room.

Dad was in his chair, and Joe was on the couch listening to the radio.

"Where've you been?" I asked.

"Picture show," Dad said.

"We saw Stagecoach," Joe said.

"What? Dad, when was the last time you went to see a movie?" I asked. He just sat there. He didn't say a word. "Just out of the blue you wanted to go see a movie?" I was a little pissed off. I didn't understand. Dad got up and walked over to the radio and turned it up.

"Did you want to see it? I'll go see it again," Joe said.

"No, it's not that." Dad walked back to his chair and sat down. I looked at him and he didn't look back. The phone rang and I left the room and headed toward the kitchen confused by my father's actions and recent behavior. I reached out my hand and grabbed the receiver off the lever.

"Elliott?" the voice said. It was Ellie. Within an hour she pulled up in the driveway, and I had just finished getting Joe's suitcase ready.

"Joe, she's here," I said. We walked out onto the front porch and headed for her car. Ellie exited the driver's side. Joe ran to his mother, and I loaded his suitcase into the backseat.

"Oh, I missed you," Ellie said as she bent down and embraced him. "Did you have fun?" she asked. The bandage was off, but she still had stitches on the side of her head just below her temple.

"I sure did!" he nodded his head and smiled, keeping our secret about him drinking a Coca-Cola. "How's your cut?" Joe asked his mom as he pointed to the side of her face.

"Good. It's getting better every day," Ellie said as she stood up. "Any trouble?" she asked me.

"Not at all."

"Good. I have to get back," she said hurriedly.

"Wait. Can't you stay for just a moment?" I asked.

"I better not. Wayne thinks I am picking him up at Mrs. Raines house. I need to get back."

"Can I see you?" I said just as Ellie turned her head slightly and I could see a bruise on her neck.

"Do you want to meet…" she started to say until I interrupted her.

"Ellie, what's this?" I asked as I moved the collar of her shirt back, revealing bruises the size and shape of fingerprints as if she was grabbed. She immediately used her hand to cover them back up.

"Joe, get in the car. Look, it's nothing," she said. Joe opened the car door and got in.

"Damn it, Ellie!" I said.

Joe rolled down the window. Ellie brought her voice down to a whisper as she stood facing me with her back to Joe.

"What do you want me to do, Elliott? There is nothing I can do. Nothing," she said as she took a step back.

"Let's get out of here. I said in a near whisper. I will get you out of here. We can go to another state." She took a step forward standing close to me keeping her back to the car. She dropped her voice even further, almost to the point that I couldn't hear her. I suppose she was making sure that there was no chance that Joe could hear.

"Did you know that Wayne's father killed people. He was a ruthless, cruel and very powerful man," she said staring into my eyes with a look that meant I had better take her seriously. "I wouldn't put it past him to come after you. It scares me."

"You don't even want to try?" I asked.

"If something happened to you, I wouldn't be able to live with myself."

She started to tear up. "I want to be with you so bad. You don't even know what it's like for me. I just don't know what to do, because I don't think anything can be done." Ellie casually wiped her tears away so as to not alarm Joe. I was steaming mad thinking that I needed to act fast and get her away from her bastard husband.

"Look, I know we can go find an attorney in Lexington or even Louisville. We explain the situation…"

"I don't want you to try to do anything. Nothing."

"God bless, Ellie, I don't want to live my life not knowing what could have been." I got a little loud. Maybe too loud and I shouldn't have.

"Roll up your window, Joe," Ellie said as she turned her head, looking him in the eye. Joe slowly rolled up the window and she turned her attention back to me. "You don't care that he could have you killed?" I could tell she was serious.

"So that's it? It's over?" I asked. She stood there trying not to cry. I am sure my angered tone of voice didn't help things. "When are you leaving?"

"I was going to call you tonight," she said.

"You were?"

"Yes, meet me at the oak tree at eleven."

"Eleven?"

"Can you make it? I don't want to talk about this right now, okay?" she said discreetly while drying her eyes.

"I will be there without a doubt."

"See you then," she said before she turned around and walked toward her car. The emotions flooding my mind and surging through my veins overtaking my body were that of rage, confusion and distress. I just felt so helpless-like the white coyote, caught in the snare with the barrel of a rife pointed at my head, just waiting for the trigger to be pulled.

23

Once again, just before eleven o'clock at night I got into my truck, drove near Georgetown College and parked on the street. It was sprinkling, and I could hear thunder in the distance. Earlier she had told me that she wanted to be with me. I couldn't believe what she had said and it confirmed that I wanted to be with her the rest of my life. I walked toward the "Big Oak" and found Ellie leaning up against the trunk like before. Once I reached her, she wrapped her arms around my neck in a hurry. She was crying.

"We are moving away. I have to be packed and on the train in two weeks," Ellie said as she buried her face in my right shoulder. "I don't want to go."

"Ellie, I don't want you to go either," I said as I pulled away and gripped her arms gently, looking into her eyes. "I don't want you to go. I want you to stay with me."

"It's impossible." Tears dripped from her eyes as she spoke. The sprinkling rain had picked up a little, but the big oak tree sheltered us for the time being. She continued to cry, and I tried to think of something to say as I held her. Eventually, after she seemed to have calmed down, I looked at her—the way a man shouldn't look at a married woman.

"Ellie, you are all I think about. Before I met you my life was training horses. Now, my life is you. You're my very purpose for being here." I had expected her to return the look that I was giving her, but instead she showed me anger and fear.

"Don't say that." The thunder in the distance grew louder, and the wind was picking up.

"Nobody can love you like I can."

"Stop it! Don't say anything else."

"Then why would you meet me here like this? Why would you even suggest to me that you want to be with me?" I said. I turned my back toward her. My heart was beating so fast I could hear it in my head. "Don't you know that saying things like that kill me? I can't be with you, yet you say these things and it tears me in half, Ellie." I was talking loud enough that I could have woken someone in one of the nearby buildings from a deep sleep. Anger had set in, and my voice was showing it.

"I can't help it. I love you," she said. She actually said it. Those words were hovering in the air between us like clothes on a line. The words waved and flapped in the wind between us, but neither of us uttered the words until that night. My back was still turned. When she said those words, my hand was on my forehead pushing back strands of hair. I removed my hand from my forehead and turned around and looked at her. Her face was briefly illuminated as lighting tore through the sky. The rain began to pelt the ground around us.

"I love you too," I said. She stood still as if she was soaking in the words as they left my mouth. The wind was blowing the strands of hair that had come loose from her ponytail. Lightning flashed, but the anger of the storm had yet to arrive. I could tell it was going to get worse.

"He is leaving for Baton Rouge at five tomorrow morning. He is packing up the car and leaving right away." I nodded my head for her to continue. She started looking around as if someone might be watching us. "When he leaves, he will be gone for two weeks while I prepare the house and get everything ready to be loaded onto the train. As soon as he leaves, I will come and stay on the farm with you if you like."

"Are you sure you want to do that? He might find out."

"He might. He might not. Maybe if he found out and I still showed up in Baton Rouge, he wouldn't care. He doesn't care about me. He just needs me to play a role."

"I don't know," I said. I wanted her to stay on the farm so bad, but I couldn't stand the thought of her taking a beating because of me. Rain had filtered through the leaves of the tree creating big drops that fell from above. Ellie looked as if she was trying to figure out a puzzle or a riddle. When she was out of answers, she looked at me with a determined look in her eyes.

"I want to."

"This town is too small. It will get back to him."

"I am willing to take the risk. It's worth it to me." Ellie's tone of voice sounded unwavering and seditious and I loved it. I smiled at her. I could feel that she wanted to be with me. It was only a moment ago that she told me that she loved me. I could already see it in her eyes and hear it in her voice.

"For how long?" I asked, not realizing what she had said before.

"Two weeks. An entire two weeks."

"So that's it? We have two weeks, and that's it? It's over?"

"It's all the time we will have. If we don't take it, we lose it." Lightning streaked across the sky. The thunder made Ellie jump, but she kept her focus on me.

"You are sure there is no other way?"

"I am sure." She was adamant. Two weeks.

"Okay," I finally said. She then walked toward me and held both of my hands in hers and gently leaned forward kissing me on the lips. We broke away, but I didn't want to and it seemed that she would have continued. We slowly separated and Ellie was the first to speak.

"I will see you tomorrow," she said.

"Okay. Let me give you a ride home," The thunder jolted our bodies and the rain came in buckets. She requested that I drop her off a block from her house and I received one more kiss before she got out of my truck and ran around the corner. I drove home thinking about the next two weeks and squinting as I tried to see past the rain smacking my windshield. The wipers on cars back then were nowhere near as good as the ones today. I drove up in the drive way and quickly got out and ran toward the back porch. My feet splashed down in recessed areas of our yard, soaking my feet through my leather boots. I walked in the house thinking of Ellie kissing me under the big oak. Two weeks. It was all I had and then she would be gone. I took my boots and socks off before walking into the dimly lit family room. I guess I wasn't paying attention or maybe I just didn't look in that direction, but my father was sitting in his chair, perfectly still.

24

I had just come in from the wind, lightning and pelting rain. My shirt and pants were soaked and it was almost midnight. I was sitting on the edge of the couch with my elbows on my knees and my head resting in my hands. I didn't see Dad when I walked in since he was sitting in his chair completely still and the only light in the room came from a small lamp near the radio. If I remember correctly, Banner had already gone upstairs and was lying on his bed of fluffy, old quilts. I was thinking about the next two weeks with Ellie, knowing it would be bittersweet. Every day spent with her would be a day closer to losing her forever and without warning, while sitting on the couch, I could feel tears running down my face.

"What in the hell is the matter with you?" Dad said. His sudden loud voice caused me to nearly jump off the couch.

"What are you doing down here? It's midnight," I said as I composed myself.

"Are you crying?" he asked. His deep-set wrinkles scrunched together in disapproval. Dad's face usually didn't show his emotions.

"I guess I am," I answered, feeling foolish.

"What in the hell for?"

"I don't want to talk about it," I said. I was distressed, but I was also furious. My voice reflected my anger when I spoke and I could feel rage building up inside me like pressure in a steam pipe. Dad continued to sit in his chair, looking at me as I continued to wipe my eyes. After a long (and uncomfortable) silence, he spoke up.

"Is it the girl?" he asked. It took me a moment, but I answered him.

"Yes."

"Is she leaving?"

"Yeah, she doesn't want to though."

"Why doesn't she stay?"

"It's a long story."

"S'pose you tell it to me," he said. I refused. I didn't want to tell him anything. I was pissed off and what did he care? I got up and started to head toward the staircase.

"Forget it," I mumbled.

"Sit down!" he yelled. He sat up in his chair and leaned forward ready to listen. I was still standing ready to leave, thinking I should just go ahead and go upstairs. Dad was inebriated anyway and would just lose interest. "Have a seat, damn it!" I didn't sit. Instead I kept standing. I walked over toward the radio and turned around and spoke to him as he sat in his chair. I told Dad about Ellie's husband and how he was abusive to her and I explained in detail about her most recent injury. I was getting angry as I spoke, pacing back in forth and raising my voice. I kept waiting for Dad to lose interest, but at the same time it felt good to say what I was feeling out loud. He never took his eyes off of me and continued to sit up in his chair. I further explained that the mayor was forcing Ellie and Joe to go to Louisiana and Ellie couldn't break away. I even told him about how she kissed me under the oak tree. Normally I wouldn't have even said a word to him about it, but I just blurted it out and I wasn't thinking clearly. I explained everything and when I was finished, I put my hands on my hips and began to calm down, slowly walking between the fireplace and the couch. After another moment of silence, Dad started to rock in his chair.

"You know, that girl reminds me of Gracie," he said. I turned my head and looked at him. He was staring at the ground in front of the fireplace. "She is full of life just like your mother. She even cooks like your mom."

Dad always referred to my mother as "Gracie" or "My Gracie." That was the first time in my entire life he used the words "your mother." I didn't know it would strike me the way it did when he said it. Up until that point, he had never acknowledged out loud that his wife was my mother. The creaking of the chair rocking back and forth sounded like an old metronome. I sat still and listened to him while soaking in the words "your mother."

"Yeah, I don't think I have had much to look forward to after your mother died." The rhythmic creaking of the chair continued as Dad stared off into the distance. "I know something about what you are feeling. It doesn't feel good, I know." The thunder roared over the house and the landscape outside could briefly be seen through the windows as the lightning flashed in random intervals. The wind was picking up as the storm was upon us.

"I don't know what I am going to do when she leaves," I said. I sat still and Dad's rocking chair stopped. I looked at him and it appeared that he had fallen asleep. I sat on the couch for about another minute before standing up to head upstairs.

"Does that man hit the boy?" he asked with his eyes closed. I stopped.

"What?" I asked.

"Does he hit the boy?" I looked down at the floor. I hated thinking about Ellie living with that bastard in Louisiana. It was tearing a hole inside me. I never saw any bruises on Joe, except from the car accident. However, Ellie had told me that Joe's father had hit him before and the thought of that grown man hitting that small boy caused me to clench my fists as I answered.

"Yes, he does."

"Nothing can be done with an attorney and a judge?" Dad asked.

"He is a political figure. It wouldn't happen," I said. The wind was beating the side of our house. Rain slammed against the windows in sheets. "He's untouchable," I said and I started toward the staircase.

"I see," Dad said, still rocking in his chair. "So that's it? She gone forever?"

"Not exactly. Her husband is going to Louisiana at five in the morning. She is coming here soon after he leaves and will be staying for two weeks. That's all I have, two weeks." I stood there with one foot in the living room and the other foot at the bottom of the stairs. Dad just rocked back and forth in his chair. "You staying up?" I asked.

"Yeah. For a little while," he said with his eyes closed.

"Goodnight."

"Yep."

As I climbed the stairs, desperate thoughts ran though my mind. What if a tornado ripped through Georgetown and sucked Mayor Evans out of his home and impaled him on a rod iron fence? Of course, my imagination left Ellie and Joe intact. If only I were so lucky.

25

The next day Booley and I prepared for the trip back to Keeneland. We loaded some extra bags of feed into the back of the truck and packed up a few extra bath sponges and soap. The sun was coming up over the horizon and I kept looking for Ellie to drive up the driveway as we walked from the barn to the main house. The sunlight illuminated the pearls of dew on the grass and created sweeping, dramatic shadows over the entire farm. As I walked closer to the main house I squinted as I looked past the darkness of the shadows across the back porch making out the faint outline of a figure on the old couch. Dad was asleep on the old couch covered up with Banner's old, nasty blanket. It was just before six that morning and it looked like he had been there all night. I walked over to him taking notice of the whiskey bottle lying on his chest moving up and down as he breathed in and out. There was still liquid in the bottle, but very little. Upon closer inspection, I could see that some of the liquid had been spilling out for some time. Every breath in and out probably rocked the liquid back and forth until the momentum caused small amounts of whiskey to slip out and onto Banner's grimy blanket. Dad was passed out and looked as if he was freezing. He had been out in the yard fooling around with his garden and more than likely he was intoxicated beyond belief as he had mud on his boots and shirt. Checking on his tomatoes in a drunken haze was nothing new and I could see that he dragged his potted tomatoes from inside the kitchen to the center of his garden, hoping to catch plenty of sunlight for the day. I signaled Booley, and he helped me get Dad's boots off. We took him inside and up the stairs to his bedroom. Banner opened one eye as he was resting comfortably on his bed of quilts, watching our movements. We got Dad into his bed and quietly closed his bedroom door. When we went back outside, Ellie and Joe were driving up in the driveway. The car she was driving belonged to the city and was meant for the servants of the mayor to pick up groceries or gardening supplies. The back seat was covered in dirt and old leaves from transporting plants and bags of soil. The exterior of the car was as filthy as the back seat. Ellie parked it on the grass on the left side of the driveway. Once again I was able to see that ponytail bobbing back and forth from behind her head with every step she took. The smile on her face grew larger as she got closer to me. When she set her luggage down she embraced me, hugging my neck tightly. I just squeezed her back. Joe spoke with Booley momentarily before asking about Dad.

"Where is Mr. Chapel?"

"Oh, he gonna be asleep for some time. He is upstairs in his bed," Booley answered.

"Oh, okay," Joe said looking a little disappointed. He was holding a piece of paper and I got the impression that he was going to give it to Dad.

"Whatcha got there, Joe?" I asked.

"Look at this," Ellie said as she took the picture from him. I could see Joe was looking at me for a sign of approval. Ellie explained, "It's a picture of Joe, you, Booley and your father and some other guy. Even Ol' Banner is in it." The picture was drawn in crayon depicting the desert with mountains in the background. It looked like we were all riding horses.

"That's The Ringo Kid," Joe said as he pointed to the unidentified man on the horse.

"Who is The Ringo Kid?" I asked.

"John Wayne,"

Back then John Wayne was best known for playing the character Stony Brooke in several movies.

"So, this is you?" I said pointing to the smallest person on the back of a horse.

"Yes."

"This is Dad, and this is the Ringo Kid?" I asked pointing out the other figures in the drawing.

"Yes and that's Banner," Joe said as he pointed to the figure that was obviously a four legged animal that wasn't a horse.

"Very good, Joe. Nice drawing," I said as I handed it to Booley. Joe spoke with Booley about the drawing while Ellie and I talked quietly off to the side.

"He left at five this morning. I was so glad to hear the engine of the car starting. I couldn't stop thinking about you all night," Ellie said.

"I have never been so excited in my entire life. I slept, but I kept waking up and looking at my watch to see if it was time to get up." We didn't hold each other's hands or kiss. We kept our distance. We did sit together in the truck on the way to Keeneland. Since Joe was transferring schools, he didn't have to go back to school until he got to Baton Rouge. He rode in the back of the pick-up truck with Booley talking about the movie "Stagecoach" and other things that interested nine year old boys. If either Booley or Joe had looked in the front seat, they would have seen me holding Ellie's hand all the way to Keeneland. Ellie talked a lot about Joe and how well he was doing in school. He had made new friends and showed the kids the movie ticket he used to get in to see Stagecoach. Ellie didn't like the fact that Dad took Joe to see a "Shoot'em up movie" as she called it, but she knew that Dad did whatever he wanted and answered to no one.

Once we arrived at Keeneland, I put the Bennett family to work in order to prepare for Mr. Wade's Tuesday visit. I then asked for Joe and Ellie to follow me to see Priced Opportunity. I explained the horse's injury to them and what Dr. Wall had said. I walked over to a supply closet and found the glass jar of ointment on a shelf. I brought it to Joe and put it in his hands.

"Joe, I am going to give you a job while you are here. I want you to apply this ointment to Price's laceration." Joe looked at me as if he was taking on a big responsibility. "When you arrive in the mornings, I want you to take him out of his stable and guide him in front of the barn, out in the open like this." I took Priced Opportunity out in front of the barn and Joe watched my every move. "Then I want you to take some of the ointment out of the jar like this." I opened the glass jar and scooped out a bit of the ointment with my fingers before moving the bandage to the side. "Just pull the bandage over and then I want you to apply the ointment like this."

"And put my hand on his cut?" Joe said looking a little dismayed.

"Well, Price needs you to take care of him and this is how you do it. When you're injured, don't you want someone to look after you?"

Joe shook his head yes. "Then you need to help him get better by using your fingers and press gently." I bent down to his level and showed him my hand. "There is nothing you can get on your hands that doesn't wash off. Men don't worry about getting their hands dirty," I said—a lesson I learned early on from my father—Joe just nodded his head as if he was agreeing with me. "Go ahead and rub that into his cut." Joe did as asked. Once it appeared that the ointment had been sufficiently worked into his skin, Joe looked at me.

"Is that it?"

"Yes, good job. You can do this again before we leave this afternoon. Okay?"

"Okay," Joe replied.

"Now go put him back in the stable," I said. Ellie and I watched him as he did as he was asked.

"You don't think the horse will kick and buck around him do you?" Ellie asked as a worried mother should.

"Nah. I was working around horses when I was his age. It's good for him."

"Well, he will sure enjoy looking after the horse. He will feel like he has a part in it."

After Joe put the horse in the stable, Ellie and Joe followed me to "The Boards" so we could watch Outpost exercise.

"The Boards" as we called them back then, were constructed bleachers on the opposite side of the track from where the spectator's seats were. "The Boards" were made with old, weathered wood and nails and were supposed to be used as regular bleachers so that trainers could sit and watch their horse's breeze around the track—however no one in their right mind would go above the second tier as they were afraid the boards would collapse. They were only twenty feet long and seven feet high, no bigger than a truck. It wasn't long after 1939 that they were torn down. Ellie and Joe sat next to me on the first tier, watching Palmer.

"He's taking him sixteen furlongs today," I said as I pointed to Outpost. "For now, Palmer will gallop him six furlongs and breeze him ten." Ellie sat on my left side and Joe next to her. Joe watched Palmer talking to Outpost, rubbing his mane, and patting him on the side of his neck.

"What's he saying to the horse?" Joe asked.

"He often talks to the horses. A lot of people don't know that a horse is often like a child. Encouraging words are generally expressed in soft tones and even gentle strokes and pats of the hand are well received, helping in their training."

"Really? I didn't know that," Ellie said.

"I didn't see him talk to them at the farm," Joe said.

"Well, he doesn't do it all the time, but he does have a relationship with the horses. The exercise rider knows the horse better than a trainer does. It is their job to tell trainers how the horses are behaving and performing."

As I was explaining the ins and outs of horse training, Dad was back at the house clutching his chest in pain. He was on the floor staring at the ceiling waiting for death to take him as he vomited the whiskey that sat in his stomach the entire night.

By the time Outpost and Ranger's Cape had finished for the day, Dad had crawled down the stairs trying to get to the phone. Banner stood by his friend and wagged his tail not knowing what was going on. As soon as Beyond The Pale and Priced Opportunity were done with their workouts, I made sure that the area around the barn was pristine and the stables looked good for Mr. Wade's visit. Before we left to return to the farm, Joe took Priced Opportunity out in front of the barn and applied the ointment to the wound using his hand.

It is difficult for me to explain the feeling that surged through my body as I walked in the house and saw Dad lying motionless on the on the floor. I compare it to being in an elevator and plummeting downward although I have never experienced it firsthand. I ran to his side and immediately checked to see if he was breathing. Banner was sitting next to him with his head resting on his friends shoulder. The slow in and out movement of his chest indicated that he was breathing which prompted me to stand up and reach for the phone.

In 1926, an ambulance was purchased by John Graves Ford Memorial Hospital. *The Georgetown Times* reported on the vehicle's arrival since the ambulance could have been purchased the previous year if the city had agreed to help pay for the much needed medical transport. Local residents complained that an ambulance would serve all of Scott County and the city should have helped the hospital with the purchase. When the newly acquired ambulance arrived for a ribbon cutting ceremony, a photographer from *The Georgetown Times* took a picture of the brand new vehicle which had a huge dent in the front of it. When asked what had happened, the man driving the ambulance replied "I hit a deer". Since then, our local ambulance was often referred to as "The Deer Hunter." After I made the phone call, The Deer Hunter, still sporting its historic dent, left the hospital and made its way to our house.

Booley and I got Dad out the front door as fast as we could when we saw the paramedics pull into the driveway. After the ambulance left, we made it to the hospital and waited while Dad was in the emergency room (back then they were called "emergency departments").

Pneumonia was a pretty scary thing back then as it wasn't as treatable as it is nowadays. When Dad was diagnosed, it seemed to us like a death sentence given his age. He tried to answer their questions as he laid there on the gurney making incoherent sounds. Except for Dad groaning, it was quiet and there were curtains all around the room dividing each patient, providing a little privacy. What smelled like ammonia, bleach, sulfur and various unidentifiable human fluids filled the air in the room, causing me to breathe through my mouth. Once it was evident that Dad was in the hospital for the night, I drove Booley back to the house and packed a small bag as I intended to stay the night with my father.

Ellie had made dinner as fast as she could so I could eat with them. Potatoes, fried okra and apple sauce were prepared and placed on everyone's plate. The potatoes were cut into small chunks and were fried in a skillet with herbs and butter. I kept thinking about what Dad had said. "Ellie cooks the way your mother used to." I was trying to eat quickly, but enjoy the flavor at the same time. Joe picked at his food as he stared at his plate. Finally, he said what was on his mind, "I used to be scared of Mr. Chapel."

"What do you mean?" Ellie asked.

"At first I thought he was scary. Didn't talk much, and he always seemed to growl at me," he said before putting an overfilled spoon of applesauce into his mouth. Booley had a question on his mind.

"How did you come to like Mr. Chapel, Joe?"

"He taught me..." Joe started to say, but Ellie made him stop by putting her hand in front of his mouth. Whenever Joe chewed, his cowlick would dance on top of his head as if it were performing a show.

"Don't talk with your mouth full," she said. Joe swallowed and then continued, so did the cowlick.

"He showed me how to stand up and not be pushed around. He taught me about fractions and who to trust and who not to trust," Joe said. Booley laughed with his mouth closed.

"Lemme guess," Booley said. "Don't trust a man wearing a suit and anyone trying to sell you something," Booley said.

"And injuns," Joe added. Even I had to laugh as I had heard my dad say that on several occasions.

"All good advice I'd say," Booley said. Joe got out of his seat and walked to the living room and came back with his drawing of the desert scene. Before he could speak, the phone rang. When I answered, a hurried female voice said, "Mr. Chapel. You had better come quickly."

I immediately hung up the phone and jumped into the truck and sped over to Ford Memorial. I had left everyone at the house and told them I would call. Once I arrived, I ran into the lobby and up the stairs to the room full of curtains. The nurse who called me came toward me with a desolate look. In her left hand she was holding a folded, brown piece of paper. Her hands rose up and touched both of my shoulders. The austere gaze in her eyes told me before she spoke.

"I am sorry," she said softly with compassion. "He didn't survive."

"What?" I said. My hand immediately covered my mouth. "He's gone?" I asked, hoping I was misunderstanding.

"I am so sorry."

"What happened? Why?"

"His lungs were failing. He was having a hard time breathing," she said. I brought my hand from my mouth to my forehead. The words stung. My dad was gone. The nurse handed me the folded, brown piece of paper and she looked into my eyes. "He asked me for a piece of paper and a pencil and he wrote a note. He said, give it to my son." I hadn't ever heard him say those words like that, "My son." He called me his son. I held the note, still letting the thought of my father's death sink in. I must have gone into a state of shock. I looked around the room unable to see clearly as my eyesight momentarily seemed out of focus. The nurse's voice faded away and my hand slowly reached into my pocket where I must have put the note without reading it. I have to tell you that it was very painful to experience it the way I did. The nurses had probably closed his curtain before pulling the sheet over his body. I could have seen him one last time, but I didn't. I am not sure why, but I guess I wanted to remember him the way I did instead of seeing his body on a hospital bed. The nurse just stood there with me and spoke to me in her soft, pleasing voice. She told me it was going to be okay and that she was sorry for my loss and at some point I regained my composure. I walked to the lobby where the chaplain's office was just off to the right side of the entrance. Brother Guthrie from the local church used the office from time to time, but he wasn't there when I walked in. I turned on the light and picked up the telephone. I was quickly reminded, as I waited for the soft melodious voice to answer, of Ellie's cold body in the back of Mr. Cooper's hearse while Doc and I put our coats over her body.

"Central on the line," the soft, familiar voice answered.

"Cooper Funeral Home please," I said. The imagery of the freezing water flowing around Ellie's body as she laid there in the creek played out in my mind. I waited for Central to connect me with Mr. Cooper thinking of how my life has changed drastically ever since I saw her in the creek. When Mr. Cooper came on the line, I explained the situation.

"I'll be right over," he said. I sat there in the lobby of the hospital waiting for that jalopy of a hearse to arrive. Dad was gone and Ellie was leaving soon. I just sat there feeling like my life was over as if I once had a purpose and something to look forward to, but once Ellie moved to Baton Rouge, I would be pointless.

"Hello, Mr. Chapel," he said as he reached out his wrinkled hand. I snapped out of my gaze and stood up.

"Hey, Coop," I said as we shook hands although I don't think I smiled. I did notice the Dobbs Dutton hat he was wearing, which he took off as he offered his condolences.

"I'm sorry to hear about your father,"

"Thanks. I appreciate your coming out here on a moment's notice."

"No problem."

"I have to get back home now. If you need anything, please call me," I said hoping to get in the truck and on my way home soon. I hated feeling like I was empty and irrelevant. I needed a distraction.

"Sure thing, and again, I am sorry," Mr. Cooper said. He shook my hand one last time, and I headed for my truck. When I got back home, Ellie and Joe were in the living room listening to the radio. Ellie was sitting on the couch when I entered the room. She immediately stood up and looked at me without saying a word. My face must have said it all as she walked over to me and wrapped her arms around my neck. I caught a glimpse of Dad's chair, and tears started to stream down my face.

"What's wrong?" Joe asked.

"Mr. Chapel passed away, sweetie," she whispered. I wiped the tears off my face. For some reason, I didn't want Joe to see me cry.

"Excuse me. I need to go upstairs for a minute," I said.

"Sure. We will be right here," Ellie replied. Joe walked over to her side and tugged on her shirt. Ellie bent over, and Joe whispered in her ear. I am sure Joe had many questions.

"I'm going to go to Booley's house after I clean up," I said out of view of Ellie.

"Okay," she answered from the other room. I walked into the bathroom and closed the door. On a shelf above the commode was my dad's shaving cream. I picked it up and squeezed a small amount of Barbasol onto my index finger. In the thirties, the shaving cream was thick instead of the light and fluffy cream that we know today. Instead of a can, it was packaged in a tube similar to toothpaste. I rubbed the shaving cream between my thumb and finger remembering the day Dad showed me how to shave.

I guess my father did teach me the necessities of life. He did teach me how to train horses, but he also treated me like hired help most of the time. I don't want to go into all the things my father did or didn't do. As I write this, I am remembering standing in that bathroom. I remember the tube of shaving cream, and I remember finding his wedding ring on the same shelf. I picked it up and looked closely at it. He had taken it off several years ago as his fingers had lost their thickness and his ring was constantly sliding off. He did wear it long after my mother's death as he had no intentions of getting remarried.

He always saw himself as being married to my mother.

I held the ring in my left hand and quickly decided it should be kept in a safer place and put it in my pocket for the time being. When I slid my hand into my pocket, my hand touched the piece of paper that I had forgotten...the note from my father which the nurse had put it in my hand at the hospital.

I pulled out the note and unfolded it. Instead of a note in a proper format, it was three lines long written with a pencil. It read:

Plant the tomatoes for the coyote

Give Booley my room if he wants it

Happiness lies between fathers and sons

At first it was confusing. My father had three final thoughts, and he wanted to write them down for me. The first line was extremely puzzling. Was the albino coyote the first thought that ran through his mind on his death bed? Did he go insane during his final moments? Then the second line made me think that he wasn't crazy. If a man like my father could have a friend and not piss them off enough to make them want to leave, it was Booley. Then the third line of the note was the most confusing of all. It wasn't his saying. It was Booley's. Several times throughout my life, my father and I heard him say that out loud, but we ignored him. It was usually when I was pissed off at Dad for being his usual self or when Dad would cuss and spit at me for doing something wrong. At a young age, I once left a saddle outside on a rack while we were away during racing season. When we got back home, Dad found the saddle after it had been exposed to the elements. Its condition was deemed worthless and Dad considered it to be a good deal of money thrown to the wind. After I received a verbal lashing from my father, Booley said as he had a few times before, "Happiness lies between fathers and sons." I didn't really know what he meant, but he picked the wrong time to say it out loud. "Shut the hell up, Booley," Dad yelled.

I held the note in my hand, looking at the words. It was odd to me that he would write that, but I suppose that was Dad's way of reconciling with me before he passed. I cleaned up by splashing cold water on my face and went into my bedroom to change clothes. Did he think I would be happy now that he was dead? Questions and thoughts arose, however I quickly dismissed the ones that were unreasonable. I put the note and the ring inside a cedar box on my dresser and went downstairs. Booley had yet to hear that Dad passed away and I wanted him to hear it from me first.

Sherlock Holmes was a live radio show that had only been on a couple times that year as it wasn't a regularly scheduled program. I could hear the dialogue and sound effects from the story *A Case of Identity.* I stood still for a moment and listened briefly while watching Joe as he sat on the floor, mourning over the death of his boxing coach. Ellie was sitting on the couch with her feet propped up in front of her. I bent over and whispered in her ear as to not interrupt Joe from the radio show.

"I am going to Booley's house and I will be back shortly."

"Do you need anything? Is there anything I can do for you?" She asked as she reached and held my hand momentarily.

"No, but I appreciate your asking," I said with a half smile.

"Let me know if you do."

I wanted to kiss her. Maybe just on the cheek but I restrained myself. As I walked toward the back door I saw out of the corner of my eye that Joe had the drawing he made for my dad laying on the floor in front of him as he listened to the radio show. I went ahead and walked outside and onto the back porch where Dad spent most of his short lived retirement days. Instead of driving to Booley's, I chose to walk.

I used to think that Dad would eventually go back to being the way he used to be, before mom died. I had always thought that he would snap out of it and stop being so angry with the world. A little naïve, I know. As I walked to Booley's house, I thought about the one thing that did seem to bother me the most and that was how he treated Joe. He helped him with his homework, took him to a movie and seemed to have taken a genuine interest in Joe. I never received any help with my homework growing up, and I was never taken to a movie or anything fun for that matter.

When I arrived at Booley's house, I knocked on the door. When he answered, he had a book in his hand with his finger marking the place where he left off.

"Hey, come in," Booley said as soon as he saw it was me.

"Thanks."

"How's he doing?" he asked as he shut the door.

"He passed away, Booley," I said. It almost brought tears to my eyes to say it out loud.

"Aw, no," he said as he set the book down losing his place entirely.

"His body gave out,"

Booley scratched his head for a moment and then asked, "Did you get to talk to him?"

"No. He died when I was on my way there."

"Gosh. I hate that for ya. I wonder what he would have said?"

I reached in my pocket to take out the note, then realizing I had put it in the cedar box with his wedding ring.

"Probably would have told me to quit allowing neighbors to use the phone," I said taking my hand out of my pocket. Booley laughed and carried on. I cracked a smile myself. "Booley, Dad wrote down three things on a piece of paper before he died," I said as I strolled over to the couch and sat down. "The nurse handed it to me just after he had passed." Booley wandered over to the fireplace and sat on the hearth, resting his elbows on his knees. "One of those things is that Dad wants you to have his room and I think it would be better for you to stay at the main house. What do you say to moving in sometime soon?" I asked.

"Elliott? You would let me stay at the main house? You mean, live there?" His mouth moved, but the rest of his body was completely still.

"Yeah. Of course," I replied. Booley finally broke his frozen stance.

"You don't know what this means to me," he said. He looked really touched at the gesture. I didn't think it would be that big of a deal. "You and your father are the most wonderful people I have ever known." I was sort of in shock at his response. It surprised me that it would mean that much to him.

"I wouldn't go that far," I said smiling. "Dad's callous nature has never been called wonderful." Booley cackled and nodded his head.

"Your father sure was somethin'," he said slapping his knee. "I will surely miss him," he added with a big smile.

"You and I might be the only ones," I said laughing. Booley got to laughing so hard his eyes started to water. I have no idea what it is about death and laughter, but they seem to go together like peanut butter and jelly. Once we settled down, I had it in mind to bring up the third line of the note as Booley was the only one who could make sense of it.

"Do you remember saying to Dad or both of us, happiness lies between fathers and sons?" I asked. Booley nodded his head.

"I sure do."

"Did you make that up?"

"No sir, I didn't," Booley said as he looked up at the ceiling of his little house in deep thought. "I believe it is from the book *The Continental Divide*, an old book written ages ago. If I remember correctly that was the first line in the book. Always stuck with me," he answered. I shifted my weight and leaned back on the couch in a more comfortable position.

"The third line of Dad's note reads happiness lies between fathers and sons."

"He wrote that?"

"Yeah, I was hoping you could make more sense of it than I can. Not sure what to make of it or what it is that he meant," I said. Booley's eyes once again glanced upward at the ceiling, deep in thought.

"I don't know. I remember him yelling at me for saying that," Booley said.

"Me too. I remember you saying it after I left the saddle outside and he cussed me out."

"Yep. That was it," Booley added. He rubbed his chin and looked off into the distance. "Why would he say that now?" Booley sat quietly for a moment and I dared not disturb his train of thought for fear I might interrupt and never hear a good reason.

"Well, I'm not sure. When people leave this life, they always want to reconcile with folks before they die. Maybe that was the only thing he could think of and he wanted to reconcile with you," he said, shrugging his shoulders. I wasn't sure that was it, but it sounded like a logical explanation. We chatted some more about Dad and talked at length about his funeral arrangements before I headed for the door.

"Your dad was very kind to me. He always treated me with respect. I just wanna say that I am grateful for him and you. Letting me stay at the main house is a blessing. The outhouse and getting up twice a night to put chopped wood on the fireplace is becoming more and more strenuous on my old and tired body."

"You're welcome, Booley." I opened the door and walked outside. "No sense in letting his room sit vacant. See you early tomorrow morning."

"See you and thank you so much, Elliott," he said. I remember the sincere tone in his voice and the look in his eyes.

I felt like I was getting the credit for it, and I didn't deserve it. I am not sure if I would have thought about letting him stay at the main house or not. I didn't mind him moving in, but I am not sure that I would have ever thought to ask him. Obviously Dad knew him better than I did.

26

The funeral was set for Monday, and I had less than a day to get everything ready to bury my father. I met with Mr. Cooper early on a Sunday morning and arranged for Paul L. Chapel to be buried next to Grace A. Chapel. I didn't have to choose a casket; in fact, I don't remember if there were any choices available to me. Mr. Cooper helped me write an obituary for the paper, and I took care of the expenses with a check. I didn't have to do much as Brother Guthrie had already been scheduled to preside over the funeral, and phone calls had already been made to people outside of town. Either Mr. Cooper was very good at his job or I received special attention. To this day I tend to think it was the latter. After the arrangements were made, I went home and called Keeneland. The manager's office was vacant when I called, so the phone rang and rang until someone eventually heard it and answered. I told the person on the other end of the line that I needed to speak with Jim Bennett; it was a full eight minutes before he was found and made his way to the phone.

"Hello?" Jim said. My intention was to inform him of my father's death, but I started with business first.

"How are things?" I asked which was followed by a laugh coming from the other end.

"Elliott? You're not going to believe this…"

In 1938 a horse by the name of Seven Chances broke the track record during a ten-furlong race posting a time of 2:03:40. A couple of hours before I spoke to Jim, Outpost posted a time of 2:03:00 in a practice session of the same distance, unofficially beating Seven Chances' record time. When Jim explained this to me, I could feel my heart start to race with excitement.

"Can you believe it?" Jim shouted. "We took on a full run with two others and he overtook them by seven lengths!"

"Are you kidding me? Who clocked him?"

"Sarah kept time on the stopwatch!"

"Holy crap! He's going to break his maiden on the first run!" I shouted back.

"I know! I know!"

It was a relief to hear good news after what I had been dealing with. I did tell Jim about Dad and he expressed his condolences. I could hear the sadness in his voice because it was my father who gave him a good job, which in turn allowed his family to eat and live a good life.

I have to be honest and say that at that point, the most painful thing was not of my father's death, but Ellie's coming departure. While it was many days away, I still had the ache in my heart which seemed to increase every time I looked at her. When I hung up, I told Ellie, Joe and Booley the good news.

Ellie fixed lunch before we helped Booley move in to the main house which wasn't that easy considering the amount of books he had. I set down a box in Booley's room and he opened it, thinking he might still have a copy of *The Continental Divide*. He dug through the box, taking out a few stacks before finding it on the bottom.

"I wasn't sure if I still had it," he said as he fished it out from the box and opened the soiled cover. He flipped past a few tarnished pages and found the first chapter. "Here it is," Booley said pointing out the line to me. He had remembered correctly, it was the first line of the book. His eyes fixed on the words and squinted as he read "Happiness lies between fathers and sons. They find themselves in each other, for when they go west they go as simple men becoming masters of spokes, rivets and sawed felloe's." I had read along with him watching his finger follow the first two sentences. "I had only said it a handful of times."

"Did he read this book?"

"No. He wouldn't have read this," Booley said as he closed the novel. "First of all it has nothing to do with horses."

"Yeah, I guess you're right."

"I don't think he ever read a book of fiction since I've been around." Booley handed it to me and I looked it over. It was heavy and looked to be about five hundred pages or more.

"What's the book about?"

"I don't really know. I only got half way through it 'cause it was as boring as a turtle racing in a one turtle race. I had to put it down," Booley explained. I handed the heavy book back to him and he put it back in the box. We talked a bit more as we drove down the dirt path to the little house and to grab the last of Booley's things.

Once we were back at the main house, Joe kept talking to his mother in hushed tones and whispers. At one point I heard him whisper, "Just ask him," to which Ellie replied in a low tone of voice,

"Later, Joe." About a half hour later, I walked back down the staircase after I had just taken the last box of Booley's clothes up the stairs.

Ellie and Joe were standing near the front door and turned toward me.

"Elliott, Joe has a question for you." Joe had been ready all day to ask me whatever it was.

"I have a friend who wants to spend the night, and I was wondering if we could camp in the backyard."

"Tonight?" I asked.

"Yeah, but I don't have any camping stuff and I was hoping that you did," Joe replied. His hands twisted and fluttered in front of him as he was a little nervous. It was obvious that he really wanted me to say yes.

"Well, I have a couple tents and lanterns. You want to camp in the backyard?"

"Since Joe won't be able to see his friend after we leave, I told him that he could spend the night with him. Only his friend lives in town and not on a farm."

"So you both want to camp out on the farm?" I asked Joe.

"Yeah, if it's okay," Joe said. His hands still interweaved sporadically in front of him.

"Yeah, but I think we can do a little bit better than the backyard."

Late that afternoon, I packed Eros and Catcher with camping gear while Ellie and Joe waited on the front porch for their guest. Eventually, Joe's friend was dropped off and Ellie greeted the parents. I was out back next to the willow tree, getting the tents packed and secured on the horses. Joe's friend was a wiry looking kid with glasses that seemed to be a bit heavy as he kept pushing them up on the bridge of his nose. His clothes weren't as nice as Joe's, but he seemed to have a permanent smile pressed into his face. All three walked toward me ready to see what adventure awaited them. Before I could say anything, Ellie started with the introductions.

"Martin, this is Elliott Chapel and this is his farm," Ellie said.

"Nice to meet you sir," Martin said as he stuck out his hand. I shook it and he giggled. "Ow," he said as if I squeezed his hand too hard. He shook it off saying, "Are those your horses?"

"Yep. This one is mine," I said pointing to Catcher. "And the other belongs to Booley, who is inside. He won't be going with us. We need to get moving if we are going to make it before sundown."

"Where are we going?" Ellie asked.

"Elkhorn Creek," I replied. "Have any of you ever been there?" They all shook their heads no. Martin was still smiling.

"Well, let's go. Martin, you ride with Ellie on Eros and Joe, you ride Catcher with me."

Once we got situated, we rode out to Elkhorn Creek which took us a little under an hour. At first, Martin was full of questions, but once we had made it across one of the main roads and into a large pasture, the scenery was enough to keep him occupied.

The sounds of individual hooves on the plush grass and firm soil paired perfectly with the orange sunlight that painted the limbs and trunks of the trees around us, effortlessly upholding Kentucky's scenic reputation. We weren't in a hurry and there was no need for trotting. Joe and I spoke off and on as I pointed out the trail ahead that took us into a heavily wooded area. Raccoons, squirrels and chipmunks darted and scurried as we made our way through the tree-covered trail. The dirt path was packed tightly and changed the sound of the hooves on the ground, which now clopped with a dull thud. Sunlight scattered, broken up by the thick trunks and innumerable limbs with buds jetting out as spring was arriving early. We exited the trail into a small pasture with Elkhorn Creek in sight. The sun had just set and dusk was fading just as quickly as it had arrived. We unloaded and set up the tents just before sunset, making our camp at a spot I was familiar with as I had been there a lot growing up. Elkhorn Creek was more like a river as it was pretty deep and it took some effort to swim across it. I have seen many fishing boats trolling the waters with lines in the creek with patient men on the other end of those lines waiting to reel in their catch.

The shore of our camp site was made up of thousands of tiny pebbles, medium sized rocks and gritty soil. Before I started to build the fire, I walked Joe and Martin over to a large tree where a thick rope was strategically tied to its enormous branches. The swinging end of the rope was wedged in a gap between two trees.

"This rope has been here since I was a kid," I said as I removed the heavy knotted rope and felt the thickness and weight of it in my hands. "The water is pretty cold. So if you feel brave enough to get in, hang on to this rope, and let go once you're out in the middle and drop in."

"Wow! I can't wait!" Joe said.

"Thanks, Mr. Chapel," Martin said still smiling. Ellie walked over to me with her arms crossed keeping warm from the cool air.

"Don't you think it's a little cold for them to be swimming?" she asked.

"I did it when I was their age. It is really cold," I said smiling. "I mean, I wouldn't do it now, but it's not too bad if there is a fire going."

The first time Joe swung out and let go of the rope, he splashed down and surfaced with raging chills stabbing his body.

"Oh! It is so cold! It's freezing!" Joe chuckled in between breaths.

He quickly made it to shore and ran over by the fire jogging in place momentarily.

"Can't be that bad!" Martin said. Once he surfaced after his splashdown, "Ahhh! It's like ice! I'm freezing!" It took Martin a bit longer to get out, but once he did he ran and stopped next to the fire. Both of their arms wrapped around their stomachs while they jolted their bodies with small jumps into the air to help bring the warmth.

"You wanna go one more time?" Joe asked Martin in a shivering voice.

"Heck no. Once was enough," he answered.

"I will put a few more logs on and make the fire a little bigger. You will warm up quicker."

"Thanks Mr. Chapel!" Martin yelled out with a smile as the chilled air caused him to shiver profusely.

"So you used to come here when you were a kid?" Ellie asked as I began to increase the flames of the fire by stacking the logs.

"Yeah, I have swung on that rope many times, and I have built many fires here in this very spot," I said as I glanced over at the rope swaying gently over the chilled water. I could almost imagine me and my friends standing in line, waiting to get our hands around that thick rope, lifting our legs and swinging out before letting go. The moments before splashdown were exhilarating and you could feel the gravity in your stomach, pulling you down into the murky water below. We did our share of plummeting into Elkhorn Creek when the water was as cold as ice, but mostly we did our plunging in the heat of summer. Many of my childhood memories were built around that creek during the hot Kentucky summers with boys and girls swimming, laughing and cooking campfire food at sunset.

"What are we eating for dinner?" Ellie asked.

"I packed hot dogs and s'mores," I answered as I walked over to Catcher, reached into the saddle bag and pulled out five hotdogs wrapped in butcher paper from Guthrie's.

"Sounds good," Ellie said. Ellie dried off the boys and made them change into warm clothes before we sat around the fire and cooked our hot dogs. Joe talked about Stagecoach while the fire cracked and popped. The conversation turned to my father, and I remember the sky being pitch black except for the silver moon and the stars sparkling above our camp.

"I am going to miss Mr. Chapel," Joe said.

"Why? He is right here," Martin said.

"No, I mean, Mr. Chapel the older Mr. Chapel. His father," Joe said pointing to me.

"Oh. So his father is the one that took you to the movie."

"Yeah, he passed away yesterday. He taught me how not to be weak."

"Well, Joe, you were never weak," Ellie said.

"Yeah, I was. Mr. Chapel told me I was a weak little kid and told me I talked like a girl." I smiled as that sounded just like my dad. "He said that I needed to be more like Elliott." This is what caught me off guard. I remember the sky being pitch black and the stars over our camp, and the fire was hot enough that waves of heat flowed over us. I even remember seeing the moon's reflection in the creek. When someone says something that you will remember the rest of your life, you tend to remember the moment and the environment.

"What do you mean, Joe?" I asked. Martin had picked up a long stick and started poking at the fire.

"He said that you were tough and didn't need anyone to look after you. You didn't have to rely on anyone."

"He said that?"

"Yeah," Joe answered as he chewed on a piece of hot dog.

"So are you weak now, Joe?" Ellie asked. Martin ceased poking at the fire with the stick and looked up at Ellie.

"I doubt it, Mrs. Evans. Joe knocked Nathan Cole's tooth out and bloodied Brandon Claypool's nose. He isn't weak," Martin said. I ignored his remark and focused on what Joe said.

"So he said I didn't need to rely on anyone?" I asked hoping to continue the conversation.

"Yep. Said you were able to take care of yourself since you was a kid." The conversation drifted to other things, but I kept thinking about what Joe had said. It wasn't long until they were both in their tents asleep, leaving Ellie and me completely alone.

"I appreciate your doing this. His father hasn't done anything with him that is fun. In fact, he isn't much of a father at all."

"Ellie, can we not talk about…" I said walking over to a pile of dry fire logs.

"I'm sorry. I'm not thinking."

"Well, now that you bring it up. Does it bother you as much as it bothers me that you're leaving for good next week?" I asked as I picked up two logs by gripping them from the top as if I were holding two big jars in my hands.

"It does, although you have to keep in mind that I'm protecting Joe. That's how I think of it. I am doing it for my son."

"I know." I leaned the two logs against the flaming stack. "Can we talk about something else?" I asked. Ellie immediately obliged.

"This is a lot of fun," Ellie said as she propped herself up against me. "It is fun. I enjoy it, but more so because you are here," I replied as I took a good look at her stitches on the side of her face. "Are your stitches holding up?"

"Yeah, I get them out tomorrow morning." She took out a white tube of ointment and was putting it on her finger before applying it to the stitches on her face. "Doc is coming over. I don't want to be at the funeral with stitches in my face." I wrapped my arm gently around her neck. I did so with one swift motion and her body shifted toward me as if that's what she wanted me to do. She put the cap back on the ointment and slid the tube in her pocket before getting more comfortable with my arm around her.

"You know he will know for sure if you come to the funeral," I said. Her head turned a little, fixing her eyes on mine.

"Who will?" she asks.

"The Mayor."

Ellie turned her head back toward the creek as she responded, "Ugh, I don't care. I don't even know if he will care. Stop thinking about it will you? This is our time."

"Sorry," I said. She immediately changed the topic back to us. She moved her hand to my kneecap and kept it there.

"You know I have been thinking that maybe someday in the future, I could come find you. You know, when Joe is eighteen and at a university I could leave my husband and come be with you."

"Nine years?"

"Well, if you could wait that long. I mean, I wouldn't expect you to…"

"I would wait twenty," I interrupted. She moved to one side and looked at me.

"I would wait thirty," she said with a smile.

"I would wait forty," I replied.

"Can you imagine at the age of seventy-five years old you hear a knock at the door and you see little, ol' Ellie standing on your door step?"

"If it takes forever, I will wait forever," I said. We continued to talk off and on until the fire had died down leaving fiery coals that generated enough heat for the camp.

Around midnight, we retired to our separate tents. I had a hard time sleeping as I kept thinking about what Joe told me around the campfire. Joe's voice rang through my head. "He said that you were tough and didn't need anyone to look after you. You didn't have to rely on anyone." I kept thinking that if Dad really thought that, then he didn't feel like he needed to preside over me. I didn't know if I was making excuses for my dad's lack of interest in me or not, but it seemed that he thought highly of me. Joe's comment had blindsided me and I couldn't stop thinking about it or the note that Dad left behind. "Happiness lies between fathers and sons." Anytime I thought about my relationship with my father, happiness is not a word I would use to describe it, but maybe he saw it differently. In mid-thought I heard something at the front of the tent. It was very dark, I couldn't see and I didn't have time to reach for the lantern. I felt a hand on my arm. It was Ellie.

"I can't wait nine years," she whispered as she made her way through the entrance of my tent. I felt her body on top of mine and her hands on my face. Her lips touched mine and I could feel her heart beating she was so close. It would be ungentlemanly of me to continue so I won't. I remember hearing an owl and what sounded like a coyote or I could have just been imagining things. I do remember waking up before sunrise with Ellie beside me. I woke her up and asked her if she wanted to get into her tent so Joe wouldn't know we were together. She kissed me with tired eyes as her unruly hair fell onto my forehead before quietly leaving. The low light of the dying campfire subtly illuminated her movements, casting a faint shadow across the fabric walls and ceiling of my tent. Once she was gone, I wished I hadn't woken her.

27

After we packed everything up at the campsite and got back home, I took care of Eros and Catcher while Ellie and Joe drove Martin home. Doc took Ellie's stitches out while she was in town and put another bandage on her cheek, telling her to take it off in an hour or so, just before the funeral. Once at the funeral home, I was prepared to greet the visitors in the only suit and tie I owned. I looked around the dimly lit home of Mr. Cooper, noticing that we didn't have a guest book and we didn't have any flowers except for a very small vase with three flowers. The vase sat next to the podium which was next to the casket and for whatever reason, the visitation was closed casket and even now I cannot remember why. I just remember the casket was closed, and there were metal bars on the side of the black coffin that allowed the pallbearers to move it with ease. I walked around the home of Mr. Cooper, looking in rooms and discovering that it looked the same back when I attended my aunt's visitation. I think that Mr. Cooper lived on the second floor and used the first floor as visiting rooms. The morgue was in the basement and there was a lock on the door leading to the stairs. As a child in elementary school, scary stories were told about the basement at Cooper's Funeral Home. None of them turned out to be true, but the stories remain with me. As I walked from room to room, the floors underneath my feet creaked and cracked, but were polished to a high shine that made anyone feel that they should have taken their shoes off before walking inside. While it was a beautiful funeral home, I could not feel at ease.

Visitors arrived to pay their respects and I knew almost everyone. There were people that attended who knew him before my mother died, and once again, I got to hear the stories of my father's joyful nature that I had never witnessed. They also spoke of the dark and dreary man that took the place of Paul Chapel after my mother died. They spoke of the despair and pain that gripped him and how he wouldn't let anyone speak to him about her death. The visitors I spoke with referred to his passing away as a good thing, so that once more, he would be reunited with my mother. I guess that was how I found peace with his death, and that was how I came to terms with him leaving the way he did.

"He once got into a lemon meringue pie fight with your mother," an old woman said to me. When I say *old*, I mean she was frail and could barely speak, let alone walk. She was accompanied by a tall man who was standing as though he was ready to catch her should she fall, and it looked as if her skin was drying up and dying right before my eyes. In a way, she reminded me of ol' Banner—the way the bottom of her eyelids drooped, exposing the watery red tissue to the air. "They were like kids at a carnival, causing a ruckus!" she explained, although I was having a hard time understanding her. She took a small step to the left as if she was trying to rest her weight on the other side of her decomposing hip when she seemed to leaned too far to the left and started to fall. The young man quickly sprang into action and I offered some assistance by holding onto her frail shoulders. She slung her purse at the man, barely hitting him in frustration for embarrassing her with his assistance. Her near fall somehow prompted her to search her purse diligently before locating what she was looking for and she removed a shiny flask with her bony, frail hand. She popped open the top of the curved bottle and took a swig. The young man rolled his eyes as she swallowed a mouthful. With an exaggerated wink of her right droopy eye, she said, "It's my youth elixir!" with an obvious whiskey odor emitting from her breath. When I was just a boy, I remember Dad and me walking through town and running into salesmen selling items out of the back of a wagon. The salesmen usually sold bottles that promised to hold an elixir of youth and people would stand around listening to the claims made by the slick-talking man standing by the wagon and holding up a bottle of clouded liquid. Dad explained that people selling something out of the back of a wagon were dishonest and to not waste my money on such things. Still, those salesmen were pretty convincing and I always wondered if those youth potions ever delivered on their promises. I did know that if this woman standing in front of me at the funeral home ever drank any youth elixirs, they didn't work. "I was part-time counter help at Fava's," she continued. Her breath seemed difficult to catch as she struggled to bring in a lung of air just so she could wheeze it back out in the form of verbal communication.

"My father? In a pie fight?" I asked.

"And your mother, sweetie. Your mom put a piece of lemon meringue on his nose, and he came back with a much larger piece of meringue and put it on her face," she wheezed. Then she coughed for what seemed like two minutes. When she regained her composure, the frail elderly lady continued. "Before I knew it, they were laughing and yelling with big smiles on their faces. Your father couldn't stop laughing." The coughing continued and then it seemed that she could no longer carry on a conversation without a nap. She wheezed and stood still for a moment until she shuffled on with the help of the man who was next to her. It could have been her son, but I am not sure.

Ellie stood close by and kept asking me if I needed anything as she frequently touched the spot where Doc had taken out her stitches. Joe was silent most of the day and stared at the coffin with a look both curious and fearul. Booley was the least quiet of the four of us as he told stories to visitors about Dad, that I either remembered or experienced first-hand.

There were a lot of horse trainers and grooms who came by. A few jockeys, but none that I knew personally. In the same way a semi truck can come out of nowhere and strike the side of your car without you seeing it, a man approached me and shook my hand. He was a large man with broad shoulders and tall frame. His hands resembled two huge catcher's mitts and his right one wrapped around mine as he shook it.

"Mr. Chapel, I'm Garret Cobbs." I knew who he was, but I had only seen him a few times. He lived in Great Crossing, KY which was only three miles outside of Georgetown. It wasn't much of a town back then as it didn't have a feed store or a grocery store. However, Great Crossing was home to several horse trainers. Garret Cobbs was one of them. "I owe a lot to your dad," he said just as he released his grip from my hand. We were standing in the hallway of the funeral home just outside the room where my father's coffin was displayed. As Mr. Cobbs spoke, he would nod his head in the direction of the room behind me when he spoke of Dad. "About ten years ago, I was kicked by a stubborn horse and was severely injured. I almost died."

"I remember hearing about that," I said. I had just gotten out of college and was helping dad on the farm when we heard the news. If you are a horse trainer, every other horse trainer is considered to be your competitor. It has always been very frustrating to a trainer for an owner to send his horse to an adjacent farm due to the owner's decision that your competitor's farm is better than yours. Mr. Cobbs continued with his story,

"My wife and kids did what they could to help out and for almost two years, we had very little income," he explained. I nodded my head listening and taking notice that this man had come to the funereal home to see me and tell me this one thing. "After the accident, I was having a hard time putting food on the table until I got a letter from Herb Guthrie. He said that if I needed groceries, that I could take what I wanted and all costs were covered." I watched as this large gorilla hung his head. It seemed that he was preventing himself from crying. He picked up his head and resumed eye contact. "I just got a call from Herb and he told me that it was your father. He was sworn to not tell me and I never knew who it was until today." I was shocked. My dad helping someone let alone a competitor was a complete and total shock.

"My dad? I had no idea."

"For two years, your father paid for my family to eat." Mr. Cobbs' eyes brimmed with tears. This large man who could probably pound a horse into the ground with one strike of his left hand was crying. His throat had clenched by the time he got around to speaking. "Your father was a good man," he said in what was a near whisper. He reached out his catcher's mitt hand and shook mine once more before turning around and leaving. I was left stunned. A lemon meringue pie fight and feeding the family of a competitor for two years...I stood there in the hall confused. He wouldn't let neighbors use the telephone and he was known in town as the man who punched the pastor in the face. Still perplexed, I glanced across the room and saw Ellie speaking with a man and a woman as if she knew them. I immediately thought about our camping trip in great detail. Strange thing about funerals, how your mind drifts off to where it shouldn't be. Maybe it's because we don't want to face the reality and that makes us think back to a more pleasant time. My head was spinning by the time everybody left. I was thinking about Dad's unexpected assistance to a competitor and thinking of him and my mom laughing while shoving lemon pie into each other's faces. The thought of Ellie in my tent kept popping into my head and I couldn't let go of it. I really only remember speaking to the old lady and Mr. Cobbs that day. Everyone else who attended is a blur.

The graveside service was at Georgetown Cemetery, and if I remember correctly, there were more people at the cemetery than at the funeral home. After the service was over, we went to Fava's to eat lunch. Ellie, Joe, Booley and I ordered lunch and talked about the funeral. I kept thinking about my father in that very restaurant, laughing while he put lemon meringue on my mom's face. I would think that she would've screamed and laughed at the same time. Then I caught a glimpse of Ellie sitting across from me with a smile that seemed to have lit up the whole room. Man, I really was in love with her, and it made me think that maybe that was how my father felt about my mother. It then occurred to me that I was about to lose the woman I loved, not in the same way my father lost my mother, but it might as well have been. I got a sudden sick feeling in my stomach and I didn't feel like eating. I lost my appetite and depression inevitably set in. That night I went to bed early. I blamed it on the day's stress which, in part, was true.

To this day, I haven't had a night like that one. I was sick, and thoughts swirled in my head making me tired, but keeping me up all night long. I think I slept off and on a total of two hours or so. I had to meet Verris Wade the next day, and I would be running on fumes. If you are ever fortunate enough to meet an American icon, I recommend you do it on more than two hours sleep.

28

Joe spoke of his job at the track as if he had a to-do list. I was sure that Priced Opportunity received more attention to his wound than was necessary, but it was good for both Price and Joe.

"Hey Elliott!" Jim yelled out as he was mixing soap into a bucket of water with Ranger's Cape standing nearby. He dropped a sponge into the bucket and came over to me wiping his hands on his overalls. "There are only a few jockeys here today. You might want to find one before Mr. Wade gets here.

"Have you seen Bull?" I asked.

"Not in town yet."

"What about Pringle?" I asked.

"Haven't seen him this year," Jim answered.

"Alright, I'll see what I can find out."

"Hey, when Mr. Wade is here, I want to see if we can get the same time with Outpost," Jim said, wiping the sweat off his brow. It was early in the morning, but Jim had been working extra hard due to the special circumstances. "It sure would look good in front of Mr. Wade," he added with a smile.

"That is a great idea. I think we can make arrangements," I said knowing that I would have to talk with the track manager. That morning I had been talking with Jim and Palmer, getting things ready

while Sarah and her kids made sure the stalls in the barn were spot-
less. Every so often, I would notice a small group of reporters hanging
around and drinking small cups of coffee, but I didn't pay much attention to them.

When the press learned that I was the trainer for Outpost, the
swarm of reporters crowded around me as I walked toward Ellie.
When I reached her, I had her walk with me to the boards as Joe had
just finished tending to Price and ran over to see what the press was
doing around his mother.

"Mr. Chapel!" a reporter yelled out.

"Is Outpost as fast as they claim?" another reporter shouted. Joe
had to stick close to Ellie as he was getting bumped into by the
overzealous reporters.

"Mr. Chapel, can we have a word?" The sudden commotion startled me in the same manner a pack of dogs would as I held a piece of
steak in the air. I tried to maintain my composure and not look like
I was put off by the sudden "hullabaloo," as Booley would say. The
reporters calmed down, although I did go blind for an instant as the
camera bulbs flashed in my direction. As soon as a photo was taken,
the photographers would pop the bulb out. Several had landed on
the ground at Ellie's feet.

"Mr. Chapel, what do you make of Outpost? Is he another Vagrant
Spender or a Zippy Chippy?" The flashes continued as the cameras
were following my every step. The used flash bulbs kept falling to the
ground as they were popped out and there didn't seem to be any effort
to pick them up. We kept walking until we reached the boards. Ellie
and Joe immediately walked up and sat down on the first tier.

"Who's the jockey for Outpost?" another reporter asked.

"Why did Mr. Wade pick you? Is it because of your father?"

"Hey!" I yelled. The questions stopped as I looked like I was about to punch one of them in the face. I walked over and picked up a flash bulb. "If a horse steps on a bulb and gets glass in his hoof, I will find you and make you take it out with your teeth!" I said as I handed one of them a used bulb. "Get 'em off the ground. Now!" The stress of Ellie leaving, my father's passing and the fact that I had to be ready to impress Mr. Wade had gotten to me. I wasn't a rude person nor would I talk to someone in that manner under normal circumstances, but lack of sleep and the stress of everything coming down on me was putting me on edge. I walked back to the boards and spoke with Ellie and Joe.

"I have to go find someone. Are you okay here?"

"Yeah, sure," Ellie said with a concerned look on her face. "Are you okay?" she asked.

"Yeah, just a lot going on," I answered. I started walking toward barn number one speaking with other trainers and grooms on the way there. Tom Preston had been training horses for twenty years and would soap up and wash his own horses from time to time. He knew Johnny Pringle and where I might find him.

"Hey, Tom, you seen Pringle around?" I asked as he dipped a sponge into a soapy bucket.

"He's here somewhere," he replied while washing the shoulder of one of his thoroughbreds. John Pringle was a jockey and didn't travel around with the others as he was older, and he hadn't won any races in a long time. He pretty much limited himself to the tracks in Ohio and Kentucky. Sometimes I would see him in New York. He raced horses from time to time, but mostly he exercised them and took in a small wage. On that particular morning, John was eating breakfast at the track kitchen. When I didn't find him at any of the barns, I walked over to the big white building which looked more like a house rather than a restaurant and walked in the front door. John was reading a newspaper and eating a plate full of eggs and bacon with a mug of steaming coffee sitting to the side of his plate. Obviously he wasn't watching his weight.

"Johnny," I said. He put down his newspaper.

"Oh hey, Elliott," he said. His helmet and riding crop sat next to him.

"Do you mind being on the front page of a newspaper?"

"Why?" he asked.

"You know who owns Outpost?"

"How could I not?" John took a sip of his coffee and showed me a picture of Verris Wade in his newspaper. That particular photo showed him riding on the back of caboose that was attached to one of his trains. His hand was stretched out and waving at a crowd of people as if he was running for office.

"He will be here pretty soon," I said. John Pringle froze holding the cup in front of his face as if he was somehow physically stunned by my words.

"Can I meet him?" he asked with eyes as big as silver dollars.

"Of course," I replied. "Actually, I want you to ride Outpost around the track for me." He set the cup of coffee down on the table.

"Are you serious?" he asked.

"I wouldn't pull your leg, Johnny. I would use my exercise rider for this, but I would prefer a jockey."

John immediately got up and walked toward the door. He was

suddenly nervous and his face looked as if it had just taken on a heavy burden.

"Is Mr. Wade here now?" John asked as he used his fingers to straighten his hair.

"Not yet."

"What am I doing?" John asked himself, suddenly realizing he had forgotten something. He went back to his table and picked up his helmet and riding crop. "Okay, what do you need me to do?" He was jumpy and looked worried. "Actually, why not use your rider?" He said. He looked fine before I told him the news.

"I want a time for ten furlongs," I said using insider talk, "We are going to use a gate on the back side. You will have the whole track, and we want you to run him with enough for the backstretch," I explained. John pulled cash out of his pocket and paid his tab. "I want someone who is lighter than my exercise rider. We are going for a timed run here."

"Everybody's going to be watching?"

"Yep," I replied.

"Holy cow, Chapel. You sure you want me to do this?" he said as he walked out the door. I followed him as he looked up at me from over his shoulder. "How much weight difference is there between me and your exercise rider? I'm not exactly tip-top here," he said as he patted his slightly pudgy stomach. By tip-top, John meant that he was about six pounds overweight. In case you're not familiar, six pounds is a big deal when speaking in terms of a jockey.

"What's your weight?" I asked.

"One twenty-two. Maybe twenty-three."

"You're much lighter," I assured him. And he was – by at least twenty pounds.

"Okay. Think I can do this?" Pringle asked looking for a sign of assurance.

"Sure. You can handle it, can't you?"

"Yeah, it's just… well, it's an honor. Thanks for letting me do this," he said.

"You're welcome. Just don't get all jittery on me." I took him over to barn twenty-one where Jim and Sarah both greeted him warmly as it had been a while since they had seen him.

"Get him set up with Palmer," I said. "Pringle needs to know how to run him."

I glanced over at the boards and saw Ellie and Joe watching the horses run around the track. Joe was pointing horses out, and Ellie was nodding her head at whatever question Joe was asking. Then I heard what sounded like a clamoring of geese coming from behind me. I turned my head and saw a swarm of reporters taking photographs of a 1932 Daimler Double Six Sport Saloon motor car. It was the most beautiful car I had ever seen with a long front end that seemed to have stretched for a mile. The wheels looked brand new as did the chrome that outlined the vehicle. I walked toward the commotion while watching the driver get out and open the door for Mr. Wade. As he exited, the reporters yelled out questions and took photographs. Two other men got out of the car and stayed behind Mr. Wade who walked in my direction.

"Mr. Chapel?" Mr. Wade yelled out.

"Yes sir," I yelled back with a wave and a smile. The reporters encircled him. He reacted as if it was a part of his life, almost oblivious to the questions from the reporters and photographers taking pictures. He was carrying a newspaper under his arm while unrolling a piece of hard candy, trying to free it from the wrapper. His suit looked new; however his shoes looked tattered and old. He wore a bow tie and a fedora hat with a black satin ribbon that wrapped around just above the brim. The other two gentlemen had similar attire except they wore regular neckties and nicer shoes. I glanced over at the barn and I could see Jim and Sarah watching Mr. Wade as they prepared Outpost for the track. John Pringle was bent over fidgeting with his high, black boots while Palmer was explaining how to handle Outpost on the turns. Mr. Wade and the gentlemen on either side of him walked toward me while the reporters and photographers swarmed around like bees to a hive.

"Mr. Chapel, Verris Wade. Nice to meet you," he said. His hand reached out and I grabbed it trying to prove my strength. I somehow thought that a man of his stature would have a strong, gripping handshake. I was right. "This is Roger Ell, my accountant, and Doug Powell, my attorney," he said as he introduced the gentlemen standing on either side of him. They looked smug and too serious as if they were all business and no personality.

"Nice to meet you all," I said above the reporters incessant questions. I shook his associate's hands and motioned over to the boards.

"We want to have a look at Outpost, and I want your thoughts on his abilities." The reporters continued to swarm Mr. Wade until he had had enough. "Hey!" he said as he put his arms up in the air. "Calm down! Calm the hell down, Christ almighty! If you can leave me alone I will give you all an interview before I leave." The reporters seemed to get the point. "Move on!" he said before making his way onto the boards.

"Please sit on the first tier only. Don't go above it as it isn't safe," I said. They did as asked and Ellie and Joe sat quietly on the end while I spoke with Mr. Wade. At that point in the day, there were about fifteen or so horses trotting and galloping around the track. The exercise riders kept glancing at Mr. Wade from the corners of their eyes as they went by.

The American icon, Verris Wade, was fifty-five years old when I met him. In those days he rubbed elbows with Howard Hughes, and before John D. Rockefeller died, he was considered a friend of the billionaire. It was surreal to sit on the dilapidated boards with a man like Mr. Wade. Unlike his business associates, he seemed very down to earth and laid back, knocking the hard candy around his mouth as he spoke.

"How's he do on the track, Mr. Chapel?" Mr. Wade asked.

"You'll see in a minute. I want to show you instead of tell you," I said. I turned my head and saw John riding Outpost to the track entrance.

"I saw in the local paper that your father passed away. I am sorry to hear that," Mr. Wade said as he continued to roll the hard candy around the sides of his teeth.

"Thanks. The funeral was yesterday."

"I never met him, but I heard good things about him." John Pringle came up to the fence mounted on Outpost. He looked professional in the saddle and seemed in control.

"What's the plan?" Pringle asked.

"He's warmed up so go ahead and gallop four, then walk him over to the gates and let him take his time.

"Will do," he replied. The other horses on the track had been moved in front of the track entry gate, away from the rail for the ten-furlong exhibition. The reporters stood next to the fence and watched Outpost trot around the track. I took a stopwatch from my pocket and held it where Mr. Wade could see it. His eyes glanced from Outpost, to the stop watch, and back to Outpost.

"The official ten furlong track record here at Keeneland is two minutes, three seconds and four tenths. I am going to time him from the gate to the finish," I said as I pointed to a white post that marked the finish line. "This will be an unofficial time, but you will get the idea." John was just taking Outpost to a gallop when Roger Ell asked me a question.

"How many horses do you train?"

"Right now I have four. This is my first year on my own. I hope to have more in the coming year."

"How many horses do trainers normally have?" Roger asked as if he was helping fill out a mortgage application.

"Anywhere from five to thirty. I have heard that some trainers carry more than thirty on their roster."

"So you are just starting out on your own, but you've been training horses for most of your life?" Mr. Wade asked. I watched John slow Outpost down to a walk and headed for the gates.

"Right. Since I was eight anyway," I said.

Mr. Wade kept his eye on Outpost as the muscular thoroughbred slowly walked to the gate with an attitude of power and infallibility. My father's custom gate at our farm track proved its weight in gold as Outpost walked into his stall as if he were a bullet, loading himself into a chamber. I could see Johnny Pringle readying his body by leaning forward, ready to take the punishment of the sheer force that was about to catapult him around the track. The gates sprung open accompanied by a loud starting bell and I started the stopwatch. Reporters snapped photographs and feverishly took notes while Mr. Wade kept his squinting eyes on his horse. As soon as Outpost passed the quarter pole, I looked at the stopwatch, taking note of the current time. *Tick. Tick. Tick. Tick.* Outpost trampled past the second quarter pole. The deep sound of his hooves thumping the track seemed to resonate in our chests. Jim and Sarah had walked over to see his run, and Booley was standing next to the reporters with his arms on the top of the fence. A few jockeys walked up to the fence and track gate, watching Johnny Pringle navigate the speeding beast around the turns. Doug Powell and Roger Ell had moved forward in their seat and focused their eyes on Mr. Wade's horse. *Tick. Tick. Tick. Tick.* I put my thumb on the stop watch button, ready to punch it as soon as Outpost hit the finishing pole. Ellie and Joe stood up as Pringle released the charging animal with repeated raps on his hind quarters. *Tick. Tick. Tick. Tick. Tick...Stop.* I hit the button as soon as Outpost's nose crossed the finish line. The stopwatch read two minutes, two seconds and five tenths. I stared at it as I turned it so that Mr. Wade could see it.

"Incredible! That's incredible," Mr. Wade said with a look of pure disbelief. His associates Roger Ell and Doug Powell managed to crack a smile as Mr. Wade laughed in excitement, slapping Mr. Powell on the back.

"What's the time, Chief?" A reporter shouted as he chewed a wad of gum, ready to write down the time on his note pad. I said the time out loud and then the commotion started. Flashes from the cameras and reporters shouting questions ensued while the crowd around the boards got bigger and bigger. When John Pringle rode over to the gate, I introduced him to the press and to Mr. Wade.

"It is an honor to meet you, sir," Pringle said as he shook Mr. Wade's hand from high atop Outpost. "You've got a hell of a horse. A hell of a horse!" Pringle added patting Outpost on the neck. A photographer assembled Outpost, John Pringle, and Mr. Wade together and made them stand still while they were bombarded with flashes from the cameras. It was a much bigger deal than I expected as I stood there with Ellie at my side. Her hand casually drifted toward mine and held it momentarily before letting go. Mr. Wade headed toward his car looking at me as he walked. He was forced to yell over the reporter's questions.

"Chapel! Meet me at the train station for lunch!" I nodded my head and waved good bye. Mr. Wade and his associates got in his Daimler Double Six Sport Saloon, and his driver took off. The reporters chased the car down the road like a pack of dogs until it reached a speed that they couldn't match. We all watched the car and the commotion following it.

"Yes sir. We're all one horse away," Booley said. Now I knew exactly what my father meant.

It was a late lunch. Noon was the time most folks ate lunch, but I didn't arrive at the train station until about one o'clock. With so much going on at the track that day, and being slowed down to run Outpost for Mr. Wade, my training schedule was prolonged a bit. I arrived at the train station alone and at the time, I didn't know why we were meeting there, but I soon found out. When I arrived at the station, I walked to the front entrance and walked inside. It was a small train station with four rows of church style pews for passengers to sit on and wait for their train. At that time the seats were empty and there wasn't anyone at the ticket counter. The interior of the train station smelled of aged oak and furniture polish as someone had just cleaned the pews and possibly mopped the hardwood floors. With no one in sight, I made my way to the platforms outside. There were a few trains parked on the service tracks, but there wasn't anyone waiting for a train, nor was there a train leaving or arriving. All was quiet until I heard someone call out my name.

"Come on in, Mr. Chapel," Mr. Wade said as he stood in the entrance of a rail car. In case you are unaware, each train station has service tracks where cars are placed for a period of time to either service the car or unload cargo. Mr. Wade travelled to Georgetown by rail car and had "parked" several of his personal rail cars on one of the service tracks.

"Come on in," Mr. Wade invited again. The first thing I noticed when I stepped into the cabin was that I was in an elegant room with a long dining table. This was no ordinary rail car. Sitting in two navy blue wing-back chairs reading different sections of the newspaper were Roger Ell and Doug Powell. The carpet was lavish with intricate designs and instead of passenger seats, there were couches and end tables with lamps. Both Roger and Doug took their eyes off their newspapers and studied my fascination with the luxurious rail car. A chef wearing a tall, white chef hat opened the back door and entered with a silver plate covered with a shiny, silver dome keeping the culinary achievement warm. Mr. Wade didn't have just one car, but four. I guess the second car was the kitchen and one of the cars must have contained Mr. Wade's Daimler Double Six Sport Saloon.

"I hope you like catfish. They were caught fresh this morning,"

Mr. Wade said as he walked over to the long, dining room table.

"Sounds good," I replied. "This is incredible," I said as I looked around the cabin.

"Thanks. I generally do not travel any other way. Mr. Ell and Mr. Powell will be joining us and I believe lunch is served, so let's have a seat. Anywhere you like," he said with a smile. Mr. Wade removed his fedora hat and threw it on the nearby sofa before sitting down. The chef removed the silver dome on my plate and proceeded to do the same with the others. The catfish was pan seared and cole slaw was positioned on my plate in the shape of a half sphere. Green beans accompanied the other side of my plate, which seemed to be the hottest item as I could see the steam rising off of their bright, vivid green surface.

"So, tell me more about Outpost. How did you get him in the condition that he is in? Seems to be in perfect shape."

"Well to start off, he has a good work ethic."

"Work ethic?" Doug Powell asked before he took a bite of the seasoned catfish. I was still having a hard time believing I was eating lunch on a private train.

"Horses have a work ethic?" Mr. Wade reiterated.

"Mr. Wade, how many horses have you owned?" I asked.

"I have had a few," he said with a smile as if I caught him not knowing a thing about horses. His candor was playful, but sharp. I remember him smiling only when a smile was warranted. He was all business, but somehow still warm and seemingly casual as if he was a family member.

"Well, a horse is much like a child," I said. "If the child wants to be good at something, he has to work at it. Do you agree that some kids are better at playing baseball than others?"

"Sure. Some hit farther; some run faster."

"Right, being equipped to do those things is only half of it. If any of those kids want to be like Babe Ruth, they have to want it. They have to work for it."

"Right. So a horse is the same way?" Mr. Wade asked.

"Very much so. Outpost was born equipped to do what he needs to do, but he has to have the desire and the heart to do it well, and he does."

"I didn't know that. I suppose there is more to training a horse than I thought," Mr. Powell said while chewing on a few green beans.

"In training a horse, I have to know the horses and what they are capable of and race them in the races that are in their class," I said. "It is a job that can take a lifetime to master, my father did it and by working for him since the age of eight, I feel I have a pretty good start. Plus I love what I do." Mr. Wade looked at Doug Powell and then at Roger Ell. I got the feeling that they were up to something. Mr. Wade set his fork down and finished what he was chewing and sat back in his chair. He spoke after he took his napkin from his lap and laid it on the table in front of him.

"Mr. Chapel, I have a friend named Samuel Bledsoe. He's from Clinton County, Kentucky and still has family there. Like me, he was into the rail business in a big way and we both love horse racing. In fact, we own sixteen horses that we have acquired over the years." He picked up a green bean with his fingers and popped it into his mouth. He chewed on one side of his mouth as he spoke. "When I purchased Outpost, I sent him to your farm because we are looking for another trainer as the one we are using in Chicago doesn't fit the bill."

"I just appreciate the opportunity," I said.

"Well I would like to present you with another one. My friend Sam, died last month."

"I am sorry to hear that," I said.

"Thank you. He was an incredible guy and really had a knack for business. My problem is that I own seven of the sixteen horses. Sam owned the rest," he explained. "Sam's family wants me to buy his horses as they really don't have any interest in racing. Now, I probably will buy them, but they will come at a price."

"I see."

"Elliott, I am looking at spending over twenty thousand dollars to buy his horses from his family and I don't want to pay that much, but I owe it to his family to give them a fair price so I will tell you what I will do." A smile slowly stretched across his face and a glint of excitement beamed from his eyes. He had been sitting back in his chair, but as soon as he paused, he leaned forward putting his forearms on the table and his hands together. It felt like I was about to be let in on a secret. "After what I saw today and after meeting you, I am seriously considering laying a bet on Outpost that will pay out twenty-five thousand dollars if he wins." I couldn't believe what I was hearing. I had heard of people making large bets at the track all my life, but I had never met anyone who had the means to do so. I just sat there and pretended to acknowledge his plan as if I was used to hearing large figures thrown out like that. Mr. Wade continued. "So, if I win I get to buy Sam's horses for free and you get to keep and train all sixteen." For a second there, I thought my heart was going to pound itself out of my chest and onto the white table cloth in front me. I kept my cool. "But if he loses," Mr. Wade added. "I will take my horses elsewhere." His smile appeared once again as if he was in his element and discussing matters that excited him. I cleared my throat.

"I see," was all that would come out of my mouth.

"So, I will have the horses put on a train in Chicago and get them to your farm if Outpost wins."

"Yes. I mean, yes, sir. But I have to ask, why me?"

"Well, horse racing for me is just a fun and exciting pleasure that I enjoy, and I am planning on enjoying it more in the coming years." He sat back in his chair and pulled out a cigar from his coat pocket. "I am closing La Grande station in Los Angeles and leaving the Chicago station to Roger and Doug here. Then I am starting a company in Ohio that designs and builds trains," Mr. Wade said as he used a cigar cutter, allowing the discarded end to fall onto his plate. "Self-contained diesel-electric locomotives are the future," he added as Doug produced a lighter and slid it along the table cloth and into Mr. Wade's hands.

"So it is a matter of location?" I asked.

"Yes. Location has a lot to do with it, but understand that I want the best in this area, and I believe I found it after what I saw today," he said as he lit the cigar. He was an experienced cigar smoker as he carefully rolled it in between his fingers, allowing the flame to ignite the tobacco rolled up in the tightly rolled leaves. He put the lighter back down on the table.

My father always told me that training a horse meant working the horse, managing the schedule and monitoring statistics. He would also say that training is a predictable series of steps with the trainer adding their discovered methods along the way. He seemed to think that anyone could do what he did, to a point. Now, I could have told Mr. Wade that Outpost was a superior horse and at that time I felt as if I didn't do anything different than what most trainers would have done. I ignored my thoughts and simply replied, "I won't let you down."

Mr. Wade leaned forward with both elbows on the table while his cigar delivered white, smoke streams that slowly crept up into the air. His fingers separated from an interlaced arrangement, moving his right hand toward his mouth while two chunky fingers and a thick, calloused thumb gripped the brown cigar and removed it from his chapped lips.

"I know. I am an excellent judge of character," Mr. Wade said with a wink and a confident smile. He leaned back in his chair with a look on his face that would imply that he just shared the secret of success. He placed the brown cigar in the corner of his mouth followed by a big smile and all I could think about was Booley saying what my father told him. "We're all one horse away."

29

A day after Mr. Wade's visit, I was in the dining room at home going over paper work. For every horse, I had a work sheet that displayed their feed schedules, exercise tables, and a list of times they posted at the track. I realized that if I acquired Mr. Wade's roster of horses, I would need a larger work sheet. Jim, Sarah and Palmer were on their way back from Keeneland with instructions to stop by the farm before going home. Ellie and Joe were checking on their horse, Eastern Express. Booley was at the feed and grain store ordering supplies and I had intended to have a meeting with everyone to tell them Mr. Wade's proposition. While I should have felt elated to be on a promising track of success, I couldn't help but think Ellie's coming departure. It was the single most depressing thought that had more than enough weight to dampen the excitement of a once in a lifetime opportunity. The thoughts of Ellie and Joe leaving were crippling, but it seemed that there was hope.

Knock. Knock. Knock. I left my paper work on the dining room table and answered the door. Sheriff Crease was standing on the front porch wiping his bottom lip. Evidently he had just spit nasty tobacco tainted saliva onto my front porch and was wiping away the excess spit that was sliding down his chin. The Grey Wolf Chewing Tobacco tin that was protruding from inside his left shirt pocket was more than evident. Guthrie's must have stocked a larger size.

"Hey, Chapel is Mrs. Evans here?"

"The hell do you want, Crease?" My right hand was balled up into a fist behind the door just out of his view and I was eyeing his gun. I didn't know what to think, but I wanted to knock his face off for throwing me off the mayor's back porch.

"I ain't gonna shoot ya, I know she's here Chapel. I need to see her."

"No," I answered. I had no intention of being polite.

"Uh, huh," he said in a cocky tone. "Where is she?" The wrinkles on his smart aleck, pudgy face scrunched together as he asked me questions.

"I don't know. Sorry," I said. Crease reached his hand up and put it flat against the door. I hadn't even tried to close it yet.

"Neighbor 'cross the street told me they saw her here this mornin' milling around the city's car." Crease motioned toward the old car sitting off to the side of our driveway that Ellie used to get here. I suppose it was Mrs. Connor who saw Ellie and told Sheriff Crease she was on our farm.

"Chapel, I know she's here," he said as he took his hand away from the door. He tried to look sociable, but I wasn't letting my guard down. "Why do you suppose she is here on your farm?" he asked. I didn't feel like answering his questions, but it did give me a chance to get under his skin.

"I am guessing that she likes it here. She feels safe here."

"With you?" he asked. I carefully watched his hand move from his side and come to a rest on the holster of his gun as if he was seeing if I would jump. My fist was prepared to come around the door and strike him in his left eyeball should he unsnap the top of his holster.

"Say again?" I asked.

"She feels at home here with you – is that what you mean?" he said in a pissy tone.

"I don't know what you're talking about," I answered.

"I'm sure you don't," he said just before he pressed his lips together and forcefully ejected another round of tobacco ridden saliva toward the front yard barely missing my front porch. "I know she's here Chapel. I am going 'round back and I would advise you not to stop me," he said, pointing his finger at me while walking up the driveway toward the side of the house. I didn't like his tone, and I didn't like the way he was asking for Ellie. I walked through the house and started for the barn. I walked briskly and looked over my shoulder every so often to see his progress. The fat, tub of guts he carried around his waist slowed him down. Too many donuts I guess. I made it to the barn way before he did. When I walked in, I gave Ellie a heads up.

"Ellie, Sheriff Crease is coming to see you," I said. She rolled her eyes and set down a bucket of feed. Joe was petting Eastern Express and letting him eat from his hand.

"No telling what he wants," she replied. "Joe, stay in the stall."

"Okay," he said.

Once Sheriff Crease came into view, he tilted the brim of his hat upward so he could see better in the shaded barn.

"Ellie, you having a good time here?"

"What do you want?" she asked in a tone that would imply that she wanted his visit to be over with quickly. Crease took his time to answer and moved his hands in front of him, hooking his thumbs in his belt.

"Got a call from an official office in Baton Rouge. They want to know when Mayor Evans is moving."

"When he's moving?" Ellie asked, sounding unsure of his question.

"Yeah, when is he going to be in Louisiana?"

"He is already there. He left days ago," she said. Sheriff Crease put his hands on his hips and stared at the ground as he thought. He looked to be a little out of breath.

"How long does it take to drive to Louisiana?" he asked.

"I don't know, never been by car. I would think two days at the most," she responded.

"How about you, Chapel?"

"Wouldn't know," I said, "I have only traveled there by train." Sheriff stood there in the entry way of the barn thinking. I am sure it took him three times longer to think than a regular human being.

"So, he left several days ago?" Crease asked.

"Yep," Ellie answered.

"When do you leave?" he asked Ellie.

"I have to be packed and have the train loaded a week from this Friday."

"Did he stop somewhere on his way to Baton Rouge?"

"Doubt it. He starts work tomorrow or maybe it's the next day. I can't remember which," Ellie answered.

"Alright then," he said. He turned around and walked out of the barn. I stood there with Ellie as she bent down and picked up a handful of feed. She reached her hand out and let Eastern Express eat from her palm.

"Wonder what that's about?" Ellie said.

"Who knows?" I replied.

"Did he say anything to you?" she asked.

"No. Except he asked me why you were here," I said. Ellie just shook her head.

"I have often thought that he was jealous because he wasn't the mayor," Ellie said. "Wouldn't surprise me if he ran for it."

"Yeah, I don't think he has the mental capacity to be the mayor."

"He is the dumbest creature on earth, and we let him walk around with a gun," Ellie said. I laughed as I was immediately reminded of one of Booley's sayings.

"You know how Booley always has a saying for everything?"

"Yeah," she said.

"Well, Booley would say that the Sheriff couldn't pour water out of a boot with instructions on the heel." We both laughed. Even Joe got the joke.

Once Booley got back from the feed store and the Bennett family made their way back from Keeneland, I gathered everyone in front of the barn by the track. Using bales of straw as seats, we all sat down and I told them the story about Mr. Wade's proposition. As I got close to the end of the story, I could see Booley smile and shake his head. I knew what he was thinking. We're all one horse away. I am sure he was hearing my father's voice in his head saying that very phrase. I never heard dad say it out loud, but then again it was un-usual to hear him speak. He spoke to Booley more than he spoke to me.

"How did you get so lucky? There are hundreds of trainers across this country and only one Mr. Wade. You somehow have the opportunity to take on the nation's biggest client," Jim said.

"Well, Mr. Wade actually sent Outpost to Dad. When I told Mr. Wade that Dad retired and that I was taking over, he told me to carry on," I said as I shrugged my shoulders.

"How big is this?" Ellie asked. "How big of a deal is it to train Mr. Wade's horses?" I was about to answer, but Jim started before I could.

"It took Mr. Chapel decades to gain the notoriety to keep and maintain a roster of thirty horses. If Outpost wins, Elliott will have done it in a few months."

"Yeah, but if it wasn't for Dad, I would never have been given this opportunity," I added.

"This is the single biggest opportunity for a trainer that I have ever heard of and I'll tell you what," Booley said as he stood up and brushed the straw off his overalls, "It couldn't have happened to a more deserving person," Booley said as he slapped me on the shoulder. He smiled and I smiled back.

"We are glad for you Elliott," Sarah said. "And for us too! We need the work," she added.

"We should celebrate!" Ellie said.

"Well, Outpost has to win first. We don't have anything to celebrate yet," I said.

"We should at least celebrate your opportunity," Ellie suggested.

"Sure. We should all go out and get something to eat for lunch," Jim said. "We never get to go out for lunch."

"Sure. That would be a treat for us," Sarah said.

"I'm hungrier than a green snake in a sugar cane field," Booley said as he rubbed his stomach.

"Where would you like to go eat?" I asked. Ellie tilted her head in thought, but it wasn't like there were a lot of choices back then.

"How about Fava's? I don't know about you, but I like eating there," she replied.

Louie Fava and his wife, Susie, left their village home in Grotta, Italy, and came to the United States at the turn of the century. Upon settling in Georgetown, Kentucky, they opened a confectionery in 1901 that was more than just a candy store. They sold homemade ice cream, fruit pies, and tins of popcorn. The most impressive aspect of their store was the selection of cigars and tobacco.

When Louie died in 1919, Susie's brother came over to the U.S. and helped run the store. Everybody in town called him "Uncle Pete," and it was known that after midnight, the guys in town would migrate over to Fava's for a late night card game. He would keep the store open until three in the morning selling sodas and cigars to his card playing patrons.

Uncle Pete altered the confectionery store's menu turning it into a counter diner serving cheeseburgers, soups and sandwiches. Fava's new business model directly competed with Guthrie's modest five stool lunch counter, but Herb didn't kick up too much of a fuss. The new menu at Fava's inspired Susie to turn it into a full service restaurant and wouldn't you know it, just before her dream was realized, she died in 1938. Louie and Susie did have two daughters that were born in Georgetown named Natalie and Louise. I don't recall seeing Louise that much, but I do remember Natalie. Just after her mother died, she graduated from the University of Kentucky and helped run the store with her uncle.

At the time Ellie, Joe, Booley and I went to Fava's, Susie's dream was a reality thanks in part to her daughter.

"Can I have a Coke, mom?" Joe asked as he slid into his chair.

"I suppose," Ellie replied. After we ordered, we talked about Mr. Wade and Outpost. Booley spoke about how he was going to have to order a new shipment of horseshoes and bridles if Outpost won. Sarah explained that we would need more help on the farm if we got Mr. Wade's horses and I noted that Dad always kept a groom for every four to five horses and I planned on following his line of thinking. I would also need to hire another exercise rider or two. Palmer suggested a fellow in Shelby County that he knew from working at Churchill Downs.

While we ate our delicious food, Booley told us another joke, and I envisioned my mother and father laughing and carrying on over a slice of lemon meringue pie. I remember what the elderly lady said to me at the funeral home. My mother put a piece of lemon meringue on his nose, and he came back with a much larger piece and put it on her face. They were laughing and yelling with big smiles on their faces, and Dad couldn't stop laughing.

"What are you smiling about?" Ellie asked. I looked at her realizing I was day dreaming.

"I was just thinking… " I answered.

"What about?" she probed.

"I was thinking……about my mother," I said. I ended up telling everyone at the table the story the frail, elderly lady told me. As I was about finished telling the story, the bell rung above the front door, it was Sheriff Crease with two deputies behind him.

"Ellie," he said. He stopped with his fat body half way inside and half out. He held the door open with his right hand looking as if he was there for one reason and one reason only. Ellie looked at him and

I had turned around to see what was going on.

"Yes," she answered.

"You better come with me," Sheriff Crease said. He opened the door all the way and motioned for her to come outside. He seemed as if he was on a mission and it seemed important.

"Stay with Elliott, Joe," she said as she got up and walked outside. I watched as Sheriff opened his car door on the passenger side with the intention of taking Ellie somewhere. I stood up and walked to the front door and opened it.

"What the hell Crease!" I yelled.

"Get back inside and stay there," he said pointing his fat finger in my direction.

"What is this about?" Ellie asked. Crease turned his head toward her and told her something. I was standing too far away to hear what he said. She got in, and they sped off down Main Street. Obviously something was wrong, but what?

30

The same day that Ellie was taken away by Sheriff Crease at Fava's, I took Booley and Joe to the farm and Jim and Sarah went home in their own car. I made a few phone calls to find out what was going on, but to no avail. I was a nervous wreck not knowing what was going on. It was nearly three-thirty that afternoon when Ellie called asking me to pick her up at her house. If there was ever a record time for driving from my farm to the mayor's house, I would have beaten it then. I got out of the truck and ran to the front door and walked in without knocking. Three deputies were hanging around the foyer as Sheriff Crease was coming down the stairs.

"She's in the living room," he said as he took one step at a time and pointed to the left. I walked in and there she was sitting on the couch biting her fingernails.

"Hey?" I said.

"Thanks for coming," she said as soon as she saw me. No hug or anything that would have showed that we were more than friends.

"What's going on?" I asked.

"My husband isn't in Baton Rouge, and they don't know where he is. I was asked to come here to inventory his clothes and suitcases to make sure he packed."

"Why can't they find him?" I asked.

"He was supposed to be there a few days ago. He hasn't called here or to Baton Rouge," Ellie answered.

Sheriff came in with his thumbs hooked on his belt looking like a law man who knew everything.

"Now we know he did pack, and he did leave for Baton Rouge." Maybe he had car trouble or something. He could be halfway or almost there, and I would suppose he is unable to get to a phone."

"What do we do now?" Ellie asked Crease.

"We have to wait a few days before we can officially declare him missing. Then I will retrace his route to try and find out what happened. If I don't find anything, then the FBI will step in."

"The FBI?" I responded.

"Used to be the Bureau of Investigation."

"I know what it is, Crease. Why would the FBI get involved?"

"He's a staff member of the Governor of Louisiana. I guess the Governor requested it. They said something about it on the telephone," he said, shrugging his shoulders. Ellie was still biting her nails, and I was ready to go. I motioned for her to follow me out the door. As we left, Sheriff made sure to make a scene out of our departure.

"Sure are getting cozy at that farm, Ellie. You might want to reconsider your arrangements when the mayor contacts me."

"Mind your business, Sheriff," Ellie responded. I could hear Crease and his deputy's laughing after I closed the front door. On the way back home, Ellie gave me the details. She spoke with her hands which I really hadn't seen her do before. She was really shook up.

"I had to show Crease where the suitcases were and where his suits were hung. I guess they wanted to make sure he really left."

"Is that it? That's all they wanted?"

"I told them that I remembered hearing the car starting up and the sound of the car driving away," she explained.

I took her back to the farm, and we talked about the situation a little more. I do remember that after everyone had gone to bed I had another night of restless sleep. I kept thinking, or more to the point, wishing that Mayor Evans was dead.

I imagined him driving along a road where a deer jumped out, and he swerved to miss the animal. In great detail, I further imagined that the car struck a tree and the mayor crashed through the wind-shield hitting the trunk of the tree head first. While my thoughts were brutal and appalling, I couldn't help but hope for that man's demise. There was more than one scenario that ran through my head that night and the only other one I remember involved a cigar. I envisioned him smoking while driving, and the wind caught the ash on the end of the cigar. The hot ash fell to his leg where he quickly tried to brush it off. Not paying attention, he drove straight toward two gasoline pumps located in the front of a store on the side of the road. Upon impact the gas pumps exploded, along with the gas tank on the mayor's car. It was these types of scenarios that kept me up most of the night. Now, you might think less of me, but back then I could only hope for one of them to come true.

31

David Crown walked along Penny Road with his tackle box and a cane pole. He had with him his old dog, named Barley that was a Hellenic hound that frequently chased small animals. Ol' Dave would make futile efforts to regain control of his dog by yelling Barley's name repeatedly, but usually to no avail. David Crown was a farmer who used to grow tobacco until he sold the farm. He then spent his days fishing in Penny Creek with his old dog resting beside him. He didn't have a lot of money nor did he have many clothes, just two pairs of overalls plus an old scraggly hat. His face could always use a shave and his shoes were long past due for the county landfill. Days spent fishing and sleeping on a grassy incline under the shade of a tree with Barley was considered "the good life" by David and I suppose Barley thought so too.

While David and his dog were walking to their favorite spot, Barley's attention was diverted from the road to a small, furry animal. The long, floppy ears coupled with the in and out breathing motion around its rib cage gave his position away in the tall grass. The bunny sensing it was in danger, darted into the thick brush and Barley chased after it disappearing from David's sight. He called for his dog as he always did once Barley had begun chasing an animal, but once again as expected, Barley didn't return. The black-and-tan dog continued to chase the bunny until Barley got caught in the thick of the brush next to a large mechanical machine. The bunny climbed onto the top of a tire. Scared and not knowing what to do, it stayed on the white wall rubber tube watching Barley struggle to get free of the brush she was entangled in.

When David had decided that he must go into the thicket, he set down his tackle box and cane pole and reached for a pocket knife in his tattered overalls. He walked through a noticeable hole in the thicket having to cut a branch here and there to get through. When he finally reached Barley, he couldn't help but notice a 1938 Buick Sedan that looked as if it hadn't been there very long. The paint was still shiny, the tires still had air, and the headlights weren't broken. The only thing out of the ordinary was a bullet hole in the windshield and blood on the upholstery. David took notice that no one was in the car and decided to report his finding. Once he freed Barley from the brush, they walked to the Sheriff's office armed with their information and the hope of a reward.

The following day, *The Georgetown Times* printed a photo and a story on the disappearance of Mayor Evans. The picture showed a tow truck pulling the Mayor's car out from the brush while a deputy held up a rifle that was found at the scene. The deputy's eyes were staring at the camera with the rifle held at chest level in a delicate manner as if the rifle were an artifact of great importance. The article explained that the Mayor had been missing for several days and that the Federal Bureau of Investigation was coming to Scott County.

Ellie and I had asked Joe to stay in the house, while we went out to the five-stable barn and read the newspaper out loud word for word. It was one of the most exciting things to read with the possibility of reading that the mayor was dead, but no such luck. The information in the article was limited, but the photo spoke volumes. We put the paper away and kept it out of Joe's sight and did our best to seem normal until we knew more. Ellie was adamant about not letting Joe know anything until we knew the details and facts, but it killed me to not talk about it as my head was racing with thoughts of the mayors demise. I had thought of calling an acquaintance I knew that worked at the newspaper, but thought I would wait until the next day and see what additional information was printed about the incident.

It was less than a week before the first race at Keeneland and I was looking over my notes from Outpost's training log. Ellie and Joe were getting ready for the day and Booley was up at the barn looking for a couple of spare halters that we had forgotten to bring with us to Keeneland. I wasn't able to think clearly as I couldn't get the fact that the Mayor may actually be dead. Blood, a bullet hole, the car hidden in the brush and the Mayor was missing. I was so excited I could barely contain myself. It was the most pivotal point in my life as I had my career depending on one horse and I desperately needed to focus. I could barely sit still in my seat as I did everything I could to try and concentrate. My mind was moving in all directions sitting at the dining room with papers spread out before me. I stood up, grabbed my cup of warm coffee and walked around taking deep breaths with the intention of clearing my head. As I was pacing back and forth in front of the staircase, something caught my eye - a car was pulling up in the driveway. I walked to the window and watched a 1938 Lincoln Zephyr 4 Door hard top park next to the house. Following the Lincoln to a stop was Sheriff Crease's car with a deputy in the front seat and another in the back. I was holding a cup of coffee when I opened the front door to five men approaching the porch. The two men that got out of the Lincoln were dressed in black suits with white shirts and black ties. They looked as if they went to the same barber as both of them had flat top haircuts with straight edged sideburns.

"Mr. Chapel?" One of the men from the Lincoln said to me. He was fatter than Sheriff Crease and seemed to waddle a bit from side to side. When he spoke, he was calm and non-threatening with a tone of voice that was matter of fact and nearly robotic. "You are under arrest for the suspicion of the murder of Wayne C. Evans. Please stay where you are and put your hands on your head."

"He's dead?" I asked as I put my left hand on my head and continued to hold the coffee in my right. The other man in the black suit was very thin and reminded me of Fred Astaire. He looked at me as he walked slightly behind the fat man, keeping his eye on my cup of coffee.

"Set the cup down on the railing and slowly put your other hand on your head," I didn't know his name, but I immediately called him Fred in my mind. The fat man and Fred stopped walking and simply stood silent, waiting for me to comply.

"Is the mayor dead?" I asked out loud.

"Where's your girlfriend, Chapel?" Sheriff Crease said, no doubt trying to upstage the visiting law men with his loud voice and left cheek full of chew. His deputies were behind him, but keeping their distance. The deputy that got out of the passenger seat was the one in the newspaper holding the rifle and as I stared at him, I realized I still had my coffee in my right hand. Before I could slowly lower the cup and set it on the railing, Ellie came out onto the porch.

"Elliott? What's going on?" she said as I had just set my coffee down and put my other hand on my head.

"Don't you move either, sweetheart! You're under arrest too," Crease said after he moved his thick wad of chew to the other side of his mouth.

"What?" Ellie said.

"Mr. Chapel, Mrs. Evans, you are both under the arrest for suspicion of the murder of Wayne C. Evans," Fred explained. "Mrs. Evans," he continued, "You might want to change into something different than a nightgown. You can either go like that or I can follow you to your room and wait outside the door while you change, your choice." I looked over at Ellie and she looked to still be perplexed at the situation. She looked over at Sheriff Crease, his deputies and then the fat man standing next to Fred.

"I'm sorry. Now who are you?" she asked Fred.

"We are with the Federal Bureau of Investigation. Sheriff is assisting us in this matter," he answered.

"The matter of my husband. Are you telling me he was found? Dead? My husband is dead?" she asked. I was anxiously awaiting the answer.

"M'am. We have questions and you must come with us. We will explain once we get to the station."

Ellie seemed to accept his answer and then looked down at her pajamas she was still wearing.

"I would like to change thank you," Ellie said in a polite tone considering the circumstances. Fred the FBI agent followed her into the house, and I could hear her talking to Joe, no doubt telling him to stay where he was and not to leave the house. Booley walked from the backyard to the front of the house as I was being handcuffed and led off the front steps.

"What's going on?" Booley asked.

"Tell you later Booley. Just get to Keeneland and work them from the clipboard. Nothing changes. Keep your eye on Outpost's gait."

"You sure you okay?" he asked.

"Yeah, just take care of everything at the track. This is just a misunderstanding."

"Misunderstanding, my ass!" Sheriff Crease muttered. "The FBI don't arrest people for no reason." Fred put me in the back of Sheriff Crease's car just as Ellie was being led out in handcuffs.

"Miss Ellie?" Booley said. His face was scrunched with worry. He looked helpless and shocked.

"It's okay, Booley. We will see you soon and feel free to take Joe with you to the track," Ellie said as she was put into the back of the FBI car.

"Okay, Miss Ellie."

We were immediately taken to the Scott County Sheriff's office where I was escorted to the back of the building. A small jail cell welcomed me with iron bars and cold, hard cement floors. Inside the iron bar cage, a table and two chairs had been placed in the middle and I was seated with the cuffs still around my wrists. Ellie was put in a room with a refrigerator and a coffee pot which was obviously the break room. At the time, I wasn't scared since I knew I had nothing to do with the mayor's disappearance or death, however I wasn't comfortable either. I do remember feeling a little excited as it started to look like the mayor was gone and gone for good. I had formed theories in my head on the way to the Sheriff's office that someone who was fed up with his back door dealings ended his life. Maybe a disgruntled business partner or an ordered assassination by a man with family ties did the world a favor. Hope was stirring inside me; hope that Ellie and Joe's biggest problem was no longer a problem. The FBI agent with the large, wide body squeezed into the cell before he wedged and packed his chunky body into the wooden chair. He grunted from the effort as his gut bumped the table. The chair he sat in was backed up against the bed, making it much more uncomfortable for his large size. There was a sheet of paper in front of him with handwritten information that I couldn't read upside down although I didn't try very hard. At that point, the excitement seemed to wither and was replaced by nervousness. Once the handcuffs were taken off, the questions began.

"Mr. Chapel, my name is Virgil Fleck. My partner and I were assigned to investigate the disappearance of Wayne C. Evans. The Governor's Office of Louisiana has graded his disappearance up to murder in order to accelerate the investigation although a body has not been recovered." His mannerisms and the way he spoke led me to believe that he hadn't ever smiled in his entire life.

"Okay," I said, hoping that I didn't sound too depressed that his body hadn't been found. Fred had been standing in the open doorway of the jail cell leaning the left side of his body on the iron frame. Sheriff Crease walked over holding a cup of coffee and studied Virgil Fleck as he questioned me.

"The reason you are under arrest is," Virgil started to say as he looked at the paper in front of him, "because we have reports of you spending time with Mrs. Evans. This simple fact gives you motive, and motive places you under immediate suspicion. This is all standard procedure."

"Coffee's ready," Crease said. Neither agent responded to him. I sat there as Virgil looked over the sheet of handwritten information.

"You found Mr. Evan's wife in a creek that divides your property with another farm, is that correct?"

"I did. She had an accident on Tenpenny Bridge and she was taken by the current down Penny Creek. I found her the same morning as her accident," I stated. "Sheriff Crease was there when we pulled her out of the creek."

"Did she stay at your farm?"

"She did."

"How long?"

"Until the mayor returned from Louisiana."

"Yeah, but she didn't want to leave, did she, Chapel? She wanted to stay with you?" Sheriff Crease interjected. Virgil closed his eyes in frustration and then opened them before continuing with his questions.

"Once she left your property, did she return for a length of time?"

"She did return."

"When was that?"

"Just after the mayor left to permanently move to Baton Rouge," I said. Virgil then took out a fountain pen and quickly wrote down information on his sheet of paper. The questions continued, and I answered them without hesitation, except for one of them. The questions about Ellie's second stay at the farm startled me. The question was asked as if it were any other question. Virgil just rattled it off as if he was asking me if I liked ice cream.

"During Mrs. Evans' stay, at anytime, did you have intimate relations with her?" Damn it, I thought. I hesitated and sat there thinking. I didn't know what to say, and I hadn't lied yet. I remember thinking that if I said "no" and she said "yes", things wouldn't look good. Then I panicked as I was taking too long to answer the question. Damn it!

"Yes," I said. Crease laughed and slapped his leg.

"Son of a bitch, I knew it! You're going to prison. Hole-Lee-shit," Crease said. Virgil seemed to have had it with him. He turned to Fred who knew what Virgil was saying without him uttering a word. Fred took Sheriff Crease by the arm and escorted him to the front of the building.

"What?" Crease said. "What I'd do? I was just sayin'." I could hear him still talking as he was seated in the front office chair.

"Stay here," Fred ordered. He walked back and leaned his slender body on the iron door frame of the cell. Virgil finished writing down my answer which seemed to take longer than the answer I gave. I glanced down at the paper, but couldn't tell what was being written down. The last two questions he asked me were the easiest to answer.

"Mr. Chapel, did you kidnap or kill Mr. Wayne C. Evans?"

"No."

"Do you know anyone who kidnapped or killed Mr. Wayne C. Evans?"

"No," I said. I answered with simple answers that needed no further explanation. Virgil removed his body from between the table and chair the same way an average sized pear would be removed from a small square hole. After a fit of wriggling and grunting, his body was free of the enclosed area. He turned around slowly and looked at me.

"I will be back shortly." He walked out of the cell, and Fred closed the jail cell door. They both walked down the hall and into the room where Ellie was being held. I sat there for the longest time, going over my answers in my head. Fear began to set in the longer I waited. What if the mayor was dead and I was blamed for his murder? I couldn't be blamed, I thought. I had nothing to do with it.

32

For the better part of the day, Ellie and I were held prisoner at the county jail under the eye of Sheriff Crease and his two guests. I certainly wasn't going anywhere being locked in a cell and Ellie wouldn't dare leave the break room. At one point I could hear muffled questioning going on where they were keeping Ellie. I could also hear a part of a telephone conversation between Virgil and his superior, but I couldn't make out what they were speaking about. I was questioned on different things throughout the day and left alone off and on until Virgil made his final appearance at my jail cell.

"Alright, here's the deal," Virgil said as Fred opened the jail cell door. "We are going to take your fingerprints and then we are letting you go, however you cannot leave town.

"That might be a problem," I said.

"Why is that, Mr. Chapel?" Virgil asked.

"I am working in Lexington right now. I am a horse trainer and my horses are at Keeneland race track."

"That's just one county, over isn't it?" Fred asked.

"Yes sir," I replied.

"How many miles away?" Virgil asked as he brought his notes in front of him, ready to write.

"About twenty-five or so," I answered. Virgil looked at Fred without saying a word and then looked at me.

"I suppose I can approve it since it is work related," Virgil said as he wrote something on his note paper.

"Thank you," I said just before exiting the jail cell. I was then led down the hall and into the room where Ellie was questioned. She was sitting at the back of the room wiping her hands with a damp cloth. I glanced at her before Virgil asked me to sit down in a chair. Fred sat down across from me and started putting on a pair of gloves.

"Place your hands on the table," Virgil said. There was a massive suitcase on the end of the table and it was opened up as if it were spreading its wings. The inside displayed various compartments and drawers that held intricate instruments and small vials of powders and liquids. Labels on each compartment were hand written on small, white pieces of cardstock, each inserted into a metal place card holder, secured by a pair of tiny screws. It also held a variety of brushes and magnifying glasses.

I watched, fascinated, as Fred carefully opened a small compartment marked *Printing Card Ink* and removed a small, black bottle. He reached for a small black square of puffy fabric that he had obviously used on Ellie shortly before my arrival. Next, he opened a small drawer marked *Pipettes* and removed an eye dropper which he inserted into the small bottle of ink. A small amount of ink was transferred to the puffy fabric. One by one, Fred pressed my fingers into the fabric and then on a special card that had been laid out before me. Each finger was printed on the card in a very quick fashion and in no time at all, he had all ten digits inked on the cardstock. Sheriff Crease had wandered into the room, this time keeping his trap shut as he gazed at the suitcase of instruments. Once Fred filed the card away in yet another drawer in the case, he handed me a damp cloth.

"Like I told Mrs. Evans, the ink won't come off completely for some time. It will take a few days."

"Are we free to go?" I asked wiping my hands.

"Yes you are," Virgil replied.

"Deputy Beaumont will drive you back," Sheriff Crease said.

"Just remember you are restricted to Scott County and your place of employment for five days," Virgil reiterated. "We may have to extend your restriction, so don't count on just the five days."

"Yes sir," I replied before leaving with Ellie. On the way back to the farm, Ellie held my ink stained hand and took deep breaths. She was obviously more shaken up than I was. Once we got to the farm, she wrapped her arms around me.

"Are you okay?" I asked as we stood on the front porch.

"Yes. Are you?" she released her arms from around my neck and looked at me.

"I am," I said as we both walked inside. I immediately went to the kitchen to see if Booley had left the morning newspaper on the kitchen table. Finding it on the counter, I quickly opened it up, looking at the front page hoping to find more news about the mayor. Before we read the article, we looked at a photo of the car being pulled out from the thicket with the deputy holding the rifle. It was basically the same photo as the one in the previous newspaper, just taken from a different angle by a different photographer.

"What do you think happened?" she asked.

"I don't have a clue," I said. She leaned toward me and reached for both of my hands. The composed look in her eyes stared at mine.

"Elliott? Did you have anything to do with this?"

"What?"

"I won't be mad, I just want to know."

"You think I killed him?" I asked.

"No, I don't know. I had to ask," she said. I guess she was right in asking. Who knew what was going through her head at that point. "I'm sorry."

"If I did it, I would have told you already," I said. We both sat at that kitchen table thinking. Then I remembered what Virgil had asked me.

"Did he ask you anything about us?" I asked with a suggestive look.

"Yes."

"About you and..." I paused for a second as it was a difficult question to ask. "...me being together?"

"Yes," she replied.

"What did you tell them?" I asked. She thought a second before replying.

"I told them yes," she said, not sure if I was going to like her answer.

"I told them that same thing. I'm just glad our stories matched up."

I heard Booley and Joe enter thorough the back door and walk into the living room. When Ellie and I walked into the room, I expected him to immediately ask us about being arrested; instead he started with, "I think there is something wrong with Banner," We immediately went out on the back porch where Banner was lying on the old couch.

"What's the matter?" I asked as I walked over and knelt down beside him. I put my hand on Banner's head and petted him.

"I put food down for him two days ago and he didn't eat anything. I didn't really think much of it other than he probably wasn't hungry. Then I noticed the bowl today and he still hasn't touched it. Joe and I looked to see if he had eaten from his bowl outside and he hasn't touched it either," Booley explained.

"What's the matter, Banner?" Ellie said as she knelt down beside me. She used her hand to stroke him from his head to his hind quarters. "Are you not feeling well?"

"I think he misses your Dad," said Booley.

"Dad used to leave all the time, and he didn't have a problem then. He would just lie out under the willow tree," I said. Joe had taken to petting Banner's long ears as Dad's faithful companion opened and closed his eyes as if he was miserable.

"I don't know, maybe not," Booley replied.

"What was all that about earlier? They arrested you?" Ellie looked at Joe.

"Joe, could you go get Banner's bowl and fill it with water? Let's see if he'll drink."

"Okay," Joe said as he walked inside.

"They questioned us…my husband is still missing."

"Missing? A bullet hole in the windshield and blood on the seat, I would figure that man for dead"

"Booley! Joe is in the other room. He doesn't need to hear that!" Ellie's eyes were wide with concern for her son. Booley pulled back under her glare.

"Right. Sorry. Uh, who were the men in the suits?" Booley asked, quickly changing the subject.

"Federal agents," I answered.

"I bet Sheriff Crease enjoyed watching you being arrested," Booley said as he rubbed Banner's head. Joe entered the room with a bowl full of water, his eyes glued to the edges of the bowl, careful not to spill any as he navigated towards Banner.

"I am sure of that!" I said.

"He don't like you very much."

"I got the feeling that the agents didn't like him."

"No surprise there. Sheriff Crease is like a big toe in a wet sock." Joe cackled nearly doubling over. Ellie and I couldn't contain our laughter either. Booley had a saying for everything. I watched him as he reached in his overalls and pulled out a piece of paper. "Jim called and said he is being bombarded by jockeys asking him about riding Outpost." Booley handed me the note.

"Thanks, I'll give him a call," I said as I patted Banner on his head.

"Should we phone, Dr. Wall?" Ellie asked.

"Let's give it a few more days," I said still petting him. "Joe, can you take Banner over to his food every once in a while and see if he will eat or drink?" I asked. I figured he was doing such a good job with Priced Opportunity that he could handle another job. He seemed to enjoy being given responsibility.

"Sure, Mr. Chapel. I'd be glad to," he responded, equal to the task.

At night I would find Banner sleeping beside my dad's chair instead of sleeping on his bed of old quilts. When I walked by, his tail wouldn't wag, and his eyes would open only to close right away. When he moved his tired body from inside to outside, he would glance at the old couch and then at the garden as if he was looking for his friend.

33

We heard nothing more about the incident in the days after the discovery of the mayor's car, although we did read an article in *The Georgetown Times* that reported on the agents investigating the case. The article explained that they were already in Kentucky when the Governor of Louisiana requested that the FBI investigate the mayor's disappearance. It seemed that the KKK was a very busy organization in the state of Kentucky in 1939 when a man named Wesley Evans (no relation to Mayor Evans) sold the organization to a Dr. Colescott and a Dr. Green. I only remember this because it was in the papers next to the ongoing reports of the Mayor's disappearance. The FBI had already sent four agents to investigate the Klan when they received a telegram asking two of the four agents to travel to Scott County. Other than that particular report, no other articles about the FBI or the mayor were printed in *The Georgetown Times*.

Once I set the paper down, more pressing matters came to me in a rush, I had to find a jockey for Outpost. If you have ever heard or even seen the way family members come out of the woodwork when a person wins the lottery, then you know what it is like to train a monumental horse such as Outpost. Jockeys, much like the family members of a suddenly wealthy individual, flock to the trainers in the hopes that they will be the one to ride the prodigious horse.

Mr. Wade arrived at Keeneland much earlier than expected and this time he was alone. The big maiden race was on Thursday and he arrived the previous Sunday. He was wearing a shirt and bow tie, but wasn't wearing a coat. His sleeves were rolled up, and his fedora hat shielded his eyes from the sun. As he walked over to the boards, a herd of reporters started his way. It was unusual for several reporters to camp out at Keeneland back then, but Mr. Wade was an important enough figure to warrant the attention. I watched as he simply held up his hand, stopping the herd of camera-toting reporters in their tracks. He sat in silence on the first tier of the boards and watched the other horses breezing around the track. Unlike Mr. Wade, I didn't have a magic hand that could stop a force of people from hassling me. I was walking toward the boards surrounded by jockeys who were giving me their wins, losses, weight, height, mounts and place records. All I could do was tell them I would make my decision later, not realizing that Mr. Wade was sitting on the first tier laughing at me and my predicament. I am sure it looked a little funny from his point of view. A six-foot tall man surrounded by twelve tiny men all wearing racing boots up to their knees. Once the jockeys got the point that I wasn't interested in talking to them at that time, I took my seat on the first tier as the jockeys scattered toward the barns.

"Morning," Mr. Wade said.

"Good morning," I replied as I brushed the dirt off my pants.

"Seems like you got a fan club."

"Yeah, they all want to ride Outpost."

"I see," Mr. Wade said. He pulled out a piece of hard candy and unwrapped it. "How does that work? Assigning a jockey to race a horse. Guess I never gave it much thought," he said as he popped the piece of hard candy in his mouth.

"Well, there are several ways and it all depends on the horse. Depends on the jockey too, but sometimes you have too many asking to ride the same horse, and sometimes you have to beg a jockey to ride a horse." Mr. Wade fiddled with the wrapper as he watched the horses move around the track. "Why are you here so early in the week?" I asked.

"I am moving everything from Chicago to my new home office in Ohio, and I thought I would take a detour and take a break for a while."

"Do you have a place to stay?"

"Yeah, I stay on my railcar."

"Oh right. Of course," I said. I could hear footsteps coming from behind me and I turned around to see who it was. It was a jockey coming to ask me about riding Outpost.

"I haven't made up my mind yet. I will talk about it tomorrow morning," I told him. The jockey just turned around and walked in the other direction.

"How are you going to choose a jockey for Outpost?" Mr. Wade asked. It felt like a dream as I sat there talking to him in a casual manner and without people surrounding us. He was an American icon and I was just talking to him the way I held a conversation with Jim or Booley.

"I usually look at their record and weight obviously, but I also try to find a jockey who really wants it. Sometimes selection of a jockey is based on instinct. Also, I know a few of them pretty well from past races."

"Is that what your father did?"

"Yep," I said. Then I suddenly remembered a story about my father. One I hadn't thought about in years. "You ever hear of a horse named White Charlotte?"

"I think so," Mr. Wade replied. "That's been ten, fifteen years hasn't it?"

"Yeah, fifteen years ago, maybe more," I answered with a big smile as I was about to tell a funny story. "Back when I was teenager and helping Dad at Churchill Downs, he was training White Charlotte who was the favorite going into a stakes race. He didn't have a jockey for the horse and he had made it known that he was looking for the one who wanted it most."

"Uh, huh," Mr. Wade said. He had turned his entire body toward me, giving me his full attention.

"So he told all of the jockeys that they would have to race for it."

"Yeah?"

"Yep, but not on a horse. He had them walk into the starting gate on the track. The track manager opened the gate and off they went."

"You mean he put all of the jockeys in the gate the horses load into and they had to race around the track on foot?" Mr. Wade said with a smile.

"Yeah! He made it a three furlong race," I said. Mr. Wade's laughter could be heard down the track. "The jockeys took off and around the turn they went. One of the grooms from another barn started calling the race, cupping his hands around his mouth and yelling as he gave detailed action of the first, second and third positions. People around the track were howling with laughter," Mr. Wade was still laughing. I saw Booley walking over to the barn with a pair of horseshoes in his hand.

"Hey, Booley!" I yelled. He came over just as Mr. Wade had settled down. "Remember that time that Dad made the jockeys race around the track?"

"I sure do. The jockey that won didn't even get to ride that horse."

"He didn't?" I asked as I had forgotten. Mr. Wade looked interested.

"Why is that?" Mr. Wade asked.

"Your Dad took the guy that came in last. The other jockeys had gotten to the finish line and were barely out of breath. The fourth jockey was sweating and breathing hard and his face was red like a beet."

"Why did Mr. Chapel choose him?" Mr. Wade asked.

"'Cause he didn't quit. No matter what, that jockey was going to finish even if it killed him."

"Did he win the race with White Charlotte?" Mr. Wade asked.

"Didn't win it, but came in second. Mr. Chapel said that was the best the horse could have done in that race anyway. From then on that jockey rode that horse. He won many times after that," Booley said as he started back toward the barn.

"Interesting," Mr. Wade said. "Very interesting. That's a good story." He turned toward me and looked at me in the eye. "You know the best way to achieve success? You make a name for yourself. Do you know how you do that?"

"How?" I asked.

"Get in the papers. Do things that no one else does."

"Yeah? You speaking from experience?"

"Sure am! Let's have a race," he said.

"You mean another jockey race?" I asked.

"Well, sure! I would love to see it," Mr. Wade said with a big smile on his face. "Tell you what," Mr. Wade said. "You take care of the set up, and I will get the press ready. I will have them take pictures and I will even offer those vultures a spiff for front page coverage."

"What's a spiff? I asked.

"I slip them a little cash if my article makes the front page," he said with excitement in his eyes. With Mr. Wade on my side, what else could I do, but say yes.

I arranged for the starting gate to be placed on the track and I notified the jockeys how I would be deciding who would mount Outpost on Tuesday. Russell Laney was our track manager back then, and when I informed him of my intentions, he agreed to officiate the race and declare the winner at the finish line.

Mr. Wade walked over to the fence and stood next to Booley waiting for the jockeys to load up. I made them run three furlongs just as my dad had set it up fifteen years ago. The press had lined up and was prepared to take photographs as the jockeys were put in the starting gate. As soon as the bell rang and the gates opened, flashes ignited from the cameras and eight jockeys sprang out and started running as fast as they could. Mr. Wade and Booley were killing themselves laughing. Mr. Wade's hat had fallen off his head, and his face had turned bright pink. The rest of the trainers, exercise riders and the grooms who watched the spectacle were tied up in fits of laughter. Benjamin J. Bull crossed the finish line first and held up his hands in victory. As soon as he did, the crowd cheered and applauded with laughter. Mr. Wade had picked up his hat and placed it on his head with a smile on his face as big as Texas. Thanks to him, if you were to look in the April 10th, 1939 edition of *The Herald* and *The Leader* newspapers, you would see Russell Laney declaring the winner of the first ever, Keeneland Jockey Race in both papers. To this day the two newspaper clippings are framed in my office. I look at them from time to time, and each time I do I think of Mr. Wade and my father.

34

Three days before the first race at Keeneland the house was filled with the aroma of buttermilk breaded pork chops, made from scratch biscuits and sliced country ham. I distinctly remember dinner that night as Ellie had purchased tea leaves and a bag of sugar from Guthrie's. She used the ingredients to brew a jug of sweet tea and poured a glass of it filled with ice. She set the amber colored beverage in front of my dinner plate, excited for me to try it and once I did, I was in love. Sweet tea has been my top beverage choice since. It wasn't until after World War II that sweet tea was available in restaurants and once it was, I opted to go out more often. While restaurants could make it close to my liking, no one could brew sweet tea the way Ellie could, she knew how to make it perfectly sweet and any sweet tea drinker knows exactly what I am talking about. While we were eating, Booley and I looked over the Keeneland Spring Condition Book. The small, orange booklet was an index of races which trainers used to decide what races the horses they are training should enter. I turned the page to the first maiden race of the year.

"So, you're submitting Outpost for the first race, what about the others?" Booley asked as he took a bite of country ham.

"I am going to run Ranger next week. I would feel better if Dr. Wall checks him over before I submit him for his first race," I answered as I cut off a piece of breaded pork chop with the side of my fork and took a small bite. I washed it down with a swig of iced tea. The burst of flavor from the sweet tea didn't overpower the taste of the buttermilk breading which isn't an easy balance. Southern cooking is an art form that Ellie had perfected.

After we all chipped in helping Ellie clean the kitchen, I woke up Banner in the living room and walked him out on the back porch and let him sit beside me on the old couch. I watched his tired eyes follow Booley's motions as he turned a metal bucket upside down and used it as a seat before he lit up a cigarette. Ellie walked over to the couch as she dried off her hands and sat down next to Banner and petted him, rubbing his ears and neck. Joe closed the door behind him as he came out of the kitchen and stood next to his mom, taking over petting Banner where she left off.

Sitting out on the back porch after dinner was a tradition my dad started. He and Booley would sit and talk business, mull over jockeys, horses and upcoming races. They didn't do it all the time, only when it was warm out and the racing season was in full swing. I still had the Keeneland Spring Condition Book in my hands, which would have been difficult to see sitting on the back porch at night, but the light coming from the window behind me illuminated the words on the page.

"What about Price and Pale?" Booley asked as he took a long draw off his cigarette. I flipped the pages of the book trying to find the next maiden race. Joe was looking at the pages and stood closer to me so he could see the book I was holding and reading from with the limited light. His head tilted sideways as he tried the read the words on the pages.

"What is the book for?" Joe asked as he stopped petting Banner on the head. I turned the book over so he could see the orange cover with the words written on the front in black ink.

"This is called a condition book and it's a list of all the races for the spring meet." I flipped to a certain page and found the first race. "See this maiden race here?" I said. Joe nodded his head. "This is the maiden race that Outpost will be entered in. I have to submit a form to the race secretary to get Outpost entered into this race."

"What's a maiden race?" Joe asked. I was ecstatic that Joe was interested enough to ask questions. I was eager to teach him the world of thoroughbreds, especially since he showed interest. Ellie was smiling and I could tell it was because I was so enthusiastic about teaching Joe the things I was passionate about.

"Come take a look, let me move up so you can see it better," I said as I sat closer to the edge of the couch. Joe stood next to me resting his weight against the front of the cushions as I held the book at an angle in front of him. The light from the window illuminated the pages and the dancing cowlick springing up from the back of Joe's head. "A horse has to run in maiden races until it wins. The horse can't get to the big money events unless it wins in a maiden class race," I explained. Booley offered his thoughts. Ellie, becoming more interested in the conversation scooted to the edge of her seat and moved forward, looking at Booley as he spoke.

"Breaking their maiden...that's what it's called when a horse wins a race in that particular class...breaking their maiden," said Booley. "Do some horses run in maiden races without ever winning?" Ellie asked.

"Some horses never break their maiden, some never win and retire having never won a race. Sure, they'll try to enter the horse in an allowance race, but they meet winners there that have more experience." Booley looked at me getting back to his question. "What about Price and Pale? I don't think you should run them until the next available maiden."

"Why not?" Joe asked. Booley inhaled the last of his cigarette before flicking the end out into the damp grass. The smoke rolled out of his nose and mouth as he answered.

"Outpost is a fast horse. Very fast. Looks like he could easily break his maiden. However Joe, I have been in this business since I was a teenager and I can't tell you how many times I have seen a horse that didn't have a chance come up and take the race by a nose. Happens all the time." Booley looked up at me. "I don't think you should risk it. You still have the other horses to worry about beating Outpost let alone two other horses on your roster," he said. I handed the book to Joe. He took it in his hands and looked it over before looking at me.

"Joe, if the April 13th race is Outpost's race, then what would be the next available race for Price, Pale and Ranger?" I asked hoping to be the first one to get Joe to use a condition book. He flipped the pages and searched the types of races available. After a moment, he handed the book to me pointing at a title of a race.

"April 19th, a race for two year old colts with an eight hundred dollar purse," he answered. Booley laughed while slapping his knee.

"That's right!" I said. Joe smiled from ear to ear. Ellie patted him on the back. There were other questions that followed that night and Booley and I took turns answering them. At about nine-thirty, Booley went inside to go to bed. Joe looked tired as well which prompted Ellie to lean in next to Joe's ear, speaking softly.

"Why don't you go lay down in our room and I will be in shortly." Joe rubbed his eyes and patted Banner on the head.

"G'night Banner," he said before going inside.

"There is so much about training horses that I never knew existed," Ellie said as she scooted closer to me on the couch.

Without hesitation, she brought it up before I did. I was thinking about it, but I was trying to not get my hopes up in the event that Mayor Evans was alive.

"You think he's dead?" she asked. I took my time before answering. I wanted to make sure I thought about my answer first.

"I hope you don't think I am a bad person by saying this, but I hope that he is dead." She leaned her head against my shoulder and crossed her arms letting out a sigh of sleepiness.

"Me too," she responded as if she was just about to go to sleep. She closed her eyes and continued, "I try not to think about it. Until I hear the final word, I don't want to think we have it made and then it be taken away, although there are reasons why people would want him dead. He has made many enemies and if he was murdered, he only brought it on himself." Her hand reached for mine. I held Ellie's hand gently, taking notice that she had removed her wedding ring. I didn't acknowledge the fact that it was missing. I was just glad it was gone.

Eventually we turned off all the lights in the house before saying goodnight to each other. I went upstairs and she quietly walked into her little room where Joe was sound asleep. I was awake for quite awhile thinking about the mayor's car and the bullet hole in the windshield and the blood on the seat. I repeatedly thought about the article in *The Georgetown Times* that there was a lot of blood, which made me think that the Mayor had to be dead.

35

Two days before the maiden race, I was sitting on the first tier of the boards as the sun was coming up over the horizon. I had been filling out a submission form under the soft orange sunlight reflecting off the clouds above. I could hear footsteps coming from behind me and I could tell that they were petite steps, the kind a woman would make. Ellie and Joe were at the barn tending to Priced Opportunity with Booley. I knew it wasn't Ellie, so it had to be a jockey. I turned around and saw John Pringle dressed in full riding gear.

"Hey Pringle," I said immediately going back to the submission form.

"Hey Chapel." He walked in front of me and patted his stomach. "I am down seven pounds."

"Really? What are you at now?"

"One sixteen. Gonna ride Bluefield in the fourth race on Thursday."

"You are? What is the fourth race?" I asked as I filled in a section of the form.

"Claiming race. Four year olds," he answered.

"You getting back into races now?" I asked taking the pencil away from the form. I looked up and made eye contact with him anxious to hear his answer as I had thought he would get back into racing since appearing in several newspapers.

"Yeah, I'd like to. Harder to keep the weight down since I am getting on in years."

"Aw, you're not that old, Johnny," I said. "That's good though. You're a good jockey."

"Thanks. I came by to tell you thank you. If you hadn't given me the chance I wouldn't have gotten so much attention. Being on the front page was the best thing that ever happened to me," he said. He looked very sincere and appreciation beamed from his eyes.

"No problem Pringle. Good luck on the claiming race," I said.

"Thanks," he replied. He put on his riding helmet and walked toward the barns with liveliness in his stride I hadn't seen before.

"Hey, Chapel!" someone shouted from behind me. I turned around and saw Russell Laney, the track manager waving at me.

"What?" I yelled back.

"Phone call!" he said pointing at the barn manager's office. I waved back at him and made my way to the small office. I walked inside and closed the door putting the phone to my ear.

"This is Elliott," I said.

Beyond The Pale was owned by a bank president and his colleagues. They all went in together and purchased Beyond The Pale from a breeder in Louisville. Phil Horace, the president of Jefferson Trust started the phone call with his sympathies.

"Chapel, sorry to hear about your dad. He was a good man," Mr. Horace said. In the summer of 1938, Mr. Horace decided to give me a chance as his trainer since my father had successfully trained three of his horses in the past. It wasn't easy as I had to make several telephone calls and a lengthy visit to his office in Louisville to get him to agree. After he saw my determination (or desperation), he gave me the chance to train the rare white horse, Beyond The Pale.

"Reason I am calling is my colleagues and I have been reading a lot about Verris Wade's horse, Outpost. Are you going to enter Beyond The Pale with Outpost in the first race?" he asked.

"No sir," I said. I was sure that he wouldn't want his horse to run against competition like Outpost. "I am going to enter him in the third race on the nineteenth of this month."

"Well, Chapel we would prefer you enter him with Outpost. We have discussed it and we like the idea of our horse racing with Wade's horse. After reading your progress reports, we think he could make a run for it," Mr. Horace explained. I didn't know what to say, I didn't want Pale running in the same race as Outpost. I didn't want to risk it.

"Mr. Horace, it is my opinion that Outpost will win. I wouldn't want to risk an unnecessary injury on the track and I feel the nineteenth is a race he can win."

"I understand, but my partners and I have made up our minds. We are making plans to come to the race on Thursday and we would like to you to arrange a meet and greet with Mr. Wade if possible. If not that's fine, but we do want Pale to run against Outpost."

His voice had the same command and authoritative tone that Mr. Wade's possessed. They both spoke with purpose and control. Once the conversation ended I found Booley near the barn looking inside a trunk of horseshoes. He was picking up each one and reading the sizes. With my hands on my hips and pacing back and forth, I took his attention away from the trunk and told him the details of the conversation with Phil Horace. Once I explained the situation, he appeared to be concerned and was quiet for sometime before speaking.

"What are you going to do?"

"I don't know. What can I do?" I asked, which was purely rhetorical.

"You could release him," Booley said. I didn't want to do that. Anytime a trainer releases a horse from his roster, it looks bad. People think that you couldn't train the horse and that you wasted the owner's money.

"Yeah I know. I'm not gonna do that."

"You don't want Pale in the race. It's too risky…way too risky" Palmer walked up to us holding my clipboard that held the Keeneland training schedule.

"Bully J. is here and we have time for him to breeze Outpost if you'd like. I'd like to give him some cues and let him get a feel on the track."

"Yeah, go ahead and prep him. I'll meet you both at the entry gate," I replied. Booley had crossed his arms and was squinting as the sun had broken over the horizon.

"Well, I'll be thinking on it. You do the same," Booley said.

"I will. Tell Jim about Pale and see what he thinks," I said before heading toward the track's entry gate.

Ellie and Joe stood beside me as I watched Outpost breeze around the track. Palmer was nearby watching intently with binoculars. He had given Bully J. cues for moving Outpost around the turns, when to hold him back and when to release him. Joe was asking questions and I was delighted to answer them.

While I was educating Joe about a thoroughbred's gait, a track employee pointed me out to a man wearing a brown suit. He looked as if he wasn't in a hurry. From the corner of my eye, I saw him strolling towards us but I still wasn't sure if he was looking for me. "Mr. Chapel?" the man asked, as he got closer. I turned and looked at him.

"Yes?"

"I am William Patterson from Patterson and White."

"Yes. Nice to meet you," I said warmly as I reached out my hand to shake his. He was close to my age, maybe a little older. His father was the founder of Patterson and White Law Firm in Lexington. They were the owners of Priced Opportunity.

"I thought I would stop by instead of calling. My father sent me to talk to you about our horse," he said. My first impression of William Patterson was that he was very passive. Most attorneys I knew were very outspoken and aggressive.

"Well sure. Are you hungry? Or do you wanna grab a cup of coffee?" I asked. It looked like a strong breeze would cause him to lose his balance.

"Coffee would be great," he said. I told Ellie and Joe I wouldn't be too long and I would see them shortly. I took Mr. Patterson over to the track kitchen and bought him a cup of unremarkable coffee. The kitchen could do a lot of things well, but coffee wasn't one of them.

"Mr. Chapel, my father and the other partners wish to sell Priced Opportunity." This was nothing new. Owners buy and sell horses all the time and I was used to it as it happened to Dad quite often.

"Okay," I said, as I took a sip.

"We are looking at a horse whose bloodline traces back to Old Rosebud," he said proudly as he took a sip of the mundane coffee. "Our interest in this thoroughbred is pending," he added. Everyone in the racing community knew who Old Rosebud was as he won many races including the Kentucky Derby in 1914. I was ten years old and it was my first time at Churchill Downs. Old Rosebud won by eight lengths, dominating the entire field and in case I haven't mentioned it before, that famous horse now resides in the field of dead horses on my farm.

"Sounds very promising," I said.

"Yes, it does. Once he is broken, we would have him sent to your farm so don't worry about us going to find another trainer," he explained. "We figure if you're good enough for Verris Wade, then we made the right decision." It was music to my ears. My association with Verris Wade seemed to already be paying off.

"Well, I do thank you for giving me the opportunity," I said as sincerely as possible without seeming desperate.

"We are looking for a private sale. Actually we think we may have a buyer for Priced Opportunity."

"Oh, good. Quick sale then," I said while stirring in more sugar.

"We think it would be a good idea to run him this Thursday in the same race as Outpost." I couldn't believe what I was hearing. I was cursing in my head. "If he wins, I think we would consider keeping him, but the partners and I know that is unlikely. Perhaps if he were to come in second of third, we would get a higher sale amount for Priced Opportunity," he said.

Damn it, I thought. The same day! Here I had two owners, two horses, in the same damn day threaten my professional life. Booley's explanation kept running through my head. "I can't tell you how many times I have seen a horse that didn't have a chance come up and take the race by a nose. Happens all the time." I did try to persuade Mr. Patterson to reconsider. He just referred to the partners who thought of the idea explaining that he had no say in the matter. We ended the conversation on a positive note and a handshake although I was still cursing in my head. I quickly found Booley and Jim and pulled them to the side of the barn to discuss the situation. I was fearful and I let them know it once I gave them the details.

"It scares me. I am not going to say it doesn't," I said.

"Can't you reason with them?" Booley asked.

"They both have clear intentions, and mostly I think they like the idea of their horse running against Mr. Wade's," I explained as I crossed my arms and leaned against the side of the barn. Jim had been brushing Ranger's Cape with a grooming brush. It was in his hands as we spoke and I watched him flick the bristles with his fingers as he considered the situation. Once he had thought things over, the flicking of the bristles stopped and he spoke up.

"What about releasing them from your roster?" Jim asked.

"Booley already mentioned it. I am not going to do that. They took a chance on me as their trainer and I am not going to disrespect them. Besides it would look bad if I released two at one time. It's bad enough when a trainer releases one."

"How about scratching one or both just before the race?" Booley questioned.

"Price does have an injury. You could scratch him at least," Jim added. I didn't want to play favorites. I stared at the ground considering scratching Price from the race, but I knew it would be unethical. I couldn't go down that road. My father never did.

"I don't think I have a choice," I said, "Besides, Outpost has the track record. I am positive he will win." I was trying to convince myself that the impossible was impossible. Booley shook his head.

"You know what can happen. You know how races are." Booley rubbed his head feeling the thinning hair on his head. "You got one horse. All it takes is one horse and here you are at that moment. You can choose to submit only Outpost, or risk losing a roster of sixteen horses just to satisfy a couple of owners and you know how owners are. They come and go. Seen 'em do it for decades. They will drop you without reason," Booley said.

He was a little distressed, but he had reason to be as this wasn't an easy position for anyone on my staff. More horses meant more money. Not just for me, but everyone. To use one of Mr. Wade's terms, I always offered the staff a "spiff" whenever one of our horses won. My dad did it and I was simply carrying on the tradition although he called it "due pay". Once I heard Mr. Wade's term, I used it for years to come.

Jim and Booley both looked perplexed and I wasn't certain on what I would do just yet. My concentration was broken when Ellie walked up pointing at the entry gate to the track.

"Palmer needs to see you." I looked over at the entry gate where Palmer was leading Outpost off the track. Bully J. was walking alongside Palmer, taking his gloves off and removing his helmet. I looked back at Jim and Booley.

"We'll meet up later," I said before leaving to talk with Palmer. Ellie walked with me and spoke with a concerned look on her face.

"Everything okay?" she asked sensing that our conversation was serious in nature.

"Well, not really. It looks like I may have to run Price and Pale in the same race as Outpost."

"Goodness. Do you *have* to?"

"Yeah. It's kind of a strange situation. Seems the owners like the idea of racing their horse against Mr. Wade's," I explained. She walked with me as I approached Palmer just as Bully J. was walking toward the locker room. He started in with his report while walking Outpost by his lead. Ellie and I walked with him, keeping up with his pace. For a short fellow, he sure walked fast.

"He's running good. Bull says he's got a lot extra on the backstretch. Could take the lead with two furlongs to go and cushion by three lengths," Palmer explained.

"Good to hear. So you think he's good to go for Thursday?"

"Without a doubt," he said with a smile.

"Listen Palmer, let me ask you," I said as I stopped him from walking. I wanted his full attention. He pulled back on the lead and brought Outpost to a halt. "It looks like I may have to run Price and Pale in the same race as Outpost. Do you feel, I mean after riding all three, that Price or Pale has what it takes to overtake Outpost on the last furlong?" I asked. Palmer squinted his eyes and looked off into the distance like he was considering the aspects of each horse before answering. Ellie looked directly at Palmer as she was eagerly waiting for his answer.

"I don't know about Price. Beyond The Pale can move though. If you had to worry about one of them, he would be the one. He doesn't waver, and his line is like a string," Palmer answered as he made a gesture with his hand moving in a straight line in front of his face. It wasn't the answer I wanted to hear. Palmer continued. "Outpost has the speed and Bully J. is experienced enough to hold and release him. I wouldn't be too concerned with a horse that has the unofficial track record. It'll be official on race day. In fact, I am going to put a honey bee on Outpost for his first race."

"A honey bee? What's that?" Ellie asked with a smile.

"That's Booley-talk," I said with a slight smile. "That's what Booley calls a hundred dollar bill. A honey bee," I said. Ellie just laughed and Palmer smiled. "That's what you get for being around Booley too long," I added. Palmer took Outpost for a cool down and Ellie walked with me to the front office where the racing secretary's office was located. I had already filled out a submission form for Outpost to enter the first race on Thursday, now I needed two more.

36

The day before a race we always initiate short, fast workouts designed to exercise the horses hard and quick, leaving the remainder of the day for rest. I watched each horse from the boards with Ellie and Joe. Instead of asking questions, Joe kept his eyes on the horses as they ran by, listening to the thumping of their hooves on the dirt track. Each time Palmer came around the quarter pole and passed us by, Joe's eyes focused. *Thumpeta, thumpeta, thumpeta, thumpeta.* Palmer was balanced in the saddle, his brow was furrowed and his hands were gripping Beyond The Pale's reins. As he paced down the track the sound of Pale's hoofs could still be heard from where we were sitting. Pale looked good and I mean really good. Everything about him emitted power and speed and it made me nervous.

When Ellie and I went to the office the previous day and I had filled out the forms necessary to enter all three horses into the maiden race, I had yet to tell anyone else my decision. Ellie was the only one that knew and I had purposely kept it from Booley. I knew he would probably throw a fit when he found out and I didn't quite know how to tell him. I suppose he didn't ask me as he was probably afraid of my answer. Once we were done for the day, I hung up the bridles and made my way back outside the barn. Jim, Sarah and their kids were waiting outside along with Ellie, Joe and Booley. Palmer came around the barn after putting the soap buckets away.

"We're curious to know about Price and Pale," Jim said. Booley was standing off to the side leaning against a post shading his eyes from the sun. I shifted my weight and crossed my arms. Instead of beating around the bush, I just came out with it and laid it on the table.

"Pale and Price are both entered and running against Outpost," I said it quickly as if I was ripping a band-aid from the skin. It wasn't what they wanted to hear, but they didn't scoff or look too upset over my decision. It was as if that's what they expected me to say. "I know I could have released them and let their owners find another trainer, but in the end I thought about what Dad would do." I shifted my weight from one side to the other as I stood in front of them. "You know, if Mr. Wade had made Dad a proposition like he offered me, Dad wouldn't have given it a second thought when asked to enter Price or Pale. He would do as asked by the owners. He was fair to everyone, never played favorites." Jim nodded his head as did Booley. It was more than just a matter of ethics to me and I think my serious tone conveyed that. "If Outpost doesn't win, then I will be content knowing that I carried out what Dad would have done." Ellie smiled looking very proud of me, which really comforted my decision even more. "I know this means as much to you as it does me and should Outpost not come in first, I apologize in advance." Jim cleared his throat before he spoke.

"Elliott, this is your decision and Sarah and I stand by it, no matter what. Win or lose," he said. Sarah nodded her head and smiled. "No apologies necessary," Jim added. Booley stood up straight, no longer leaning on the post.

"Your dad…" Booley said as he looked right at me, making full eye contact, "…I think, would be proud of you." That was all I needed. It was just as good as if I were to hear it from Paul Chapel himself. It wasn't that Booley or Jim had been thinking in an unfair manner. It wasn't their job to work with owners. I had to think like a trainer, which meant thinking ahead and building a good reputation and acting in a fair and ethical manner. Booley and Jim only thought about the horses, as that was their job. I had a much higher responsibility and after that day I felt qualified to be a trainer, but more importantly, for the first time in my life, I felt like my father's son.

We all chatted about the race the next day before we parted ways that afternoon. Palmer talked a bit about the honey bee he was laying on Outpost and Booley ribbed Palmer for using one of his sayings. I received a hug from both Jim and Sarah as they wished me good luck and I thanked them for all their help.

The spring air was cool and the sun felt good on our skin. Booley and Joe decided to ride in the back of the truck while Ellie and I rode up front. On the way back to Georgetown, we stopped at a gas station to fill up the tank. Gas stations back then only had two pumps and one attendant, at least in our area of Kentucky. The attendants were always around to check your oil, gas up your tank and sell you auto parts when necessary. Some of the owners lived at the gas station and it wasn't unusual to be serviced by the entire family that lived there. The attendant that day was checking the oil when Ellie asked him if he sold newspapers.

"We get some in every once in a while. I'll go check," the attendant said as he turned around heading back inside the small building attached to the one car garage.

"Oh, if you have yesterday's and today's I would take both," Ellie said politely as she fished a dollar bill out of her pocket. The man nodded acknowledging her request as he went inside.

"Did you not see yesterday's?" I asked her.

"No. I am hoping there is more info," she said with a knowing look in her eyes. She added with a whisper, "Maybe he was found dead and we don't know it yet." Ellie turned around and looked in the back of the truck. Both Joe and Booley were leaning up against the back talking. "What are they talking about?" she asked. I shrugged my shoulders and cracked the window on my side and listened. His voice was muffled, but I could make out what he was saying.

"He's been playing with the Padres and the Millers and hit more home runs than anyone on the team. They say he hits a homerun nearly every time he is at the plate. I mean this guy must be huge!" Joe said as he gestured big biceps on his arm. "They say his eyesight is better than an eagle. He can read a record while it's spinning in circles." Ellie looked at me rather confused.

"Who is he talking about?" she asked.

"There's a new guy coming up to the majors and the news reports say he's the best hitter baseball has ever seen," I answered. Every time I turned on the radio in the thirties, I would inevitably hear about how Ted Williams was going to reach a four hundred batting average like Bill Terry. Back then I didn't believe the hype, who knew?

The gas station attendant came out holding two newspapers.

"We don't have any for sale, but these are mine and I am done with them," he said handing them to Ellie.

"Oh well thank you! Thank you so much!"

"No problem," he said as he went back to checking the oil. Ellie began rifling through the papers trying to find news reports on the mayor. She handed me the paper from yesterday and I began searching the articles. The attendant finished up and rattled off what I owed him.

"Anything?" I asked as I handed the attendant cash telling him to keep the change as I started the engine.

"No. I don't see anything," she said in a frustrated voice.

"Me either," I said.

"Maybe there will be something in the paper tomorrow," Ellie said in a hopeful tone. Instead of driving directly home that afternoon, I made a quick stop at the newspaper office to speak with a woman named Darlene Dolan. If there was any new information, Darlene would know. She was the secretary at the local paper and was famous for never missing the autumn potluck at the local church. Her husband died many years ago when I was a child and I remember dad refusing to go to his funeral even though they were friends before I was born.

I pulled into the parking space in front of the newspaper office and went inside. Without fail, one could walk into the newspaper office and get the latest news from Darlene. She loved to tell people what was going on before they could read it in the paper. Women who patronized Hagan's Beauty Salon would get the extended versions of stories printed in *The Georgetown Times* whether they asked for it or not. When Ellie and I entered, Darlene was sitting at her desk looking at recipes written on index cards that were stacked in a small pile. Her fingers showed her age with thin wrinkled skin and her taste for gaudy jewelry was evident by the size and number of the rings seated above her bony knuckles. Her smile was contagious and her eyes seemed to glow behind her thick glasses.

"Howdy!" she said greeting us with wrinkles on both sides of her smile. Later in life, Minnie Pearl would remind me of Darlene Dolan.

"Hello Mrs. Dolan, do you know Ellie?" I asked.

"I sure do, but I am guessing you don't know me," she said with a smile.

"I am sure I have seen you around town," Ellie said returning a warm smile of her own.

"I am certain. What can I help you with?" she asked as she fluffed her gray hair with her wrinkled fingers, either trying to keep up her appearance or showing off her gaudy jewelry. I wasn't sure which.

"What have you got on the mayor?" I asked as I leaned forward and spoke in a hushed tone. She leaned in close to respond.

"The FBI are staying at the East Washington Inn and have been investigating and asking questions around Corinth Lake."

"Who are they investigating?" Ellie asked.

"Not sure," Darlene said. She looked back at the office where the editor of the paper was sitting. She watched him take a bite of a sandwich before turning back around. "Heard that they were up at Bullock Lake too," she said in a near whisper.

"Bullock Penn?" I asked.

"Yep," Darlene said nodding her head.

"Is that it?" Ellie asked.

"Everything else has been printed in the paper," she said. I looked at Ellie and she looked back at me.

"You wanna go to the Washington Inn?" I asked. "We could go after dinner, ask them questions."

"No. I think I would rather let it play out and not interfere," she responded.

"If I hear anything else. I'll give you a holler," Darlene said with a smile.

"Sounds good. We appreciate it," I said.

That night after dinner, Ellie and I stayed up after Booley and Joe went to sleep. I was resting on the old couch when Ellie came out onto the back porch after tucking Joe in for the night. She positioned herself on the couch so that she was lying beside me with her head resting on my chest.

"If we are able to be together, what do you think our lives will be like?" I asked.

"I almost don't want to talk about it. I feel if I even think about it, I will hear the next day that he's alive and everything I had thought of was a waste of time."

"So you don't think about it?"

"I do. I tell myself that I wasn't thinking about it when I really was. I catch myself. I just don't want to give my hopes up, counting the chickens before they're hatched."

"I count the chickens every day," I said making Ellie laugh. After a brief silence, I asked, "Do you like this farm?"

"I love this farm," she said as she wrapped her arm around my stomach. She closed her tired eyes. "I don't ever want to leave," she said softly. I was glad to hear her say it out loud. My hand rested near her head and I ran my fingers gently through her hair.

"I can imagine going to different race tracks with you by my side. Watching our horses win, taking you to the Derby. I will buy you a dress, gloves and a matching hat. We'll go on vacations together and watch Joe grow up and go to college. I could take him to baseball games and teach him how to throw a curve ball. We can sit on this back porch and drink sweet tea and watch sunsets together, ride our horses to Elkhorn Creek and camp out as much as we want," I said these things with Ellie's eyes closed, not knowing if she heard me. I laid there for about a minute in silence thinking she had fallen asleep.

"I could want nothing more," she said in both a meaningful and sleepy tone of voice.

Outpost was the key to my career and I had allowed two strong competitors on my roster to threaten my professional life. I had two dreams then. The bigger of the two was Ellie. As long as I had her in my life I would be happy, no matter what. The second was Outpost. I needed him to win. If he didn't, at least I would have a reputation of being ethical and fair. I could hear Booley's voice in my head "We're all one horse away."

37

Thursday, April 13th 1939, was the first day of the spring meet at Keeneland. People lucky enough to have a grandstand seat were in the shade while the people that paid a quarter to get in stood out in the sun without a chair. I was helping Jim and Sarah clean up around the barn while Ellie and Joe waited for me nearby. I didn't want them to get dirty as they were both wearing nice clothes. I could hear the crowd from the barn, and I couldn't have been more excited. Outpost looked fantastic and I had already turned away several reporters who wanted interviews. The reporters were small potatoes compared to RKO Pictures, which had scheduled an interview with Mr. Wade in front of the barn that held Outpost. I was sweeping the straw away from the front of the barns and Jim and Sarah were stowing soap buckets and filling up hay nets trying to make the barn look orderly. We had just finished cleaning up when Mr. Wade came around the corner followed by his entourage, a crowd of onlookers and two men from RKO Pictures.

"Okay, I think we're good," I said to Jim and Sarah as I put the broom away. I looked over at Ellie and Joe, "This shouldn't take long," I said as I walked over to Outpost's stable. I had been instructed to bring him out in front of the barn as soon as Mr. Wade arrived.

"Power, speed, agility, intuitiveness and work ethic. It's all the components to a great horse and this one has it all." Mr. Wade spoke over his shoulder as he walked, using his hands to make grandiose gestures. I opened the stable door and brought Outpost out in front of the crowd. The gentlemen from RKO Pictures had a movie camera with them and had begun setting it up while Mr. Wade asked everyone to stand back for his interview.

"How about moving back a little? Give these guys some room to set up and get the camera going," Mr. Wade said as he smiled. He was very commanding, yet kind and courteous. "Thanks, that's great. Just want to make these fellas comfortable."

Before television, Americans were updated on current events via newsreels in movie theaters. While radio and newspapers provided the majority of the reports back then, newsreels offered sound and motion. I remember many times before a movie started, a newsreel would run and report on topics of interest. In spring of 1939, Mr. Wade was of interest and his horse was the topic. I just stood there holding onto Outpost's lead and smiled while Mr. Wade did all the talking. I kept thinking how fascinating it was going to be to sit in a theater and watch a newsreel that featured my client, and hopefully I would be seen on the silver screen. One of the gentlemen from RKO Pictures got behind the camera and turned a ratchet key as if he was winding up a small motor. When he pressed a button, a shuffling sound emanated from the camera while he looked through the viewfinder. The reporter asking the questions was of average build and his moustache was remarkably thin. He wore a gray Fedora hat with a small, white card tucked into the band that wrapped around his hat. The small white card simply read, *Press*.

"Mr. Wade, you purchased Outpost who was sired by Vagrant

Spender. You must have paid a pretty penny for this bloodline?" Mr. Wade was asked many questions that day and he answered each one, injecting humor where he could. As he spoke, the crowd surrounding him grew bigger and bigger. By the time he answered the last question, there were nearly a hundred people peeking in on the icon who spoke like a preacher on a soapbox.

"This is only the beginning. You can't hold back a thoroughbred who wants it. A horse who fights for it. A champion who has heart and the ability to compete for it. The finish line is the goal and the goal will be reached today and every day after!" The cheering and applause of nearly a hundred people was heard throughout Keeneland. The sudden noise turned heads and the crowd grew even larger. The man operating the camera ceased the motor with the press of a button and collapsed the tripod with ease. The reporter turned to Mr. Wade, "Mr. Wade, it's rumored that you're placing a sizeable wager on your horse, care to take RKO with you to the betting window?"

"Certainly. You're gonna want to get this wager on film," Mr. Wade said. He looked over into the crowd and hollered out. "Roger! Come over here." Roger Ell, Mr. Wade's accountant walked over, excusing his way through the crowd. Onlookers took notice of the man who was called upon by Mr. Wade. Every time I saw Roger Ell, he was dressed like an accountant. Somehow you knew what his profession was; just by the way he dressed. I watched as Mr. Wade put his arm around Roger and asked him in front of everyone. "You bring the money in?"

"I sure did. It's up at the count room locked in a cage," Roger said gesturing toward the grandstands.

"What's the wager?" The reporter from RKO asked.

"If Outpost wins, I will collect over 25,000 clams!" His boisterous voice and his demeanor continued to work the crowd. "Oohhs" and "Aahhs" emitted from the people around him. He took a few steps toward me and put his arm around my neck. "And this is the trainer who's gonna make it happen!" Mr. Wade could create excitement. It was a gift. Even I got caught up in it, cheering along with the crowd.

Once the spectacle was over, Ellie, Joe and I left for the grandstands. Ellie's face was stuck in a state of amazement.

"That was incredible!" Ellie said. "You think you will be in the newsreel?"

"I don't know. That would be pretty neat huh?"

"You would be famous!" Joe said as Ellie reached out and held his hand. We were approaching a large crowd leading up to the stairs of the grandstands. "You could be seen before a John Wayne movie!" Joe said above the noise of the crowd.

"You really could be famous, standing next to Mr. Wade like that. The world might see you on the silver screen!" Ellie said as she held Joe's hand tightly while following me through the crowd. I waved off the famous talk as it certainly wasn't my style.

We found our seats and sat down just before the nervous tension began to creep over me as if a bucket of thick tar was being poured over my head, slowly running down the sides of my face. It was hitting me that in less than an hour, my life would be different—for better or for worse. Ellie and Joe were looking around at all the people while I was thinking of Price and Pale. I could envision them racing down the track past the final pole and overtaking Outpost at the finish. It was entirely possible. My concentration was broken when I caught a glimpse of Mr. Wade making his way to his seat after placing his bet on Outpost. Other businessmen who looked to be employed by Mr. Wade were seated around him, telling jokes and occasionally talking about money. Mr. Wade was holding his tote ticket firmly between his thumb and index finger, which would net him over twenty-five thousand dollars should Outpost win.

"You okay?" Ellie asked. Evidently, the stress on my face was easy to see.

"Yeah, I'm fine," I said.

"Mr. Chapel! Mr. Chapel!" a boy yelled as he raced up the steps toward my seat. He looked frantic as if something was seriously wrong. I didn't know his name, but I seem to remember that he was a stable boy and worked at several barns at Keeneland.

"What is it?" I asked.

"Come quick!" The boy yelled as he turned around and headed in the other direction. I followed him through the sea of spectators walking behind him all the way into the jockey's locker room where a crowd was gathered around a bench. Lying on the bench was Benjamin J. Bull in pain. With tears in his eyes and his face contorting from the pain, Bully J. was grunting with his teeth clenched. I knelt down by his side while the other jockey's surrounded him.

"What happened?" I asked. The track physician was looking him over as he answered me.

"Kicked by a horse. Right in the back," the physician replied as he examined Bully J's neck.

"He gonna be okay?" I asked.

"Don't know. He won't race today for sure," the physician said. I stood up thinking about Outpost. Who was I going to get to ride him?

"ARRRGGHHH!!!!!" Bully J. screamed.

"Okay Bull, okay. We're gonna need to get you to the hospital," the physician said. "Gonna need help gettin' him outta here!" he yelled. The jockeys around Bully J. sprang into action and brought a backboard over to the bench. I helped the other jockeys carefully move Bull from the bench to the board. From there, they carried him out the door following the physician to an ambulance waiting outside. Fear set in and I frantically searched my mind for a replacement jockey for Outpost in the first race. Palmer ran into the locker room and saw the panicked look on my face.

"Is he out? I heard he was out?" Palmer said.

"He's out," I said standing there.

"Oh great!" He said rolling his eyes. "Who can you get?" I walked over to a sheet taped to the wall. The names of each jockey present were handwritten on the white piece of paper. Beside each name was the race they were in and the times they were to report to the paddock. I skimmed the names. Gordie Jones. Willy Yarberry. Ian Hanford. I looked at the registered weights while Palmer headed for the barn.

"I'll have Outpost ready. Just bring a jockey to the paddock ready to ride, but hurry up 'cause I need a little time with him. I have very specific instructions!" he said before bolting out the door. I looked back at the jockey sheet and saw the name staring me in the face. Johnny Pringle. I knew Palmer could get him briefed before the race without a problem. Where was he? I looked around and didn't see him. As jockeys began filtering back into the locker room from carrying Bully J. to the ambulance, my eyes scanned the short statured fellows.

"Where's Pringle? Johnny Pringle!" I asked to whoever was listening.

"He's here somewhere," a voice said in the crowd. I needed to find him fast and get him to Palmer. Where was he?

"Pringle!" I shouted. I walked briskly toward the shower room and came upon a jockey wrapped in towel. "You seen Johnny Pringle?" I asked. He pointed over his shoulder.

"He is in the shower," he said continuing on his way. I ran inside and found the only closed curtain with water splashing against the concrete floor. I ripped open the flimsy, white curtain. Pringle immediately screamed and turned around. His naked, wet, soapy body was a shock. He looked even shorter without clothes. That was the first and last time I ever saw a jockey naked. He did his best to cover himself, but I didn't care. This was an emergency.

"Bully J. is out. I need you for Outpost. Get Bull's silks and get dressed as fast as you can and get to the paddock," I said before leaving. I ran back to the grandstands and found Mr. Wade. As I walked up to him, he was telling a joke in his boisterous voice.

"He said they go out to eat twice a week, candlelight dinner, a dozen roses. So I say, that's the secret to a long marriage? He says yeah, I go Tuesdays and Thursdays and she goes Mondays and Fridays." The crowd around Mr. Wade erupts with laughter. I interrupt to tell him the news.

"Mr. Wade, may I see you for a moment?" He excused himself, walking out into the aisle, giving me his full attention.

"Our jockey got kicked in the back. He won't be able to race," I said. I just came out with it. No need to sugar coat the news.

"Is it serious?" he asked.

"I don't know. They took him away in an ambulance."

"Goodness. You got another jockey?"

"John Pringle. The same jockey that took him around the track, breaking the record."

"Sounds good to me. Can't see how it could hurt," Mr. Wade said. As I was speaking to him, I saw Phil Horace waving at me trying to get my attention. I suddenly remembered I was supposed to introduce him to Mr. Wade. I waved back signaling him to come on over.

"Me either. I just wanted you to know. Mr. Wade, I have a client that owns Beyond The Pale and his horse is racing today along with Outpost. Would you mind meeting him? He asked me if I could introduce him to you," I asked cautiously.

"Sure. No problem," he said in a nonchalant manner while slapping me on my shoulder. Phil Horace walked over with several of his colleagues standing behind him in the aisle. Once I made the introductions, I was anxious to get to the paddock and make sure Palmer spoke with Johnny Pringle.

In my old age, I have since forgotten the names of the jockeys who mounted Priced Opportunity and Beyond The Pale. I do remember seeing them at the paddock with Booley and Jim, but my attention was focused elsewhere. I quickly found Palmer standing next to Outpost, walking him by his lead around the paddock walkway. Pringle was right by his side. As I walked closer, I heard Palmer speaking under his breath. Pringle was listening intently.

"He's got a lot extra on the backstretch. Could take the lead with a furlong to go and cushion by three lengths. Keep that cushion. Don't let him ease up for nothin' and get on it all the way to the line. Seriously, don't let up. He's got it and he'll use it for sure."

I looked over at Jim helping the jockey mount Priced Opportunity and Booley had already hoisted the other jockey on Beyond The Pale. Pringle was the last of our group to sit in the saddle and take the reins.

"That's it," Booley said, "It's up to them now." I looked over at Palmer who was wiping the sweat off his forehead.

"You put down your honey bee?" I asked him. He removed a hundred dollar bill from his pocket.

"Nope. I am headed up that way now." I headed to the grandstands with Palmer, parting ways at the betting window to sit with Ellie and Joe.

Ellie was looking at the racing form with Joe when I found them.

"Did you bet on Outpost?" Joe asked.

"No, I don't ever bet on them."

"Why is that?" Ellie asked.

"A trainer already has a lot of time and money on their horse, so if we bet money on them and they lose, it's like we lost a lot more than what we bet. Plus it's a superstitious thing. Most horse trainers don't do it as it's very bad luck."

"Oh well, you gotta stick to those superstitions. Especially today!" Ellie said. "This is so exciting!" she added as she playfully clapped her hands. I explained what happened to Benjamin J. Bull and that Johnny Pringle was riding Outpost. He was such an unlikely choice since he could barely run his tired body down the stretch if he had raced against the other jockeys. But he did break the track record with Outpost and I suppose him losing weight could mean that Outpost could set another record. I suddenly got nervous. I glanced over and saw Mr. Wade chatting with his accountant and attorney. When

Outpost walked out onto the track with the other horses, Roger Ell pointed at Mr. Wade's horse and looked at his racing form with Doug Powell.

Joe sat on the edge of his seat watching the thoroughbreds make their way to the starting gate. I started to sweat as the first horse was loaded. One by one they walked into their predetermined slot escorted by the valets. The air became still and the noise of the crowd dwindled down to a soft murmur. In the middle of a deep breath, my heart leapt as the gates sprung open accompanied by a bell. All nine horses bolted forward as the crowd sat still watching their exit, all strong and powerful with an apparent will to run. Several people were hollering and yelling out, but no one was losing their cool just yet. The slow turn of the hats on the heads of the spectators were following the nine thoroughbreds closing in on the first turn. Outpost was in second place behind Cooperstown. Priced Opportunity was in last place and gaining. After the first turn, Beyond The Pale slowly crept up to first place with Outpost taking third. Mr. Wade was sitting still in his chair following the race with a pair of shiny brass yacht binoculars pressed against his eye sockets. Roger Ell and Doug Powell squinted with anticipation a they quietly watched the race. At the half mile mark, Outpost was passed by Red Dock, a horse making a move for the lead. Pringle was holding Outpost, keeping the horse underneath him on a tight and easy pace. No need to rush. Palmer had given strict instructions. After one mile with four furlongs to go, Outpost overtook Red Dock, and had taken second place. The horses hooves slapping against the dry track beneath them could faintly be heard in the stands...*thumpeta, thumpeta, thumpeta, thumpeta*...Beyond The Pale held his position in first. Priced Opportunity bypassed Red

Dock and Centuple, taking the fourth position...*thumpeta, thumpeta, thumpeta, thumpeta*...approaching the final turn, the spectators started to stand up. The hollering and infrequent shouts became a mass of screaming and fierce yelling with tote tickets being waved in the air. Mr. Wade had risen to his feet while he clutched his racing form in his tightly made fist while shouting for Outpost to release. The screaming in the stands was almost unbearable. "Red Dock!" "Barrell down!" "Run Pale run!" "Go six, go six, go!" I was completely silent. My eyes fixed on Mr. Wade's horse. Outpost made a move for first position overtaking Beyond the Pale with his feet kicking up clods of dirt into the crowd of horses behind him. Outpost sprinted toward the finish line as the grandstands became louder and louder...*thumpeta, thumpeta, thumpeta, thumpeta*...Mr. Wade had both hands in the air as Outpost, in first position, took off toward the finish line with two lengths separating him with Beyond the Pale in second. The crowd jumped up and down, raising their fists in the air. Flashes from cameras ignited as Pringle gripped the reins and repeatedly encouraged the saddled beast with his riding crop. I placed my foot on my seat and stepped up, getting a better view as I screamed with both of my hands cupped around my mouth!

"Go Outpost go!" Outpost crossed the finish line with Beyond The Pale second and Priced Opportunity taking third. All three horses placed and Ellie threw her hands up toward the sky as she screamed in pure elation. I stepped down off my seat with a smile on my face that stretched from ear to ear while Joe was jumping up and down yelling,

"He won! He won!"

"Remarkable finish!" I heard someone say. "Just remarkable!"

I looked over at Mr. Wade who was scanning the seats to the right of him. He was looking for me and once his eyes found mine, he pointed and screamed at me with his winning ticket in the air, "Twenty-five thousand dollars!"

I grabbed Ellie's hand while she took Joe's. We made our way through the crowd toward the winners circle, walking on tossed tote tickets, weaving our way past gentlemen dressed in hound's-tooth jackets and ladies in ruffled dresses with umbrellas.

"Elliott!" I heard someone say above the crowd. I looked around and didn't see anyone. "Elliott!" I heard again. I turned and looked directly behind me and saw Booley, Jim and Palmer coming toward us.

"Hang on!" I said to Ellie and Joe. I let go of her hand and walked up to Booley who had the biggest smile on his face.

"All three horses! Can you believe it? I mean, I just can't, can you believe it?" Booley yelled as he put his arm around me. Jim and Palmer patted me on the back.

"That was incredible!" Jim said, "Ain't seen nuthin' like it!"

"I shoulda put down two honey bees!" Palmer shouted with a smile. I propped up my elbows on both Booley's and Jim's shoulders and looked at them with a grin.

"You know, I never had a doubt!" I said, causing a riot among the three of them as they laughed and pushed me back and forth between them like a pinball.

"Awwwwww! You liar! You're tellin' stories!" Booley said with a chuckle as he pretended to punch me in the stomach.

Once we calmed down, we all walked over to the winner's circle and stood around Outpost and Mr. Wade. I made sure Ellie was standing next to me as we prepared for the onslaught of photographs. Even RKO Pictures had set up and filmed us waving and smiling while Johnny Pringle was screaming with both hands in the air. Mr. Wade was standing next to me posing for the cameras while stretching his arm around my shoulders, he spoke through his smile.

"Chapel, come to the train tonight for a celebratory dinner. Bring whoever you wish."

"Yes, sir!" I replied, immediately thinking I would bring Ellie, Joe and Booley. Mr. Wade reached up and shook John Pringle's hand as the photographers continued to snap away. Although Outpost didn't quite break the official track record that day, he did win by a few lengths. RKO Pictures walked over to Mr. Wade and the reporter began asking questions with the camera pointed in his direction. Pringle's face was painted in pure elation as he smiled and patted Outpost's neck. A photographer yelled at him while changing out the flash bulb in his camera.

"Hey Johnny! You just won big man Wade twenty-five thousand bananas on the horse everyone will be talking about tomorrow. Show us how you feel," the man said as he held the camera's viewfinder up to his right eye. Johnny raised both fists into the air and yelled at the top of his lungs with Verris Wade by his side. The flashes ignited and captured the excitement on Pringle's face. Instead of winning a maiden race, you would have thought he won the Bluegrass Stakes.

38

"You okay back there? It's starting to rain!" I shouted over the sound of the engine.

"Yeah, just hurry!" Booley replied. I was driving to the train station with Ellie in the front seat. Joe and Booley were riding in the back of the truck when raindrops hit my windshield. As soon as we got to the train station we ran on board the railcar just as the downpour began in heavy sheets.

"Just in time," Mr. Wade said as he got up from his chair to greet us. Roger Ell and Doug Powell were playing a casual game of checkers on a small table across from the couch, opposite from where Mr. Wade was sitting. "Chapel, who have you got with you?" he asked. Ellie was the first one in the railcar as I got her out of the rain the quickest. I wasn't quite sure how to introduce Ellie and Joe to Mr. Wade so I just explained that they were my friends.

"Mr. Wade may I introduce you to my friend Ellie Evans and her son Joe," I said trying to sound proper.

"Ellie, my pleasure. Make yourself at home," he said. Ellie's eyes scanned the luxurious interior of the railcar.

"This is incredible Mr. Wade. Very pleasant."

"Why thank you Ellie. It is my home away from home," he explained. "And Joe, it is very nice to meet you," Mr. Wade said as he reached out his thick hand. Joe's eyes were dancing about, taking in the interior.

"This is the most incredible train I have ever seen!" Joe exclaimed shaking Mr. Wade's hand.

"Why thank you Joe. Trains are my favorite way to travel." Booley was standing near the exit being very quiet as he stared at the textile pattern on the ceiling.

"And this is my assistant trainer Booley," I said as I looked in his direction. Booley took his eyes off the ceiling as Mr. Wade walked toward him. The casual manner in which he approached his guest was familiar to Booley as if he was at the feed store telling jokes and meeting a fellow joke-teller.

"Now Booley, is Chapel here the real deal, or are you the man behind the man, making him look good?" Mr. Wade said in a playful tone. Booley answered without missing a beat.

"Well it takes a team to train a horse and let's just say without me, you would have lost a lot of money today." Booley's response caused a deep and contagious laugh from Mr. Wade. Fast friends, he slapped Booley on the shoulder and motioned over to the dining table.

"Well come and have seat, have a seat anywhere you like and don't be shy. My railcar is your railcar!" He chuckled.

The same chef with the tall white hat entered with prepared food on the silver plates. On the menu that night: Porterhouse steaks with mashed potatoes and steamed asparagus. Ellie was impressed by the presentation with the silver dome being lifted up in front of her revealing her plate. I acted as if I had seen it a thousand times.

You would think that Booley would feel timid being that he was outnumbered by white people and being around a wealthy man. In-

stead he told jokes and cut up as he always did. I am sure that it was
Mr. Wade who made him feel comfortable, offering him rolls and
passing the butter as if he was a member of his family. Back then it
was rare to see a man of power treat someone like Booley the way he
did. Nothing but polite conversation and Mr. Wade was very good
about including everyone whenever he spoke.

"About three years ago I was in Newark, New Jersey waiting for
Howard Hughes to land. You see, we had spoken to him about nine
hours before while he was in Los Angeles." Mr. Wade set his fork
down and used his hands to tell the rest of the story. I will always remember him being very animated when he spoke. "He left the airport
in LA and in nine and a half hours later he landed in Newark, setting
the record for the fastest transcontinental flight."

"How amazing!" Ellie said.

"How did he do that?" Booley asked.

"When I asked Howard how he did it he said all he did was sit
there. The engine did the work!" Mr. Wade said. We all laughed and
carried on. Even Joe was sitting up and paying attention, getting the
punch lines and having a great time.

More stories followed, and the table was cleared. Dessert and coffee was served before we left the train that night. I distinctly remember that night as it was the first time in my life I had ever eaten a
dessert called Boston Cream Pie. While it looked more like cake than
pie, after I ate two pieces, I didn't care what they called it!

When it was time to leave, Ellie and Joe stepped off and looked
at the exterior of the train up close. Booley and I turned to Mr. Wade
thanking him one last time.

"No thanks required, Elliott. I am leaving for Los Angeles in the morning and then to Chicago. The horses will be transported in a few days and will arrive here at this station. I will have someone give you a call and I won't be available until October so I will see you then."

"Okay. Travel safe," I said.

"Will do, and in the meantime if you need to get a hold of me for any reason, call my secretary. You have the number. Let me know how my horses do in the races."

"Certainly," I replied. I stepped off the train and we walked back to the truck and drove home. Having Mr. Wade as a client proved to be a long lasting relationship, but more on that later, Ellie was about to be visited by two FBI agents.

39

On Saturday morning, I received a telegram explaining that Mr. Wade's horses were boarding in Chicago and should arrive at the Georgetown Train Station on April 17th. I had two days before they arrived and I needed to add to my staff as soon as possible. When the newspaper office opened that morning, I called Darlene Dolan and asked her to type up a help wanted ad for a few different positions available on the farm. If Dad were alive at that point and saw that I had already expanded to twenty horses and a larger staff, I wonder what he would have said. "Congratulations?" "Well done?" "Can I go back to sleep now?" I was excited at the idea of having a big operation where I trained horses and sent them to different tracks to run in different races, just as my father had done. I imagined receiving phone calls that this horse took first or that horse took second. Prize money would come in, and owners would seek out my services instead of me having to seek them out. It all sounded good, but I still didn't have what I wanted. Ellie was supposed to be leaving soon, but then her husband was still unaccounted for. Maybe he was dead. I hoped and prayed...however I didn't think God liked the fact that I was praying for a man to be dead. For the most part, I just hoped.

The following Monday, I waited at the train station with Ellie, Booley and the Bennett family. Mr. Wade's horses had been traveling for a full day, and we were anxious to get them to the farm. I had a letter with me that was sent by Mr. Wade's secretary which explained the date and time of arrival along with a manifest that included rail car numbers. I held it in my hands as I watched the large mechanical beast of a train steam to a stop.

"I see the ramp down yonder," Booley said as he pointed down the tracks. We could see the ramp being lowered on rail car 27 and 28 which held all sixteen of Mr. Wade's horses.

"Let's go ahead, and start walking to the rail cars," I said. "Booley, can you bring the trailer to the side of the station and back it up to the gate? Jim, let's wait until our trailer is loaded and out of the way before you back yours in, okay?"

"Sure thing," Jim answered as he headed to his truck.

The on-board freight manager—a wispy, reserved gentleman with a handlebar mustache—obviously had special instructions from Mr. Wade as he had most of his crew readying the horses to disembark before tending to other matters. He kept his crew working and started the process of moving the horses off the rail cars. He hopped off the train with ease and he was no taller than Joe and could have easily been confused for a jockey.

"You, Chapel?" he asked with one eye open. The other eye blocked out the sun that was close to setting. His thin, tree limb arm reached out and I shook his bony hand.

"Yes. I'm Elliott Chapel."

"Nice to meet you," he said as I handed him the manifest. He looked it over and seemed to read every word of it. "Yes sir, I have 'em all here. Ready to go." On the side of the train station was a half acre that was fenced in. It was meant for horses, but sometimes we would see cattle in there or even pigs. Luckily, when Mr. Wade's sixteen horses arrived there weren't any livestock in the corral.

"We'll escort them off the car and if you can help us get them to the corral, that'd be a great help," he said as he handed the manifest back to me and went to work.

"No problem," I said.

That afternoon was spent traveling back and forth from the train station to the farm until all sixteen horses were in the twenty stall barn. A stack of paperwork came with them which listed their current track exercises, feeding schedules, and miscellaneous information from the previous trainer. Some had raced in ten to twenty races thus far, and I was to pick up where the last trainer left off.

The next day I had gotten up early in the morning and fixed a cup of coffee. I walked into the living room finding Banner asleep on the floor next to Dad's old chair. I sat down on the couch and unfolded that morning's newspaper. As I did, I looked at Banner and noticed that he didn't look right. It was as if every muscle in his body had completely relaxed. I got up off the couch and set my coffee down before walking over to him. I put my hand on his head and felt the chill of Dad's old friend. Banner had died sometime in the night next to an empty rocking chair. I left him in the living room and once everyone had gotten up I told them the bad news.

When Joe learned of Banner's death he came to me with a very distraught look.

"I took Banner over...I took him over to his bowls of food and water...he didn't eat...I tried to..."

"I know you did, Joe, but I believe it was Banner's time. It's not your fault," I said as I patted Joe on his shoulder. I had thought briefly of burying Banner in the field of dead horses, but decided on the willow tree out back.

"When your Dad was away, it was his favorite place to sleep," Booley said. I agreed. With the reverence and manner in which we buried him, you would have thought this funeral was for a human being. I brought the old quilts down from Dad's old room and wrapped Banner up before placing him in the hole. It was more delicate than putting a horse into a grave. I was able to lay Banner into the hole gently although I did strain to do so. Booley and I shoveled the dirt over his body as the branches of the willow tree brushed over the tops of our heads.

"I will miss you, Banner," Joe said as he held a picture he drew of him. Once the burial was complete, we stood there in silence before Booley shared his thoughts.

"You know Banner was old, but I don't think that's why he died," he said. No one said anything. We all just stared at the grave and listed to him speak. "I think he died when your Dad died. Or at least he didn't see any reason to live," he added. We all thought about what Booley said, and I added my two cents.

"Kind of like when my mother died, Dad probably felt the same way."

One thing was for sure, the Paul Chapel everyone knew, died the day my mom passed away. It seemed that Banner lost the life inside him when my father passed, and I couldn't help but think that I would die in the same way if Ellie was taken away from me. I had hope and I wanted nothing more than for Mayor Evans to be gone for good.

Before we left Banner's grave, Joe tugged on my shirt.

"Would it be okay if I carved Banner's name into the tree?"

"He would like that," I said as I took out my pocket knife and handed it to him.

"You be very careful Joe. Very careful," his mom said. She couldn't help it. When we went inside I remember washing my hands when the phone rang. I picked it up and heard Darlene Dolan's voice on the line.

"FBI are on their way to your house," she said in a near whisper. Before I could say anything, I heard a knock at the front door.

"I think they are already here," I said before thanking Darlene and hanging up the phone. When I answered the front door, Virgil Fleck and Fred were standing on the porch. Sheriff Crease's car wasn't in the drive nor did I see his pudgy body dallying about and spitting all over my front lawn.

"Sorry to bother you, Mr. Chapel," Virgil said in a very polite manner. "Is Mrs. Evans here?" he asked. Obviously he wasn't going to arrest us again. His demeanor was passive and polite.

"Come in," I said and guided them to the living room. "She is out back, I will get her for you." As I went to get Ellie I heard them whispering, but I couldn't make out what they were saying. I went outside on the back porch where Ellie was watching Joe carve Banner's name into the willow tree.

"The FBI guys are here," I told Ellie in a hushed tone.

"What do they want?"

"I don't know. They don't seem like they want to arrest us, but they asked for you," I said as I reached out and held her left hand out of view of Joe, should he turn around. "Do you want me to go with you?"

"Yes, please," she said as she squeezed my hand before letting go.

We went inside and walked into the living room.

"Is it okay if I stay?" I asked Virgil.

"We were going to speak to you and Mrs. Evans separately, however, if it is okay with Mrs. Evans you can stay and we'll speak to you both."

"It's fine," Ellie said. Virgil flipped open a notepad and glanced at his notes as he spoke. Ellie continued to stand up, unable to sit down. I was hoping for good news.

"Mrs. Evans, I am sorry to tell you that the federal government is listing your husband as deceased. We believe that foul play is involved in his disappearance although because of the condition of the evidence, we are unable to either verify leads or construct any new leads."

"What about the evidence? I'm sorry, I don't understand," Ellie asked. Virgil looked at Fred who responded.

"The fingerprints on the rifle are useless. It was handled by many people and many of the prints were smudged before we could take them off the surface. Rain, mud and other debris have contributed to the breakdown of the fingerprints."

"However, we do have prints of one unknown person that are on the driver's side window. We have not been able to locate anyone whose prints match and they do not belong to you, Mr. Chapel, or your husband.

"We believe that this is the person who either killed or kidnapped Mr. Evans," Virgil's partner explained.

"So my husband could still be alive?" Ellie asked.

"Our investigation concludes that he did lose a lot of blood and without medical attention, he would not have survived. All area hospitals have been searched and we have found nothing. Since there does seem to be foul play involved, the state has declared Mr. Evans as murdered," Virgil answered. I looked at Ellie who was taking the information in. She didn't look like she was going to cry, but she didn't look happy either.

"Is that it?" Ellie asked.

"It is. We have to catch a train to Baton Rouge tonight and file our report tomorrow morning and meet with the governor. The case will remain open. Local and state authorities will get a copy of our report and follow any new leads," Virgil said as he put away his notepad, "I am told that you will receive a death certificate issued by the state." Looking like they were ready to leave, I walked to the front door and they followed. I thanked them both and closed the door behind them. Once the door was closed, I walked back to the living room and embraced Ellie for it was at that moment we both knew that we would be together from then on.

"Elliott," she whispered. "I am with you. I am with you for good." Her hand moved up my back to my neck and held me tightly as if she were hanging on to me. "I love you. I love you so much," she added. My arms were wrapped around her when I whispered back, "I could want nothing more."

"You are the best thing that has happened in our lives. Joe wanted to be a son so bad. And now, he is...he has a father."

"He does, Ellie."

It was an exciting time for me as my career was just beginning, but the real excitement came from knowing that I would have Ellie and Joe in my life. The thought of getting married, having a baby, celebrating birthdays together and the sheer joy of having a real family under the house my father built was exciting. It was as if the gray cloud that hovered over our farm was gone and gone for good.

Before my story ends, I have one more thing to share with you. It is the sole reason that I wrote this book, and it revolves around the deep, personal secret that I have kept for almost 50 years.

40

In September of 1943, Eastern Express took a turn for the worse. Although America was heavily focused on World War II that year, most racing continued except for tracks in California and Florida. Booley had already left for New York with three members of our staff to enter eight horses at Belmont while I stayed at home with Ellie in her delicate condition.

Eastern Express passed away due to a form of colic that Dr. Wall fought with everything he had until the thoroughbred succumbed after lying down in his stall. Ellie and Joe had given him four years of extra life living in the pastures on our farm while being fed the occasional apple or carrot. The summer of 1939 was when we discovered Eastern's love of peppermints and even kept an old milk bottle on top of the refrigerator. We all chipped in and deposited peppermints into the bottle we accumulated from restaurants, candy stores and the penny jar at Guthrie's. Eastern always seemed grateful to Ellie and Joe for their kindness and I know it is a funny thing to say, but if you've been around horses long enough you can sense what they are feeling.

I staked the maple and oak frame into the ground and attached the pulleys to the wooden frame and Eastern's body. After carefully inserting Eastern into his grave using the pulleys, I covered him up with a tarp after adding the powered chemical needed to abide by local burial regulations. In no time at all I filled in the grave with the tractor and took out my pocketknife. Since I had buried Eastern near the back fence, it was just a short walk away from where the names were carved. Anytime I was out there in the field, I would often look at the names of the horses, reminding myself of the great ones who were buried there. That day, I took the time to read the names engraved on the wooden fence: *Old Rosebud, Star Banner, Preeminent, Challedon, Speed Chronicle, Comet's Tail* and many others as my eyes scanned the list. Although there was one name in particular which caught my eye. I was holding the pocketknife in my right hand; the sun was shining toward the fence casting my shadow on part of a name. I didn't know what I saw at first, but as I walked closer it became clear. Carved on the fence was the name *Untouchable Mayor*. I didn't know what to think at first. I walked closer to the fence and traced the letter "M" with my finger. It shook me in the same manner as if I had woken up from a deep sleep only to see a massive, black train headed directly at me. If you'll recall the stormy, rainy night I had come home from meeting Ellie at the oak tree, my father saw me crying in the living room. I didn't realize he was there until he spoke:

"What in the hell is the matter with you?" Dad asked in his gruff tone. His sudden, loud voice sent a shockwave through my nervous system—jolting my entire body.

"What are you doing down here? It's midnight," I said as I tried to compose myself, bringing my shoulder to my face, wiping the tears with the fabric of my shirt.

"Are you crying?" he asked. His deep-set wrinkles scrunched together in

disapproval. Dad's face usually didn't show his emotions.

"I guess I am," I answered, feeling foolish.

I remember explaining everything to him that night and what I remember the most was Dad's question about the situation.

"Nothing can be done with an attorney and a judge?" Dad asked as he sat in his chair, rocking back and forth.

"He's a political figure. It wouldn't happen. He's untouchable."

"I see," he replied.

As I stood there in the field of dead horses, tears started to stream down my face as I realized what my father had done. He had left the house that night and waited for the mayor to drive down Penny Road early the next morning. I imagine that it went something like this.

Once Mayor Evans saw that a man's vehicle had broken down, he slowed his vehicle so that he wouldn't hit the bystander. Then he came to a full stop once my father stepped out in front of his car. The limited light and the rain probably helped disguise the rifle my father was holding. A swift action of positioning the barrel toward the head of Mayor Evans through the windshield was probably the hardest part. He had to be accurate when he pulled the trigger firing the bullet through the glass and ultimately into the skull of the public official.

I never thought to look closely at the rifle the deputy was holding in the photograph on the front of *The Georgetown Times*. Later, I would go to the porch and find the spot where my father kept his Remington M37 Rangemaster only to verify that it was missing. I imagined that it was sitting on a shelf somewhere with an evidence tag attached to it. That rifle never saw the Chapel Farm again.

When Dad was sure that Mayor Evans was dead, he pushed him out of the car and drove the 1938 Buick Sedan into the brush – either leaving the rifle or forgetting it entirely. Then, my 67-year-old father picked up the mayor and slid him onto the bed of the truck. No easy feat for a man of his age, but he wasn't weak by any means as his biceps were bigger than most men twenty years his junior. Once he was in the field of dead horses, a long burial ensued with a lot of digging in the rain soaked soil and rolling the body into the hole before covering him up, one shovel full at a time. Later that morning when Booley and I found Dad on the back porch, he wasn't passed out from drinking; rather he was passed out from exertion. The mud on his boots wasn't from milling around his garden in an alcoholic haze, rather it was from the field. The cold rain and high level of activity nearly shut his entire body down. A physician might think that he died from pneumonia and that might be true, but I think it was his time and he knew it. I believe that he wanted to move on.

I looked around the field of dead horses to see if anyone was looking at me or could see me. I don't know why, I just suddenly felt like I was being watched. Then I searched the field with my eyes, scanning for the Mayor's grave. There was no telling where he was buried. The elements of nature had concealed his final resting place forever. I wiped the tears off my face and stared at the name again. Over time, people would see the name "Untouchable Mayor" on the fence and think nothing of it...just another horse's interesting name. I find it interesting that until now, people in the racing community had always thought of the field of dead horses as a resting place for great thoroughbreds. Now you know it does contain legends of the race track, but also one public official who was placed there by a man who gave his son the most precious gift. I never told Ellie or anyone else what happened. I guess the first time anyone in my family will hear about it will be after I am gone.

The same day I found out the truth about the Mayor's demise, Ellie and I were resting on the old couch late in the afternoon. The sun was setting and Ellie had fallen asleep as pregnant women often take naps during the day. I had one arm draped over her as I drifted in and out of sleep while the soft breeze floated over us. The reason I tell you this is because I remember opening my eyes and seeing the white albino coyote eating a ripe tomato off the vine. It was one of my father's final requests on the same sheet of paper where he wrote "Happiness lies between fathers and sons" and it was then that the note made complete sense.

As I write this, it is Christmas Eve morning and the house is full of sleeping grandkids. I am a very old man and I intend to leave behind what I have written when I depart this earth. I am writing this in my study with a fire crackling in the fireplace and wearing a tattered, plaid robe that I am sure will be replaced when I open gifts tomorrow morning. I am surrounded by book-shelves filled with books about training thoroughbreds along with a few trophies that mean a lot to me. I never won the Kentucky Derby which has always been a coveted prize, but I am sure Joe will have opportunities to bring that one home.

Mr. Wade was my most generous and favorite client. We became fast friends and in his retirement years, it wasn't unusual to see him at the Chapel Farm every so often, doing menial chores such as cleaning out a stall or refilling hay nets. He was a man who was not above hard work and he seemed to take pride in even the smallest task. That man loved horses more than most owners and he made more money than most owners due to his fearless mind-set of taking risks and placing bets all for the thrill. I attended his funeral when he passed in 1967 from a heart attack and took notice that carved into his grave marker was a thoroughbred horse running next to a speeding train. Without a doubt, I owe my career to Mr. Wade and Outpost.

"We're all one horse away." I can hear Booley say now as if he was in the room with me. Speaking of Booley, he passed in 1954 from what they call old age. I miss him…his good heart and his entertaining phrases. I use his sayings and have a good chuckle when they occasionally pop into my old head. Recently one of my grandchildren came up to me holding a broken toy. I fidgeted with the toy in my worn, wrinkled hands before finding two separated, plastic hinges. I popped the hinges into place and the toy was functioning again. "Thank you grandpa!" my granddaughter said. I simply responded, "You are as welcome as the flowers in May." I smiled thinking that Booley would have said the same thing without missing a beat.

The year following 1939 was an election year, and Sheriff Crease lost by a landslide. He spent a lot of time in his dark house spitting out Grey Wolf Chewing Tobacco and drinking as much as he could. After two years of tobacco and alcohol, he was found dead in his kitchen with his face in a half eaten bowl of oatmeal. His funeral was held at Mr. Cooper's funeral home and it was reported in *The Georgetown Times* that no one attended.

I have a big picture window in my study that allows me to see the beautiful landscape, which is currently covered in pure white snow. We moved in 1955 to a nice sized house and even nicer sized farm outside of Louisville. Churchill Downs became our home track where Joe and his son now spend a lot of their time. Joe's son is named Elliott Chapel, after me of course, but he didn't take the same path as I did as he is a bloodstock agent, or at least just starting out in that particular field.

As for Ellie, she and I lived a life that wasn't meant to be. I have never loved anyone the way I loved her, and it pains me to say that she died last spring. Even now, I feel exactly like I did the day at the hospital when I lost her. I am not the same person anymore, just as my father wasn't when he lost his "Gracie." It hurts every day. The thing that gets me the most is that my dad lost Mom when they had yet to live a full life together. The fact that he didn't get to live that life with my mother is why I think he was so mad at God and the world. I am now living each day without Ellie and each day that goes by I feel that I didn't live it at all. I feel like ol' Banner sitting on the old couch on the back porch without any reason to live.

My intention is not to depress you, but to explain that a man who I never understood growing up, gave me a gift of decades with the one that I fell in love with. "Happiness lies between fathers and sons" the note read. My father knew that I could have a life that he never had. I made Ellie laugh and did things that made her smile. I chased her around the bedroom and would pull her into a doorway when she wasn't expecting it, making her scream and laugh. I took her to places she never thought she'd see and I covered her in kisses every chance I got. My father gave me the gift of love, and I lived my life taking advantage of it every day. I think about the old farm and every so often I try to imagine our life had my mother not died during childbirth and the better life that my father would have had. I think about my mother and how I wish I'd truly known her instead of learning about her in other people's stories. I can't lie and say I don't think about it and shed a tear from time to time.

Although I no longer live in Georgetown, I still own the old farm, leasing it from year to year. If you're ever in the area, look for a tattered sign on a fence that reads *Chapel Farm*. If you were to travel down Main Street today in Georgetown, you would still find Fava's open for business, owned by a different family of course. Guthrie's closed decades ago and as I get older, I think back to the thirties when I would buy a sandwich wrapped in wax paper and an ice cold Coca-Cola from Guthrie's. The Coke bottle would rest between my legs and I would take a bite and take a sip while the warm summer air would flow into the cab of the truck.

I remember seeing Ellie entering the church in her wedding dress. She was so beautiful. I continually reach back into the far corners of my mind and remember when Ellie and I would go to the Kentucky Derby and she would wear a beautiful dress and long white gloves along with a brand new hat. She was enchanting. I miss Booley's laugh, his sayings and his attention to detail when it came to training a horse. Anytime I think back to eating at the dinner table with Ellie, Booley and Joe, I can feel my heart beating. I become very warm and excitement runs though my old, worn veins like hot chocolate through a crazy straw. I will never forget the night when I told my father that Mayor Evans was "untouchable." Turns out, he wasn't.

Should you ever visit Georgetown, Kentucky I recommend you eat at Fava's and imagine my mother and father playfully fighting with bits of lemon meringue pie on their faces. Drive five minutes past the old Guthrie building and you'll see the Chapel Farm on the right. Wander over to a large fenced in pasture and look for that certain name in the field of dead horses.